Author: **Crumley**, M.M.
Title: THE IMMORTAL DOC HOLLIDAY, HIDDEN.
ISBN: 9798740527215
Target Audience: Adult
Also available in this series
THE IMMORTAL DOC HOLLIDAY: COUP D'ÉTAT (Book 2)
THE IMMORTAL DOC HOLLIDAY: RUTHLESS (Book 3)
THE IMMORTAL DOC HOLLIDAY: INSTINCT (Book 4)

Subjects:
Urban Fantasy/ Horror Comedy

D1522173

LONE GHOST
Publishing

Never Give Up The Ghost

Also by **M.M. Crumley**
**Urban Fantasy**

## THE IMMORTAL DOC HOLLIDAY SERIES
BOOK 1: HIDDEN
BOOK 2: COUP D'ÉTAT
BOOK 3: RUTHLESS
BOOK 4: INSTINCT
BOOK 5: ROGUES
BOOK 6: EMPIRE
BOOK 7: OMENS
BOOK 8: CHASM
BOOK 9: FERAL

## THE LEGEND OF ANDREW RUFUS SERIES
BOOK 1: DARK AWAKENING
BOOK 2: BONE DEEP
BOOK 3: BLOOD STAINED
BOOK 4: BURIAL GROUND
BOOK 5: DEATH SONG
BOOK 6: FUNERAL MARCH
BOOK 7: WARPATH

Writing as **M.M. Boulder**
**Psychological Thrillers**

THE LAST DOOR
MY BETTER HALF
THE HOUSE THAT JACK BUILT
MY ONE AND ONLY
WE ALL FALL DOWN

www.facebook.com/LoneGhostPublishing
www.loneghostpublishing.com

# THE IMMORTAL DOC HOLLIDAY

## Book 1:
## HIDDEN

### M.M. Crumley

*For Doc...*
*Because I still have a crush on you.*

LONE GHOST
Publishing

*Never Give Up The Ghost*

# 1

"Wake up, you filthy hedonist!"

Doc Holliday ignored the nagging voice because he was in the middle of a particularly nice dream and he didn't want to wake up just yet.

He'd just been dealt the winning hand; which he knew because he could always feel it when he was about to win. The man he was playing against was a hotheaded imbecile who didn't really understand how to play the game; and if Doc was lucky, which he usually was, the hothead wouldn't take losing well, especially since he was young and playing with money he'd stolen from his father. If Doc was very lucky, the hothead would pull a gun.

"Wake up!" the voice snapped again. "It's time!"

Doc rolled away from the voice, intent on finishing his dream, and controlled all his facial expressions as he threw in his chips and called the hand. The hothead was sweating now, chewing his lip anxiously. Doc held back his grin as he laid his cards face-up on the table.

The hothead's face went white. He sputtered for a second

before tossing his cards onto the table and demanding, "How'd ya do that? You're cheatin', ain't ya?" His face wasn't pale now; it was bright red.

Doc smiled very slowly, leaning back in his chair as he did. "I don't need to cheat," he drawled. "I've the devil's own luck."

"Gimme a chance to win it back!" the man suddenly pleaded.

"No."

"You gotta!"

"I don't have to do anything," Doc mused. "If you can't afford to lose, you shouldn't play. That's just a good rule to live by."

The hothead's hand twitched, moving closer to his gun. Finally, Doc thought, smiling a little wider.

"WAKE UP!!!"

"Goddamn it!" Doc sputtered, sitting upright in bed. "I was just getting to the good part."

"Two women or three?" Thaddeus asked solicitously, accent making his words crisp.

"No," Doc grumbled. "It wasn't that kind of dream."

"Ah. The old 'I'm going to kill you to get my money back' dream?"

Doc grinned lazily as he stretched. "Something like that. Where's Ana?"

"How should I know? Fortunately, I'm not her keeper. Unfortunately, I appear to be yours."

"I think you have that backwards, Thaddy, old boy." Doc stepped from his bed, picking up his silk robe and slipping his arms through it. "Which reminds me, have I watered you lately?"

"Have I watered you lately?" Thaddeus mocked softly. "Why let me think. It's been approximately five years since you invited Ana to come have a stay. In all that time you've watered me... Wait, it'll come to me. That's right, twice."

Doc chuckled as he ran a finger over one of Thaddeus's shiny green leaves. "It's a good thing you're so low maintenance."

"Humph," Thaddeus snorted. "It's a good thing Rosa comes. That's the maid, if your addled brain will recall. If it wasn't for her I'd be dead. She, at least, waters me regularly. She's quite frightened to come into your bedroom, you know," he added slyly. "She believes you're a Tlahuelpuchi."

"Really? Now, how ever could she have gotten that idea?"

"I do get bored," Thaddeus grumped. "And I may have told her a fairytale or two."

"I hope you educated her, instead of feeding her prejudice," Doc said softly. "I once spent a very pleasant summer with a Tlahuelpuchi."

"But you're not an infant, are you, so you weren't in any danger of being drained dry," Thaddeus pointed out.

"That's just a myth," Doc said, stretching his neck. "Any type of blood will do."

"Oh, well, that's certainly less frightening!" Thaddeus snapped.

Doc shrugged and poured himself a glass of whiskey.

"It took me two years to get Rosa to even talk to me," Thaddeus muttered. "She's extremely superstitious." He was quiet for a mere second before he added, "It's not easy living as a plant, you know. Especially when my only source of conversation decides to take a five-year, vampire-induced hiatus."

"My, you are grumpy." Doc poured himself another shot of whiskey, then tipped some into Thaddeus's pot. "Maybe some whiskey'll take the edge off."

"Goddamn it, Doc! You know I can't handle whiskey!"

Doc's eyes widened innocently. "You can't?"

"I don't know why I try. You're not worth it."

"That's what they all say. Are you going to tell me why you ruined my dream?"

"You told me to, you worthless wretch." Thaddeus's crisp words were starting to soften. "It's time. Señora Teodora."

"Oh."

Doc blinked, and his plush hotel suite faded away, replaced with the memory of a different hotel room. Not as plush, not as clean, and filled with the scent of death.

He was lying in the bed, staring at the cracked ceiling, coated in sticky sweat, sheets soaked from his constant perspiration.

He hadn't planned to die this way, not like his mother had, drowning in her own blood in a filthy bed, slowly giving in to the consumption. He'd planned to go out in a blaze of glory. One card game too many. One card sleight too obvious. But he had the devil's own luck. Except in anything that mattered.

Another cough racked his broken frame, and he welcomed it. Welcomed death. Asked it to come, but it didn't.

"Whiskey," he rasped.

Kate shook her head, sorrow making her eyes huge. "Whiskey isn't good for you. You know that."

"I'm dying!" Doc spat. "What the hell do I care? Get me some goddamn whiskey!"

She must have taken pity on him because she stood and left the room, hopefully in search of the best whiskey they had to offer. Not that he'd be paying for it.

He rested his hand on the cool ivory handle of his six-shooter. It would be faster to just eat a bullet, but he rather liked his face and he didn't want to ruin it. No one would attend his funeral if his face was a bowl of mush. He laughed softly, trying not to trigger another coughing fit.

The door opened, but it wasn't Kate returning with the whiskey; instead a rather old woman entered. She didn't particularly look old. Her face was lined, but not wrinkled, and her hair was thick with only a few streaks of grey. Her eyes were sharp as a hawk's, and he knew from experience her hands were strong enough to squeeze the life from a man's neck, not to mention his other parts.

"Señora Teodora," he wheezed, "come to make sure I die?"

"No." She sat beside him and studied him with the eye of a woman used to death. "You haven't much longer."

"I should expect not," he chuckled, gesturing towards a pile of bloody linens in the corner. "I can't imagine I have much blood left."

"You still do not take life seriously."

"Why would I?"

"I have forgiven you for seducing my granddaughter."

"Is that why you're here?" Doc laughed dryly. "To absolve me of my sins?"

She spat contemptuously to the side, then said, "Do not speak to me like I am one of them. They destroyed my culture, my people, and if they knew what I was they would burn me and think nothing of it."

"Then why are you here, Señora? I'm dying, and I'm afraid I don't have time for games."

"You've never had time for anything but games."

"True enough."

"Do you regret it? Do you wish you'd done something else?"

"You mean marry like my brother did?" Doc retorted. "Have children, then die, leaving them grief stricken and fatherless? I'd rather relive my own life over and over and over again."

Doc's heart clenched, thinking of Francisco. He hadn't

been with him when he died, and he should have been. He didn't have many regrets, but that was one.

"If you lived past today, would you choose a different path?" she asked.

"No."

Doc blinked, returning to the present, and looked around his elegant suite with a grin. He was Doc Holliday. There was no other path.

"Why can't you drink brandy?" Thaddeus slurred.

Doc laughed heartily. "Because I'm a whiskey man, Thaddy. Always have been."

"I utterly despise you."

"Shall I lose you in my next game?"

"Only if you lose to a nubile young nudist."

"Male or female?"

Thaddeus made a strange noise which Doc assumed was a growl. Sometimes he wished Thaddeus at least had a face. It wasn't easy reading a plant's moods.

"I'm back," Ana sang cheerfully as she sauntered into the bedroom. "Doc!" she exclaimed. "You're upright!"

"Yes. I'm afraid our staycation has come to an end." He kissed her fondly, grazing his hands over her slim form.

"But we were just starting to have fun," she pouted. "One more night?"

He pushed her away gently, stepping backwards so her fangs couldn't touch his skin. "A night with you, my dear, turns into a hundred."

She smiled widely, fangs glinting for a second before receding into her gums. "I will miss you," she said, licking her lips seductively.

"It's never a goodbye, Ana," he said, yearning to sink into her arms for just another minute or two. He couldn't though.

The time had come, and he needed to be clear headed, not drugged into lust and happy dreams by the lovely sedative she injected into his veins every time she was near him.

"Go," he insisted. "Before I give into temptation."

"Call me anytime," she murmured throatily, tracing her fingertips over the tattoo covering his naked chest before turning and leaving the room.

"I'll miss her," Thaddeus muttered drunkenly. "Her hips were perfect."

"Indeed. But we have work to do," Doc said.

"You have work to do. I'm taking a nap."

"Sleep well, old boy," Doc whispered, pouring another bit of whiskey into the clay pot before throwing open his heavy brocade curtains and gazing out at the city beneath him.

He hadn't been outside his suite in five years, but at a glance, not much had changed. Another building or two perhaps, but it still looked like Denver. Modern Denver, not Denver as he'd first seen it. That was an entirely different thing. He couldn't have imagined back then that Denver would ever turn into this sprawling, towering mammoth.

He opened the window, letting the breeze brush over his chest. He hadn't been hiding so much as taking a break. Every now and then he needed a break to remind himself how much life there was left to live.

There were more hands of cards to be played. There were more women to be thoroughly bedded. Hell, there's more whiskey to be drank, he thought as he took a sip and breathed deeply.

If living forever meant he had to take a breather every now and then, it was a small price to pay. Thirty-six years just hadn't been enough. Now that he was heading towards two hundred, he could honestly say he'd lived. If Death came to collect him tomorrow, he might not even fight it. Well, not tomorrow. He had to take care of something first; then he wouldn't fight it. Maybe. He'd just have to see.

Doc chuckled softly, amused at himself, and then indulged in a leisurely shower. After he'd dried, he studied his clothes and carefully picked out a white shirt, dark grey vest, and black trousers. As much as he'd enjoyed being naked for the last several years, it felt good to get dressed.

He'd missed his knives more than anything. He strapped a small knife around his ankle and one around his thigh that he could access through his pants pocket. After he'd donned his shirt, he buckled his special knife harness across his chest. His vest hid it completely, but he had easy access to both knives, the one under his shoulder blade and the one in the center of his chest.

He buttoned his vest, enjoying the feel of the buttons between his fingers, rolled up his shirtsleeves, and slipped on his bracelets. He had five for each wrist, and each one was made of horse hair, or something more exotic, and held a stone meant to block psychic or magical attacks.

He hadn't lounged around doing nothing the last hundred and fifty years. He'd acquired knowledge, he'd found friends, lost friends, and collected more than a few enemies. He'd honed his skills; he'd learned new skills; and he'd endeavored to understand the world in which he lived. Both worlds, the regular one and the Hidden one.

But unfortunately, he still wasn't ready. For everything he knew, there were a hundred things he didn't. A hundred and fifty years, and he'd only scratched the surface.

For the first time in decades, there was a very small part of him that was nervous. Señora Teodora had entrusted him with a task, and he was very much afraid he was going to fail.

# 2

Doc stepped from the elevator into the hotel lobby, glancing around and noting the small changes. The rugs had been replaced, there were a few more exotic potted plants, and the front windows had been switched out with stained glass.

He searched the lobby for the shadow of his ever present hotel manager, startling slightly when Jervis spoke from right behind him.

"Delightful to see you once more, sir," Jervis said dryly.

Doc grinned. He'd missed Jervis's dry German accent. He'd missed his lack of humor. He'd missed his sharpness.

"No need to lie on my account," Doc chuckled, turning to face him.

"I never lie," Jervis said.

"What about that one time when you told Mrs. Hasmire that she'd lost weight due to the heat?"

Jervis raised an eyebrow. "That was mostly true. Blood thins when it gets hot so I may have taken just an itty bit more then I intended."

Doc burst out laughing. "I've missed you," he said merrily.

"I've been here the entire time, sir."

"I know," Doc said, voice sincere. "I depend on it."

In addition to managing Doc's hotel, Jervis managed every single aspect of Doc's life; and Doc really did depend on him to do it. He would have never spent five years in his suite making love to Ana if he hadn't known Jervis was here, doing what Jervis did.

"How are things?" Doc asked.

"If there was a problem, I would have let you know." Jervis replied. "However, I should mention that Mr. Jury's been by."

"Really?"

"Yes. Every week for about a year now."

Doc grinned slightly. "I'm sure he told you not to tell me."

"Most emphatically."

"My lips are sealed," Doc said cheerfully. "Jervis, good man, give yourself a raise."

"I already did, sir."

"Excellent. You certainly deserve it."

Jervis studied the lobby with a critical eye. "I certainly do."

"Keep up the good work," Doc laughed as he walked out the door and into the sunshine.

When he stepped out onto the sidewalk, the sound of passing traffic was a little overwhelming for a second. It probably wasn't any worse than it had been five years ago, but he'd been ensconced in his soundproof suite for so long, away from the noise and chaos, that for a moment it was staggeringly loud.

Modernity was nice in its ways, but sometimes he missed the relative simplicity of his mortal days. Each advancement seemed to come with twice as many complexities and irritations. He'd trade his cell phone for the anonymity of the olden days and the ability to change his name from town to town without paying to do it. He'd trade his indoor plumbing for a high-rolling, gun-filled, whiskey-soaked saloon. But it was what it was, and there was no point in wasting his time mourning what wasn't.

Doc meandered along the sidewalk, observing the store fronts, the traffic, the people. Not much had changed. One restaurant had been replaced with another; the cars were even more generic, if such a thing was possible; and the fashion had shifted again, and not for the better. He'd rather enjoyed the fashion of the twenties and the fifties.

He subtly observed a pair of women striding down the sidewalk towards him. They may as well have been naked. Even dance hall girls and prostitutes had worn more clothes. He supposed it was all right on a purely visual level, but he preferred a little mystery in his partners. He liked the unexpected; he enjoyed making calculated guesses; he reveled in both the win and the loss.

The women smiled as they passed him; women usually did; and he gave them a solicitous nod and kept walking, wishing he hadn't had to send Ana away.

He turned down a side street and ambled among buildings nearly as old as he was. It was here that the entrances to the Hidden world were found. Sure, there were other entrances in newer sections of the city, and there were entrances in poorer sections of the city as well, but the oldest and most powerful cryptids lived here. As well as a few well-placed norms.

He stopped in front of a narrow four-story house situated in between two taller buildings. It wasn't hidden; it was visible to all who walked by, and a bronze plaque engraved with the words "Graves, Graves, and Graves. Hunc Quaesitorem" hung beside the door.

It was a clever trick norms sometimes used to advertise to the Hidden. A regular Joe isn't likely to knock on a door marked "Graves, Graves, and Graves. Hunc Quaesitorem", but they might knock on a door labeled "Graves, Graves, and Graves. Investigator."

Doc had used the same trick fifty or so years ago when he'd renamed his hotel Dulcis Requiem. It was the equivalent of hanging out a welcome sign for cryptids. It annoyed Doc that it wasn't quite the proper arrangement of Latin, but dulcis requiem sounded somewhat more prestigious than reliqua dulce, and he knew Pliny would understand. Especially if Pliny was a cryptid as some lore seemed to suggest.

Doc walked up the narrow steps and pulled the bell pull. It was all very upper class. Nothing as pedestrian as doorbells or knockers. He waited patiently, evaluating each person who passed by, and before long a wizened old man cracked open the door.

"What do you want?" he demanded.

"Losing your good humor, I see," Doc chuckled. "If I were Virgil, I'd have put you out to pasture years ago."

"I was counting on you being dead," the man sneered.

"No such luck," Doc replied. "How much did you bet on it?"

"Only a thousand."

"Easy come, easy go," Doc shrugged. "Is he in?"

"He always keeps his appointments," the man grunted, opening the door wider to let Doc pass.

"Thank you, Magnus. It is truly always a pleasure."

Magnus snorted, and Doc grinned widely as he walked through the hallway towards Virgil's office.

"Doc!" Virgil boomed when Doc pushed open the door. "Right on time!"

"I strive for perfection," Doc drawled.

Virgil laughed and motioned for Doc to sit as he poured them both a glass of whiskey.

"Well?" Doc asked when Virgil sat.

"I'm sorry. I still haven't been able to find her."

There was that feeling again. That wave of imminent doom. Failure. He could not fail. He couldn't. He wouldn't.

"I've had people working on this for the last six years, but to be honest, you didn't give us much to go on."

"I gave you everything I have," Doc said.

"I know," Virgil replied. "But it's hard to say if we're even looking in the right areas. A witch, for all intents and purposes, should look just like a norm, or at least your witch should. She could function in the normal world just like you do. She might need somebody to forge new paperwork every now and then, just like you, but other than that, she could be completely off my radar."

Virgil frowned, eyes clouded with irritation. "The Teodora line just stopped in 1994, but there're no death records for the three remaining Teodoras, none of which were named Sofia." He refilled Doc's glass and said, "We're only working with three facts. Sofia is of Mexican descent, she's a witch, and she lives in Denver. Talk about looking for a needle in a haystack. We don't even know if she goes by Sofia."

This was not good. He was running out of time. Perhaps his staycation had been ill-timed after all.

"Keep looking," Doc said. "I have to find her."

"I have my best man on it," Virgil said with a grin. He pressed a button on his desk and said, "Please come to my office, Tessa."

"But Tessa's just a..." Doc paused. Time had a way of passing when he wasn't paying attention. He remembered Tessa as a small girl with curly brown pigtails, but he supposed she'd grown when he wasn't watching.

The door opened, and a lithe, fit woman walked in; a woman who only vaguely resembled the girl he used to know.

Doc stood and took her hand with a smile. "Tessa Graves," he drawled. "You are definitely not a girl anymore."

"Doc," Virgil growled.

"I was merely noting that some time has passed," Doc said cheerfully, not looking away from Tessa's intelligent eyes.

She grinned and said, "And yet, you look exactly the same."

"The curse of being forever young," he said regretfully.

"Such a curse," she laughed.

"You'd be surprised," he replied, feeling a pang of sadness for the friends he'd watched grow older and older and older until one day they were just gone.

"Unhand my daughter and sit," Virgil commanded.

"Don't be silly, Daddy. Doc and I are just catching up," Tessa said. "I'm sure he has a dozen women waiting for him at home. He doesn't need another."

"They aren't nearly as gorgeous as you," Doc said. "But alas, I still remember you holding my hand while I walked through that terrifying wax museum. The statue depicting me was so... revolting, if you hadn't been there to save me, I don't know what I would have done." He brought her hand to his lips with a sudden flare of Southern gentility. "As lovely as you are, my dear, you are perfectly safe with me."

"Sit," Virgil growled.

Doc sat, winking at Tessa as he did. She laughed cheerfully, then perched on the edge of her father's desk, facing Doc.

"I've pretty much exhausted the cryp world," Tessa said. "Unless you think it's possible she's not in Denver?" Doc shook his head, and she went on, "I'm sifting through norms right now, but it's a long shot. I'm not sure I'll be able to find her."

Doc nodded. "I'll have to search using other means then."

Virgil's face tightened. "Watch your step, Doc. You don't want to cross any lines. There're rules in place for a reason."

Doc lifted one shoulder in dismissal. "And when have I ever been known for following the rules, Virgil?"

His meeting with Virgil taken care of, Doc wandered back out into the city. There was something he had to do before he could continue his search. Something that couldn't be put off any longer.

The payment for long life, he thought with a chuckle as he drifted into another memory.

"There's a price to pay," Señora Teodora had said as she sat patiently beside his sick bed.

"There always is," Doc replied.

"It will put a heavy weight on your soul."

Doc considered that for a moment. "Do you believe in hell?" he suddenly asked. He'd wondered a few times lately if hell really existed. He wasn't interested in anyone's version of heaven, but he wasn't sure he looked forward to burning in brimstone either.

"I don't," Señora Teodora said firmly.

"So what happens, and why should I care if my soul is burdened? If it's not between me and god then it's between me and me."

She studied him for a moment, carefully wiping the blood from his chin when he succumbed to another coughing fit.

"I cannot answer your questions. For myself, I agree. I do not judge myself by anyone else's standards, only my own. And when I die, my mother, the earth, will open her arms and take me back inside her womb. Perhaps to be born another day, perhaps to sleep, perhaps to fuel the strength of others. I cannot say."

"So why warn me?"

"It is up to each to decide. I know you as a man who does not shirk from death. Many men have died at your hands, and I do not think you feel guilt or sadness for them. That is just one of the many reasons I ask this of you."

Señora Teodora had been right. He didn't feel guilt or sadness about killing people. In fact, it didn't weigh on his soul at all. In his more philosophical moods, he considered it a service to society as a whole.

Doc whistled cheerfully as he turned into the area known as Five Points and checked the address his go-to man Bennie had texted him; it was just ahead.

Jim Phillips. Single. Forty-five. Convicted rapist and child-molester. Out on probation due to overcrowding in the prison system. It would be a privilege. No, it would be a pleasure.

Doc enjoyed his women. Truly he did. But he'd never forced his attentions or affections on anyone. Not ever. He didn't need to, but even if no woman would have him, he wouldn't. It took a twisted man to find pleasure in the act through pain and force. If his partner wasn't pleased, neither was Doc.

And to prey on children? Doc couldn't even comprehend it. So yes, he considered it a service to society as a whole, and it didn't matter to him what anyone else thought.

The neighborhood abruptly changed. The careful, neat

yards and house fronts faded, replaced by broken windows and brown weeds. An air of neglect and disuse permeated the street, even though cars and pedestrians still traveled back and forth.

Doc glanced at the house numbers. Just another block. And not a moment too soon. He hadn't fed in over five years, and his self-control was stretched a little thin.

He saw the house up ahead and decided the front door approach was best. He ambled up the sidewalk and opened the door. It hadn't been locked, but even if it had been, it would have been no match for his strength.

"Mr. Phillips?" Doc called out, closing the door behind him. "Are you home?"

"What the fuck?!" someone, presumably Phillips, yelled from further inside the house.

"It's time for your appointment with the doctor," Doc laughed, pulling out one of his knives and dragging it along the wall. "Have you been exercising and eating all your fruits and vegetables? That's essential to quality of life, you know."

A large man, bulky and broad suddenly appeared at the end of the hallway. His face was red with anger, and a vein throbbed rapidly on his forehead.

"You are Mr. Phillips?" Doc asked. Not that he really cared, but it was always good to know.

"I am, but who the fuck're you?" Phillips demanded, hefting a baseball bat in his meaty hands.

"Oh good," Doc drawled. "I was so hoping you would put up a fight."

Phillips rushed down the hallway, but Doc easily ducked the swinging bat, slicing a thin line across the man's belly as he did. Not a deep line, just a shallow one so he'd bleed. Doc didn't want the fight to end too soon.

"You'll pay for that, you son of a whore!" Phillips screamed as he spun around.

"Tut, tut. My mother was definitely not a whore. Your mother, however..." Doc left the sentence hanging as he backed down the hallway and into the living room.

Phillips roared with rage and crashed down the hallway after him. He burst into the living room and charged after Doc, swinging his bat like a sledgehammer. Doc waited until the last second, then stepped nimbly to the side, cutting a figure eight into Phillips' arm.

"Goddamn you!" Full of rage, Phillips started swinging wildly, knocking a lamp off its stand and decimating the huge television that dominated the room. Doc moved about the room, effortlessly dodging Phillips' blows, striking with his knife when and where he wanted.

After a minute of frantic attack, Phillip paused, heaving with exertion, and demanded, "Who the fuck're you?"

"I'm the devil, and I've come for your soul." Doc smiled widely, then stepped quickly forward and shoved his knife through Phillips' throat. Blood pumped around the knife, running down Phillips' neck and staining the front of his filthy shirt. His eyes went wide, fluttered a few times, then he fell to his knees.

Doc stopped him from falling on his face and held Phillips' chin, gazing into his nearly dead eyes. "Give it to me," Doc whispered.

Doc's chest grew hot, and he closed his eyes as the energy or soul or whatever it is that makes a man a man, pulled out of Phillips and flowed into Doc's tattoo. Doc shuddered with pleasure as the power rushed from the tattoo into his limbs, filling him with power and strength, with life everlasting.

When the transfer was complete, Doc removed his knife and stepped away from the dead man, letting him drop with a thud to the floor. "Prognosis grim," Doc said softly, before turning on his heel and heading for the door.

# 3

"A pleasant appetizer," Doc texted Bennie. "But what about a main course?"

"Greedy bastard, aren't you?"

"I haven't eaten in five years; if you'd like I can swing by and see you."

"Keep your panties on."

Bennie was a Worm. Literally and figuratively. As a shapeshifting cryp, he alternated between a man and some sort of worm creature. But on top of that, Bennie just couldn't be trusted. Doc was convinced he'd sell his own mother if she was around and someone was buying.

That's why Bennie was so useful. If it was out there, he could find it for you. And if it wasn't for sale, he'd find someone who could acquire it for you. He didn't have any loyalty or allegiance though, so if someone wanted information on you, he'd sell it in a heartbeat.

In spite of Bennie's lack of loyalty, he wasn't stupid. Just like a courtier, he knew how to measure strength, aptitude, skill, and probabilities, and he would align himself with the strongest players on the board. He hadn't crossed Doc in years, but that probably meant it was coming.

Doc's phone beeped, and he checked it. Another name, another address. Not a convicted criminal, but a conman under investigation. Doc scanned the information. Dr. Jonas Higgins. A doctor promising an alternative miracle cure for cancer. His target of choice: the elderly.

Hunger flared; not in Doc's stomach, but in his being, his whole self. Rough and tumble men like Phillips had a sort of primal energy or power. Consuming their life added a layer of strength to Doc's already considerable power.

White collar criminals, however, had quite a different sort of energy. Their strength was in their cunning, in their mind. When Doc consumed a person like that, it made him feel like he'd plugged his mind into an amplifier.

"Dr. Higgins," he murmured. "I hope you have room on your schedule for one more."

He hailed a taxi, stepped into the back, and gave the driver the address. Dr. Higgins' office was located out in Brighton, and it was rush hour, so it would take a while to get there, but Doc didn't mind. He just laid his head against the seat, closed his eyes, and slipped into another memory.

"Why don't you do it?" he rasped, lungs working harder than he'd ever felt them work before. He could feel it now. Death was creeping outside the door.

"I am old," Señora Teodora said with a slight shrug. "I have lived a good life. I have loved, had children, watched them grow. I have lived, Señor Holliday. I will not die for many years yet; I can see this, but I am ready to die whenever my mother calls me home. I have no fear."

"This isn't about fear," Doc struggled to say.

"No. I can see you are not frightened to die. Even now,

drowning in your own blood, you face it like a warrior, brave and confident." She wiped the blood from his lips. "But you must choose. You have not long to make up your mind. Yes or no?"

Doc refocused on the city surrounding him. He hadn't been ready to die then, not at a mere thirty six years of age. Even with as much as he'd done, he'd felt like he'd barely lived, just scratched the surface of the possible. And he had wanted more. It wasn't about fear; it was about greed.

Mortals were strange to him. They lived a fraction of his time, showing very little lust and greed for the life they were given; and when death came knocking, they met it with fear, fighting it tooth and nail; not at all like Señora Teodora. What they didn't understand was that it wasn't really about how long they lived, it was about how well. If they'd just been a little greedier, a little more engaged, taken a few more risks.

But they didn't. They just let life pass them by, and when they reached the end it came as a shock, like they hadn't seen it coming. They'd been so focused on the road, they hadn't noticed the drive.

And in their panic, they turned to men like Dr. Higgins; and he used their fear and hope against them, stealing what was left of their life. Doc had met plenty of men like Dr. Higgins, and he'd killed most of them.

"Here's your stop," the taxi driver suddenly said. "Want me to wait?"

Doc glanced out the window. He was in a fairly new area, surrounded by glitzy business buildings. It would be a slum in another twenty years; nothing ever stayed glitzy for long. There were no taxis here though. Too suburban.

"Sure," Doc said. "I won't be long."

He paid the taxi driver, then headed towards Dr. Higgins'

office, excitement thrumming through his blood. He'd missed the hunt, the kill, the feeding. It was good to be back.

"I have a special appointment to see Dr. Higgins," he told the secretary, using his most Southern voice and smiling charmingly.

She twittered, just like he'd known she would, and said, "Let me just check with him, Mr...?"

"Doc," he said. "Just Doc."

"Oh, are you an associate of Dr. Higgins?" She leaned towards him, generous bust pressing forward until he was certain her shirt might burst from the pressure.

"Something like that." He winked, and she giggled.

"Why don't you go on back? He's free right now."

"Thank you so much, Marcia," he drawled, brushing his fingertips over the back of her hand. "I'll see you on the way out."

Her eyes widened, and her cheeks flushed. He winked again, then headed back towards Dr. Higgins' door. Doc pushed open the door, startling a thin man with a thick head of wavy hair.

"Dr. Higgins, I presume?" Doc said, just managing to keep the laughter from his tone.

"Who are you?" Dr. Higgins sputtered. "I don't have any appointments right now. Did Marcia let you back here?"

"We have an appointment, don't you remember?" Doc said with a feral grin. "You're the doctor of lies, and I'm the doctor of death."

"What?" Dr. Higgins glared at Doc with confusion. "Is this some kind of prank?"

"Just for clarification," Doc said, because Bennie was a worm, and he wouldn't put it past Bennie to send him an innocent's information. "What exactly do you do here?"

He grabbed Dr. Higgins' hand before he could press the buzzer on his desk telephone, and Dr. Higgins stared at him, eyes wide with fear and stuttered, "I... um... I help people."

Good old Bennie. "How so?"

"I devised a treatment for terminally ill cancer patients. I can add three to five years to their life expectancy. It's all above board, I swear."

Dr. Higgins was sweating profusely. Not something honest people typically did. Not to mention that honest people didn't normally feel the need to swear that their practice was above board.

"Three to five years," Doc murmured. "That's astounding. What's your success rate?"

"What?" Dr. Higgins stuttered.

"Success rate. Surely you have the numbers."

Dr. Higgins swallowed nervously. "Of course I do. They're in my filing cabinet. I can get them for you."

"I think I've heard all I need to hear," Doc said. He reached out his other hand and pulled Dr. Higgins' tie tight around his neck. "Statistics is such a numbers game," he remarked conversationally as Dr. Higgins' eyes grew wider and wider. He clawed at Doc's hand, but Doc barely felt it; he was watching the life fade from Dr. Higgins' eyes.

Suddenly Dr. Higgins stopped fighting. He shuddered violently, shaking his desk, then abruptly ceased, eyes frozen in horror.

The tattoo on Doc's chest began to heat up, burning him with its intensity. He could feel it pulling the life force from Dr. Higgins, stealing it, taking it before it could return to the earth. It infused Doc, filling him with energy and alertness, making him feel like he'd just wooed a beautiful woman into his bed.

He grinned slowly, letting it seep into him, then he loosened Dr. Higgins' tie and called for Marcia. "Marcia! Come quick! I think Dr. Higgins has had a heart attack!" Doc injected panic into his voice, and as soon as Marcia rushed into the room, he exclaimed, "I'll call nine one one; you administer CPR!"

He exited the room, leaving a frantic Marcia behind him, flicked the phone off its base, then strolled out the door and climbed back into the taxi.

"Union Station," he said evenly.

"Sure thing, boss."

Doc stepped out of the taxi at Union Station and paid the driver before sitting at one of the many tables along the street. He leaned back in his chair and studied the station.

It had changed since he'd first laid eyes on it in 1882. He'd been surprised at its size then. Not because he'd never seen a building so big, but because he had been surprised to see one so big out here, in the untamed West. Now it looked small in comparison. Like an ant hill surrounded by mountains.

"Is that you, Doc?" a weathered voice said. "I swear you haven't aged a day."

"Darius, old friend, how are you?" Doc asked, smiling as a bent over man approached his table, wooden box tucked securely under his arm.

"Haven't had a good match in years," Darius chuckled. "About five or so."

"Shall we remedy that?"

Darius didn't respond, just sat and started setting up the chessboard, wrinkled brown hands shaking faintly. "I'll let you play white," he said. "Since you're rusty and all."

"How do you know I'm rusty?"

"You just told me."

Doc laughed lightly. "We shall see."

For the next hour they played silently until Doc finally said, "Check mate."

"Well done," Darius said happily. "I haven't been beat since the last time we played."

"You are a world champion," Doc stated.

"Was. Just an old man now."

"No one is ever just an old man," Doc said seriously, his experience with Dr. Higgins still fresh in his mind. "You're an amazing culmination of events and experiences. You're a story, a legend, a key to the future and a glimpse at the past."

"Nice poetry, but it doesn't make it any easier when death starts hunting you down."

"Don't be scared of it," Doc said emphatically. "It's just another chapter of your story."

"How do you know though?" Darius asked, brow lined with concentration.

Doc smiled wistfully. "I once heard it from a witch."

"A witch?!" Darius exclaimed. "A real witch? Like spells and magic?"

Doc frowned, memories swirling in his mind, reminding him of things he had forgotten. "Actually, I'm not sure that's right," he murmured. "I've never been clear on the difference, but now that I think about it, she might have been a shaman."

Maybe that was the problem. Maybe Virgil was looking for the wrong thing. "I'm sorry, Darius," Doc said, standing abruptly. "I need to see a man about a witch."

# 4

It took Doc a day or two to find Thomas Jury, mostly because Jury had gone out of his way to hide. Which meant that if Doc didn't play his cards just right, he was going to have to grovel.

"How did you find me?" Jury demanded irritably when Doc finally showed up on his doorstep.

"Nice to see you too, old friend," Doc chuckled.

"We are not friends," Jury snarled.

"How can you say that after all we've been through together?"

"Been through, yes. Together, no," Jury growled.

"That really pains me," Doc replied.

Jury shrugged carelessly. "I'm not the one who locked himself away for five years without a word."

"So that's what this is about?" Doc said solemnly. "You missed me."

"Did not!" Jury retorted. "I'd be happy to never see your ugly face again."

"I have it on good authority that my face is quite delightful."

Jury snorted.

"I didn't come here to argue," Doc said, stepping past Jury and into his spartan loft space. "I like the new place by the way. Could use a little brightening up though. How about a plant? I have a really nice one, and it doesn't need much water or care."

Jury shuddered. "No. I do not want Thaddeus."

"Doesn't hurt to offer," Doc said with a shrug.

"Why're you here? Better yet, how did you find me?"

Doc cringed. "Let's skip that question."

"Let's not."

"Suffice to say I sacrificed my body and skills to a powerful scryer."

"That makes no sense," Jury argued. "A scryer looks into the future."

Doc shrugged. "I asked her where you'd be today at eleven o'clock, and here we are."

"Give it to me," Jury growled.

"Give what to you?" Doc replied innocently.

"Whatever you gave her to focus the scrying."

"What?!" Doc exclaimed. "You can focus a scrying? How do you do that?"

"Don't play dumb with me, Doc. Give it to me, or I'll find it my own way."

Doc laughed softly and held out a shiny tooth.

"Are you serious?" Jury snapped.

Doc shrugged. "It seemed a shame to waste it; especially since I went through all that trouble to knock it out."

Jury snatched his tooth from Doc's hand with a glare. "Do you know there's an 'I hate Doc Holliday' club? I'm considering joining it."

"You should," Doc chuckled. "Last time I checked there were only ten members. If you join, I'll be inclined to take them more seriously."

"I swear every time I see you something gets broken or stolen or..." Jury sighed. "It'd be better not to say. I don't want to jinx anything."

"As my grandma used to say," Doc grinned. "Don't go borrowing trouble."

Jury rubbed his forehead. "What is it you want?"

"I have a question."

"If only it were ever that simple."

"This time it is," Doc said cheerfully. "I think."

Jury gestured for him to sit, poured them each a cup of coffee, and sat across from Doc, black eyebrows raised in question.

"I once met a witch," Doc said. "I mean to say I thought she was a witch. But then I realized there's a subtle difference between a witch and a shaman. At least that's what someone once told me."

In his mind the room shifted, and Doc was standing beside a campfire listening to two men argue. The younger man exuded more power and strength than anyone Doc had ever met, and there was a very small part of him that wondered what it would be like to eat his soul. Not that he was going to try. He'd just started living, and he was in no hurry to die.

"I don't like 'im," the older man growled.

"You don't like anyone," the younger man replied with a laugh. "Is there any particular reason this time?"

"No."

"Well, that's the same thing you said about Janey, and look how that turned out."

"I said you couldn't handle her, and you can't."

"I handle her just fine, thank you very much!" The

younger man paled suddenly and burst out, "I did not just say that! Don't you dare tell Janey I said that!"

Doc hadn't introduced himself yet, mostly because he hadn't decided whether or not to use his real name or an alias. But at the mention of a Janey... The world was really much smaller than it seemed. Especially the West.

"Pardon the interruption," Doc drawled. "The name's Doc Holliday."

The younger man turned, eyebrows high. "THE Doc Holliday?"

"The very one," Doc said with a grin.

"You know my wife," the man stated.

"Jane Falke?"

"The very one." The man stepped forward, grinning widely, and extended his hand. "Andrew Rufus. I heard you were dead."

"I was. For a minute."

Andrew seemed to accept that easily. "This is Doyle," he said pointing towards the grumpy older man. "He's the grumpy one. That's Joe." He pointed at the man sitting by the fire playing a harmonica softly. "He's the good-looking one. And that's Charlie. He can find anything."

Doc nodded towards them, thinking Andrew was a little bit strange; he'd never heard anyone introduce people like that.

"You're a gambler, right?" Andrew asked, sitting down beside Joe and motioning for Doc to sit as well.

"A gambler?" Charlie said, suddenly sitting forward, black eyes alert.

"Yes," Doc said.

"You good?"

Doc controlled his grin and merely shrugged a shoulder.

Part of the reason he was so good is because he never gave anything away.

"Poker?" Charlie asked eagerly.

"We playing for money?" Doc asked casually.

"Oh hell," Andrew groaned. "I can't watch. Doyle, make me coffee!"

Doc stared at the fire in his mind, soaking in that moment, the moment he'd first met Andrew. He had soon become one of Doc's closest friends; for a time, at least. Couldn't be friends forever. Death always felt the need to intervene.

"What exactly is your question?" Jury demanded, bringing Doc back to the present.

"What were we talking about?"

"This is your conversation. Why should I keep track?"

Doc laughed softly. Apparently Jury was still a little irritated. "Is there a difference between a witch and a shaman? My witch could walk through dreams, and that's apparently a big deal."

"Are you certain?" Jury asked.

"Yes."

"What else could she do?"

He'd never told anyone except Andrew and Jervis the whole truth about Señora Teodora. He'd told Thaddeus a little about her, but not all the details. It was a memory he kept for himself. He considered lying, but he needed Jury's help; and he knew from experience that Jury didn't like it when people lied to him.

"She made me into..." Doc searched for a word, but couldn't find one, so he finally said, "Whatever I am."

Jury's eyes were sharp now, intent. "How exactly did she do it? It has to do with your tattoo, right?"

"I can't tell you. She warned me that if I told others or

tried to change anyone else, the consequences would be dire."

Jury dismissed that with a careless wave. "Witches are always saying things like that."

"You would know," Doc muttered.

"It's not like I'm going to change anyone; I just want to know how she did it," Jury insisted.

"That's what they all say," Doc chuckled.

"But I really mean it! Who would I change anyway?"

"Your mother?" Doc suggested.

"God, no!"

"Then can we get back to the point?"

"What point?"

"The difference between witches and shamans."

"Right." Jury was silent for a moment, but he finally said, "I don't know what your definition of shaman is, but in the most clear-cut context, witches, such as myself, cannot traverse the dreaming. We are bound to the earth and the elements. People who can travel the dreaming are connected to an entirely different power source. Some call it the ether. Others call it the psychic realm. Still others call it the life force." Jury shrugged. "But who really knows?"

Doc shook his head irritably. He'd been looking for the wrong thing. All this time he'd thought she was a witch, so he'd been looking for a witch. He'd never paid much attention to the distinction.

"Do you know any?" Doc asked.

"Shamans?"

"People who can traverse the dreaming?"

Jury shook his head. "Even among the Hidden there are some things it's not wise to admit to. The BCA keeps a tight watch on certain... powers. To make sure they aren't misused, of course," Jury added derisively. "If I could travel the dreaming, I'd probably try to exist outside of the Hidden."

Doc stared into his empty coffee cup for a moment, thinking about what Jury had just said. He'd always considered the Hidden a safe place, a home for those the normal world would cast out or hate. He'd never realized there were dangers there, not like Jury was suggesting.

"I told you all I had was a question," Doc finally said, grinning widely.

"Sure... So this is the last time I'll see you? For what, another five years?"

"I don't think it'll be that long," Doc said carefully.

"You never do," Jury huffed.

Doc sighed, wondering how long it would take Jury to forgive him this time. "Thanks," Doc said as he stood. "I owe you one."

"That's a favor I hope I never have to cash in," Jury muttered.

"At least you know I'm good for it."

"Get out," Jury ordered. "And don't tell anyone you spoke to me. The BCA has been sniffing around lately, and I don't want anything to do with them."

Doc nodded solemnly. He was a cheat and a liar. He was a murderer and a thief. But he was loyal. And he never sold anyone down the river. Even if they were annoying.

"You could have told me she was a shaman," Doc said as he poured himself a glass of whiskey.

"I assumed you knew," Thaddeus retorted.

"Have you been out on the deck lately? I could put you up on the ledge; let you get some fresh air?" Doc threatened.

"I'm sorry," Thaddeus ground out. "I honestly didn't realize you didn't know."

"This is out of my skillset," Doc mumbled. "She should have realized that when she asked me."

"She knew you as a clever man who was unafraid to take risks. That was enough."

Doc waited for Thaddeus to go on, to add the insult, but he didn't. "I swear that's the nicest thing you've ever said to me," Doc said in surprise.

"Don't get used to it," Thaddeus snapped.

"Don't worry."

Doc rubbed his forehead. He never had actual headaches, but right now he felt like his head should hurt. "It's all really muddled. Jury said the Bureau of Cryptid Affairs likes to keep a watch on certain powers, but I thought the cryps were protected from surveillance by the original bylaws," Doc puzzled.

"Yes, governments are always quite scrupulous in following their own treaties and policies."

"You got me there," Doc sighed. "I don't know what I was thinking."

"Furthermore," Thaddeus intoned, "'keep a watch on' is code for 'lock up and study'."

"Lock up and study? That's insane! The Bureau is a governmental... Goddamn, what am I saying?"

"Yes, it is quite shocking how naive you still are."

"I'm not naive," Doc grunted. "I just... prefer to pretend that people are..."

"Basically good?" Thaddeus mocked.

"Now that's taking it a bit far."

"Nice?"

"Definitely not."

"Kind?"

"Alright, I get the point. I don't know what I was thinking.

I guess I'm a little off my game."

"Vampire venom has been known to affect the mental state," Thaddeus said.

"Worth it," Doc said cheerfully. "Ana is—"

"I know exactly what Ana is," Thaddeus snorted.

Doc sighed, remembering Ana's soft body and sweet kisses. It had been five years well spent, even if he was a little slower on the uptake. Not that he was. He'd just forgotten how revolting people as a whole were.

He paced the room for a moment, then said, "My shaman should be human, or at least humanoid, so she could exist as a norm. How am I going to find her?"

"You'll just have to get more creative."

"You are no help."

"I'm a plant! What do you want?"

"Yes, but you're an incredibly smart plant!"

"Fine. Back in the day, now this was two hundred and fifty years ago, mind you, I theorized that different creatures and people had different energy signatures. This was before electricity, you understand. I was working on a device that could measure these signatures so I could categorize them. Jefferson was funding my research, but obviously something went wrong." Thaddeus's voice trailed off, and Doc assumed he was lost in a memory.

He pondered Thaddeus's words for a minute, then said, "Unfortunately, that doesn't help me, old boy. For one, I'd just have to walk around testing everyone I came in contact with; and two, we have no baseline. I wouldn't be able to tell what any of the signatures meant."

"I did warn you."

"I need to clear my head," Doc said, pouring some whiskey into Thaddeus's container.

"Damn you, Doc!"

"Hush, it's good for you," Doc laughed.

Before long, Doc was sitting at a faro table dealing the cards. Faro had gone out of fashion a hundred years ago or more, but the House of Banshee had revived it as a personal favor. The table only ever operated when Doc was there to run it, but since he was something of a celebrity among the cryps, the faro table was always busy.

"You seem annoyed," Aine whispered.

"You're supposed to be counting the cards," Doc said. "Not lecturing me."

He deftly took one player's bet and paid out another player's.

"You've been gone for five years," she hissed. "Some people thought you were dead!"

"Some people betted on it," he laughed. "I hope you didn't."

"Doc!" she exclaimed. "Are you okay?"

"I'm fine, Aine darling, but honestly, you have to focus on the game. You missed the last two cards."

Aine huffed irritably, but turned her focus to the counter. After a couple hours of play, Doc held up his hands. "That's it for tonight, my friends."

Several of the players groaned, and Doc grinned. "If you need a chance to win back your money, check out one of the poker tables."

"Talk to me, Doc," Aine said. "I came to see you."

"You shouldn't have."

"I was worried about you."

"You shouldn't be."

"Doc!"

"I'm fine," he said, cupping her cheek gently and smiling

into her deep green eyes. "And you should know that. If I ever do die though... would you mourn me?"

"Don't make jokes," she whispered.

"I'm not. I'd prefer that you did." He smiled suddenly, good humor back in place. "So you missed me?"

She rolled her eyes. "I missed the business you bring to the tables."

"As if you need me," he laughed, gesturing around the large room. Every table was surrounded by both humanoids and cryptids, losing money, making money, and gaining favors. Somewhere out there Bennie was likely slithering around, collecting information to sell; and more deals were conducted among the tables and in the backrooms than in a hundred corporate boardrooms during the day.

The House of Banshee was the place to go if you were anyone in the Hidden. If you didn't have access to the House, you may as well fold and go back to bed. Certainly there were plenty of cryps who would never step foot near the House, and there were norms like Virgil who had full access.

The world of the Hidden was no different than any other. It had hierarchies and classes, but mostly just the haves and the have nots.

"I should go," he said, feeling droll once more.

"You can stay," Aine said hopefully.

"I'd better not." He kissed her hand, as he always did, and slid through the crush towards one of the side doors.

For once, time was not on his side. He'd made a promise, and he had every intention of keeping it. So he'd find a way.

# 5

Doc opened the House of Banshee's side door and stepped out onto the sidewalk, glancing around casually. No one noticed him; no one ever did. It seemed to him that if he just suddenly appeared on the sidewalk, someone should take notice; but Jury had once told Doc that the human mind ignored what it couldn't explain. Doc wished he could ignore it as well because it certainly had never made sense to him.

The House of Banshee was hidden, and when norms looked over, they saw two norm buildings. Actually, since this was a side door, even someone with the sight couldn't see it from the outside.

The only visible door was the front door, and if you had the sight and you were walking down the street, you might not even realize you were looking at a Hidden entrance except for two small details.

Most Hidden doors looked nothing like norm doors. They were typically ornate and made of materials like steel or brass or intricately carved wood. Very distinctive. In addition to that, all Hidden entrances were required to be marked with a bronze plaque, not unlike the Graves' plaque, noting what the entrance was for.

A team of witches worked for the Hidden government shielding new buildings, checking the shields on old buildings, giving and redacting eyes to see, along with a whole slew of other things Doc was certain he was better off not knowing.

Cards he understood. Chess he understood. He understood people and lust and greed. He understood loyalty and making love. But he didn't understand magic. Whenever he tried to focus on it, tried to understand it, his mind turned fuzzy. It was like trying to look at something you only glimpsed from the corner of your eye. Turn to face it, and it was gone.

The idea that someone could hide a building between two other buildings was completely foreign to him. He knew they'd done it; he simply couldn't understand how. Someday he'd ask Jury to explain it again.

He chuckled softly and rolled Jury's tooth over the top of his knuckles. Jury would be plenty irate when he realized he'd snatched a peanut, not his tooth. He may have magic, but Doc had sleight of hand. He laughed out loud, imagining Jury's face, and turned to walk towards his hotel.

The night air was dry and hot. Sometimes he missed the hot, humid air of the South, but every time he thought of it, a latent urge to cough stirred in his lungs. He breathed deeply, reminding himself that those weren't his lungs anymore. His lungs were strong and powerful, not feeble and full of blood.

A memory stirred, and he let himself be drawn into it.

"I've met my descendants," Señora Teodora said, gently holding a cup of water to Doc's lips so he could sip. It astounded him that he was so weak he couldn't even hold a cup of water. He'd done every man he'd ever killed a favor. At least they'd died on their feet.

"All of them," she added. "I meet them in dreams. Sofia is the last of them, my very last descendant, but something has happened to her, something unnatural, like a hand snatching her from the world."

"Like death?" Doc suggested, struggling to subdue a coughing fit that wanted out.

"No. Death I can sense. This is different."

"What does that have to do with me?" he asked.

"I need you to find her and save her."

He laughed fitfully. "Have you seen me? I'm nearly dead."

"Ah, but you needn't be."

The main door of Dulcis Requiem slid around Doc as he entered the lobby, returning him to the moment. Jervis told him constantly that revolving doors had long gone out of fashion, but Doc enjoyed it, so it stayed.

He strolled across the subtly elegant lobby and stepped into the elevator, smiling at the women who entered after him. "I do hope you're enjoying your stay," he drawled, words dripping with Southernism.

The younger woman blushed and twittered. "It's been lovely."

Doc took her hand and slowly kissed each of her knuckles. "I'd love for you to join me for dinner," he said.

Her eyes widened. "I... I don't even know your name!"

"My apologies. Holliday, John Holliday. Shall I stop by your room at say..." He pulled out his pocket watch and glanced at the time. It was already nine o'clock. "I suppose it's a tad late for dinner. How about dessert?"

Her lips moved, but no words came out. "I'm headed up to my suite now," he murmured. "What shall I have them send up? Chocolate? Strawberries? Wine?" She still didn't respond, so he said, "How about a little bit of everything?"

"She'd love to!" the older woman finally cut in. The elevator doors slid open, and the older woman grabbed the other woman's hand and pulled her into the hallway. "Just give us a moment, please."

"I'll hold the door," Doc chuckled.

"What on earth are you doing?" the younger woman hissed.

"Listen, Ferny, that's the legendary John Holliday. I have a friend who caught his interest, and she said it was the best thing to ever happen to her."

Doc grinned. It was nice to know his fame had spread.

"He is... a master in the bedroom," the older woman whispered.

"I'm getting engaged tomorrow!" Ferny exclaimed.

"Oh please. It's not as if you and Richard are pledging true love. It's a business deal. This is your chance to... I don't know, but if it was me he was asking, I'd already be up there!"

"Aunty Ruth! You're married!"

"I dare say even Howard would understand."

"I don't know," Ferny hedged.

Doc glanced at his watch. He was being rather indulgent, taking time out to play, but Ferny's silvery blond hair had caught his eye, and he just couldn't help himself. After all, what was the point of living if you didn't have fun?

It didn't bother him that she was engaged because there were two types of women in the world, available and unavailable. Things like marriage or age didn't factor into it in the least. He could tell within five seconds if a woman was available or not by the subtle shifts in her posture when she responded to his opening words.

"Ladies," he said, interrupting their tête-à-tête, "I'm sorry if I caused offense. I confess I'm feeling a bit lonely tonight and seeking some companionship, but I'll seek it elsewhere." He bowed slightly before turning back towards the elevator.

"No!" Ferny exclaimed. "I'd be honored... I mean, I'd love to keep you company for a spell."

He grinned. Worked every time. "I am the one who is honored," he said, turning and holding out his arm to her. "You remind me of a fairy slipping out into the moonlight."

She ducked her head, blushing furiously. Doc winked at Aunty Ruth and said, "I'll have her back by midnight."

"Don't rush on my account," Aunty Ruth said, grinning broadly.

And so it wasn't until the next morning that Doc remembered to text Tessa Graves to request a meeting.


"So this is your place," Tessa said as she circled Doc's living room. "It's very... modern."

"What did you expect?" Doc chuckled.

"I'm not sure. Old West posters? Skins on the floor? Guns on the wall?"

"I keep my guns in a safe," he laughed. "I'm not a fixed point, Tessa. You don't honestly expect me to be the same man I was a hundred years ago, do you?"

"No, I suppose not. And I've met enough immortals that you'd think I'd know that, but most immortals aren't memorialized in movies and media the way you are. You know what I mean?"

"Whiskey?" Doc asked instead of answering her question.

"It's ten in the morning."

"Can't hold your liquor?"

"What does that have to do with anything?" she exclaimed.

"What does the time of day have to do with anything?" he retorted.

She burst out laughing and said, "I guess I see your point."

He motioned for her to sit and sat across from her. He was never fully sated, and despite what he'd said the other day, she was a very beautiful woman. Sadly, he valued Virgil's work too much to cross him by sleeping with his daughter.

"Have you been searching for a witch or a shaman?" he asked.

"A witch."

"Are you aware of the difference?"

"I'm not sure how you mean it, but I am aware there are two different types of magic wielders. The ones who use earthly elements, and the ones who use spiritual elements."

"Sofia is the kind who uses spiritual elements."

"Ah." She was silent for a moment before saying, "That might complicate things."

"How so?"

She glanced around her, and Doc realized her mannerisms had shifted abruptly. She was nervous. Perhaps even a bit scared.

"You can speak freely here," he said softly.

"Are you certain?"

"Quite."

She licked her lips, and part of Doc wished she'd done it from arousal instead of fear. "Dad wouldn't like me talking to you about this."

"I won't tell him if you won't."

She smiled, but didn't laugh like he'd hoped. "There's been a strange movement over the last decade or so. The BCA has been... Well, that's the thing. Nobody really knows. Occasionally someone within the Hidden goes missing, and if they're traced, the trail gets lost somewhere near the BCA's back door."

She stood and started pacing. "You wouldn't believe how many people have gone missing either; in Denver alone over a hundred cryps have been reported. Things like this aren't supposed to happen!" she exclaimed. "The BCA's supposed to help keep the peace between norms and cryps. They're supposed to defend and help the cryptids, not..." She shrugged in frustration and said, "Whatever it is they're doing!"

"That's not entirely true," Thaddeus said from his perch on the end table.

Tessa shrieked softly, whirling around to look for the voice.

"Calm yourself," Doc soothed. "It's just Thaddy."

"Thaddeus Whythe, at your service, my dear."

Tessa was still frantically searching the room, so Doc stood and turned her to face Thaddeus. He honestly hoped she was more composed when she was investigating because right now she was nearly hysterical. He assumed it was because she was talking so freely about the Bureau.

"Tessa," he said, gesturing towards the plant, "this is Thaddy. My plant."

"Your plant?" she stuttered just as Thaddeus exclaimed the same thing.

"Yes. I water it; I feed it; I give it whiskey. That makes it mine."

"I hate whiskey, you libertine!"

"I know. That's why I give it to you."

Tessa was staring at Thaddeus with wide eyes. "Your plant talks," she whispered.

"Yes; unfortunately. Now, what do you mean about the Bureau, old boy?"

"Not unless you do something for me."

Doc sighed heavily and made a note on his mental to-do

list. Find a way to restore Thaddeus's body so he could run his own damn errands.

"What do you want?"

"Brandy."

"That's it?"

"Yes."

"Done! I'll have Jervis send it right up."

"I want the good kind!"

"Jervis will know which kind to get. Now tell me about the Bureau."

"Jefferson was a brilliant leader, but perhaps not the kindest man," Thaddeus said slowly.

"Oh hell. Is this another one of your history lessons?"

"Bear with me, and you might actually learn something for a change."

Doc sat back down with a sigh. "Settle in," he told Tessa. "We'll be here for a while."

"Cryptids have been around since time immemorial," Thaddeus said, dry voice refusing to inject any enthusiasm into his words. "So have witches, shamans, shapeshifters, both born and made, immortals, and frankly a whole menagerie of other creatures that defy classification.

"Among norms, the term cryptid simply refers to a creature that has not yet been studied, such as the supposed Bigfoot and Loch Ness monster, you understand?

"But within the Hidden, cryptid is a rather broad term that refers to any creature who is not a human. Even a witch is considered a cryptid, regardless of whether or not they are humanoid in form. A line has been drawn in the sand, if you will. Cryptids on one side. Humanity on the other."

This was why Doc avoided politics. Too many terms, too much classification, too many perceived differences.

"Many cryptids and other creatures can pass as human and have been doing just that for millennia," Thaddeus went on. "Some, however, cannot pass as human; but even if they are not humanoid, they often seem to possess humanlike thoughts and desires; and as such, they tend to migrate towards cities, build homes, and seek after the same things humans do."

"What do you mean?" Tessa demanded.

"I'll get there," Thaddeus rebuked.

"You have to just let him tell it in his own way," Doc said, pouring himself another glass of whiskey. "You can't hurry him along or ask questions, so don't even bother trying."

"But—"

"Hush," Doc said.

"As I was saying, before I was so rudely interrupted," Thaddeus continued. "When these creatures first arrived in the colonies, they hid, existing on the outskirts of society. But it doesn't take long for a smart man to realize how useful a cryptid can be. A norm is really rather pathetic in comparison to most cryptids or creatures of power. A witch, for instance, has control of the earthy elements. If a ruler is not a witch, he would like a league of witches at his command."

"But what does this—" Tessa began.

Doc lifted his finger to his lips to silence her. "Patience," he mouthed, rolling his eyes.

"I can see you, you know," Thaddeus snapped.

"Please continue, Thaddy. I'm on the edge of my seat here."

"Humph. In any case, rulers have been using cryptids for their own purposes since the beginning of it all, and the colonies were no exception. Washington used a small band of banshees to frighten and rout the British soldiers several times. In exchange for their cooperation, they were promised a safe haven. You can imagine how that turned out."

Doc certainly could. As Thaddeus had already reminded him, the government was not one to keep its word.

"Jefferson, however, devised a plan that would give these creatures what they so desperately wanted, in exchange of course, for their help when called open. Like an open favor, if you will."

Doc shuddered. He was well aware of the dangers of open favors.

"He negotiated a deal with the chieftains. Of every main city, they could have ten percent of the real estate, outside of government control, as long as they stayed hidden and never revealed their existence to the general public. A special government unit was formed, consisting of a norm ambassador and a cryptid ambassador. And that was the extent of it. Unless the US government called in a favor, and then it was up to the Hidden to deliver."

Doc suppressed a yawn. He'd learned many years ago, that the less interest he expressed, the longer the history lesson continued.

"It stayed this way until the Bureau was formed in 1985. The Bureau—"

"Wait," Doc interrupted, fully realizing that he'd pay for it later on. "You were already a plant long before the Bureau was formed. How do you know anything about—"

"If you would allow me to speak," Thaddeus broke in, "the answers to your question might become clear. Up until the mid-nineties I lived inside the office of Davis Brenner."

"Ah," Doc said.

"Who's Brenner?" Tessa asked.

"The original head of the Bureau," Doc said. "Please go on, Thaddy. Pins and needles."

"My throat is rather parched," Thaddeus complained.

"You don't have a throat, and your brandy is on its way."

"Fine. On the face of it, the Bureau is an extension of the ambassadorship. A way for the Hidden to interact with the world more fully. But the Bureau's true purpose is to study that which has not yet been studied and to find a way to harness all those vagrant powers. To use them. To forge them into the ultimate weapon."

For a moment, Thaddeus's words faded, and Doc stared at the small talking plant, fighting off that feeling, that horrible foreboding feeling. The feeling of eminent failure.

# 6

Three tedious hours later, and Thaddeus finally wound down. "And so, that is a very brief history of the actual purpose of the Bureau."

"Brief indeed," Doc murmured. "How about I take you into the bedroom now so you can be alone with your brandy?"

"That would be quite refreshing."

Doc picked up the plant, winking at Tessa as he did, and carried Thaddeus into the bedroom. "Here you are, old boy," he said, tilting quite a hefty portion of brandy into the pot.

"Now that's a gentleman's drink," Thaddeus sighed.

"Enjoy. You earned it."

Doc closed the door behind him, then sat across from Tessa once more. "We'll have to play a hand or two of cards," Doc said cheerfully, "before I can talk about serious things again. Thaddy tends to ramble, and I confess my mind is quite worn out. Do you play gin rummy?"

"Not well," she confessed.

"Then I shall help you become better."

He pulled a deck of well-worn cards from his vest pocket and began to shuffle.

"Are those pin-up girls?" she asked hesitantly.

"Certainly."

"Odd choice."

"I won them in a poker game."

"What's it like to live so long?"

"Are you this curious with all your clients?" he questioned as he swiftly dealt them each ten cards.

"No. But I didn't hold most clients' hands as a young girl either."

"Fair enough." He studied his cards briefly, categorizing them in his mind without moving them, and said, "It's interesting. I've seen more than I expected. And certainly made more love than I expected."

"Dad says it's all a game to you."

"Not true at all," he laughed.

"It's not?"

"Of course not. Games have rules." He drew and discarded, inserting the new card to the left of his hand.

"Life has rules," Tessa sputtered.

"It's your draw," he reminded her.

She drew and threw down a random card. He could tell because she didn't even look at her hand when she did it. She had no talent for distraction. Interesting.

He drew again. Discarded. "Your draw."

"Life has rules," she insisted again.

"Only if you let it." He smiled at her and laid his cards on the table. "Gin."

"What? How did you... But they're not in melds!"

"Sure they are," he said, deftly rearranging them.

"Oh." She stared at his cards for a moment, before placing her cards face-down on the table.

He stacked up the cards; but instead of dealing again, he put them away, and leaned back in his chair, kicking his feet up on the table.

"Back to the case," he said. "If I understand Thaddeus's unspoken subtext, although how he could have left anything unspoken I do not know, it would appear I'm looking for a shaman that the Bureau might also take an interest in. Which makes it imperative that I conduct my search quietly and quickly so I can find her before they do."

Tessa visibly paled. "But if you go against the BCA, your sight could be redacted. Not to mention—"

"Never mind that," he interrupted. "I know a fellow. And furthermore, if I don't find Sofia... I need to find Sofia."

"Why's she so special to you?" Tessa asked.

"I made a promise," he said, still remembering the moment like it was yesterday.

"Don't forget," Señora Teodora had said insistently, "her name is Sofia."

"I know," Doc replied, impatient now to get on with life. A life without death hovering over his head. Where should he go first? California? The old country? The jungles of Africa? "You wrote down everything," he reminded her. "The year, the city, her name, and everything else you thought might help. I read it. I know it by heart."

It was true. He didn't have to read something more than once to remember it. Unless it was worthless, in which case, he sometimes could force himself to forget, but he'd burned Sofia's details into his heart. He would never forget. He wouldn't fail. He would save her, and his debt would be paid.

"You must not go too long without feeding," she reminded him, worry making her forehead crease. "If you wait too long, you will lose control; but the longer you live, the better your control."

"I understand," he said, breathing deeply again and again. The last time he'd breathed like this had been so long ago he couldn't even remember it now. He felt like a new man. He was a new man. His only regret was that he couldn't say goodbye to Kate or Wyatt. They thought he was dead, and that was for the best.

"You have my eternal gratitude," she said sincerely.

"You'd better save it," Doc replied. "I haven't done anything yet."

"I don't understand," Tessa said, interrupting his memory. "Who did you make a promise to? You've never even met Sofia."

He studied Tessa's face for a moment, noting her pursed lips and crinkled eyes. As a child, she'd idolized him. She'd thought his sleight of hand nothing short of magical. She'd begged for stories of the old West. She'd asked him to teach her to ride a horse. He hadn't ignored her or told her to go away; instead he'd patiently indulged her inquisitive nature.

Tessa wasn't a little girl anymore though; she was a woman, but there was still a part of her that idolized him, wanted to know him, wanted to see what he saw. As a girl, it had been harmless. As a woman, it was deadly. He'd have to step very carefully.

"Tessa," he said suddenly as he stood. "You're off the case."

"What?!" she exclaimed.

"I don't want you crossing paths with the Bureau. I'll handle this on my own."

"But Doc, I can do this. I'm not scared of them."

"I never said you were." He smiled gently and took her hand to lead her towards the door. "You're anything but a damsel in distress, my dear; however, this search requires a different sort of means."

"I can help you—" she started to say, but he closed the door in her face and locked it behind him.

Not only was she dangerous to be around, but she also couldn't help him. She had access to Hidden circles, but anything she did would be noted, and if she bandied about, no matter how discreetly, that he was searching for a shaman, things were bound to get messy.

He needed a different sort of help entirely. He shuddered at the mere thought. Even if Tessa didn't bandy it about, things were about to get messy.

Doc gazed out his floor-to-ceiling window at the street far below. It had been nearly an hour since he'd kicked out Tessa, but he hadn't done anything except stare. If he was going to do this, he was going to have to get drunk. Really, really drunk.

Which was a bit difficult. He'd built up quite a tolerance in his time. Quite a tolerance indeed. He honestly couldn't remember the last time he'd been drunk.

He pulled out his phone and texted Jervis, "I need whiskey, and lots of it."

"Define 'lots'."

"Ten bottles." He wasn't sure that would do it, but he also wasn't sure he could drink more than that in one sitting.

"Certainly, sir."

Doc continued to stare out the window. If he wanted to find Sofia without arousing suspicion, he needed someone who could travel through dreams. Perhaps he was oversimplifying things, but that seemed like the easiest route. And he only knew two people with that kind of power.

One was a shaman whom Doc already owed a favor, and Doc wasn't keen to remind him of the unpaid debt.

The other was... a very, very enthusiastic succubus.

He was going to need to feed as well, because if he wasn't careful, she'd take more than he had to give.

"I'm feeling a bit peckish," he texted Bennie.

"Real shark, aren't you?"

"I suppose I can take my money elsewhere."

"What're you in the mood for?"

"Surprise me."

In less than half an hour, Doc had a name. Maggie Rubins. She'd gone to trial for murdering her husband and three kids. There was no doubt she'd done it. Her neighbors had called the police after hearing her angry screams, and when the police arrived they'd had to pull her off her dead son. She'd been carving holes in his chest with a fork.

She'd been found not guilty by reason of insanity. She'd claimed her husband was drugging her, although no evidence was found; and, after her acquittal, she'd been committed to a mental institution for a short time before being released.

Since she'd already been tried and acquitted, she'd gone on to write a book about her experiences entitled *The Freeing Power of Murder.*

Doc knew all about the power of murder.

Within the hour, Doc was sitting outside Maggie's house, watching the picketers parade back and forth.

"You should pay for your crimes!" one woman screamed.

"Your hands will never be clean!" one of the signs read.

It was disorder and chaos, and all they were accomplishing was feeding her fame.

Doc drove his red McLaren F1 a block further, then parked along the street behind Maggie's house. He exited his car, tossing a stern glare at the punk eyeing it from the corner. Something in his manner must have translated because the punk turned tail and ran.

Doc walked along the back of the houses until he reached Maggie's lot. He strolled through her yard and opened the back door, breaking the lock as he did.

"It's time for you to stop living vicariously through me," he heard a husky female voice say. "It's time for you to take the plunge."

"I don't mind killing my wife," a man's voice complained, "but do I have to kill the children? Can't I just sell them on the black market or something?"

"This isn't about money," she reprimanded him. "It's about power."

Doc grinned happily and muttered, "Two for the price of one."

"When you take their lives," she said, "you'll feel power like you never dreamed. You'll be reborn."

"She's lying," Doc drawled easily from the doorway of Maggie's library. "When you kill a man, you just kill him. There's no power there. If you want power, you have to do it my way."

"Who are you?!" Maggie demanded. "Are you one of those protestors? I'll have you and your whole bunch arrested!"

She reached for the phone, but just before her hand reached it, Doc's knife buried into it, destroying the electronics and pinning it to the desktop.

"Tut, tut," he said. "You believe in empowering others through murder, and I'm here to show you how it's really done. Aren't you the least bit curious?"

She was. He could see it in her greedy eyes. Her power was through mind control, not through murder.

"Shall I show you?" he murmured, eyes never leaving hers.

"Yes," she breathed.

Doc slowly unbuttoned his vest and shirt, revealing the large circular tattoo on his chest.

"Maggie," the man stuttered, "what's going on?"

"Be quiet," she ordered.

Doc grinned slowly as he stepped closer to them. "Death is essential," he said. "Without death, you can't have the soul."

Maggie's eyes were wide, and when she bit her lip, Doc knew he had her. His eyes didn't leave hers for a second as he pulled out another knife and shoved it into the man's quickly beating heart. He hadn't murdered his wife yet, but he was planning to, and that was good enough for Doc.

Blood poured through the man's shirt all over Doc's hand, but Doc didn't let go. Instead he used the knife to hold the dying man upright, waiting for the moment when his tattoo would begin to burn.

Maggie's eyes suddenly dropped to Doc's chest, widening even further; and Doc knew the tattoo had begun to glow. Heat pooled as it pulled the man's essence from his being and into Doc. Then it spread, flooding Doc with raw energy.

He pulled out the knife, and the dead man dropped to the floor. "Now that's true power," Doc confided, stepping close enough to touch her.

"Show me again," she whispered.

"It would be my pleasure," he said, smiling as he thrust the bloody knife into her belly.

Her eyes shifted from pleasure to confusion, and she tried to pull away from him. "No," he said, holding her closer. "I want you to feel it. I want you to suffer. Just like your children suffered."

She clawed at his chest, but he didn't budge, just watched her face pale more and more as she realized she was going to die. She was going to die, and she was powerless to stop it.

"My mother loved me," he whispered in her ear as her body began to shake violently. "That's true power."

She stopped fighting him, and in another moment he was holding dead weight. His chest grew hot, and he felt her essence flow into him, adding another layer to his inhuman strength.

"Too easy," he murmured as he let her fall to the floor like a broken doll. "I prefer it when they put up a fight."

# 7

"I can't believe I'm doing this," Doc murmured, words barely slurred. "I've drank all ten bottles, and I'm scarcely drunk. She nearly killed me last time; I need to be completely off my game."

"That makes no sense," Thaddeus said sanctimoniously.

"For every one thing you think you know," Doc declared, "there're a thousand things you don't. Silbu is a succubus. She's a dream walker who feeds off sex."

"Sounds right up your alley."

"In theory, but the more satisfied she is, the more she feeds. And in my case, for instance, if she was very, very satisfied... Well, you get the idea."

Something happened then that rarely occurred. Thaddeus started laughing.

"It's not funny," Doc grumped.

"It really is," Thaddeus laughed.

"I still have some whiskey left."

"I don't even care!"

Doc sat on his bed and stared wryly at the plant. Even

after all these years, it still unsettled him to hear and respond to a disembodied voice. He knew it came from the plant. He could hear it coming from the plant, but he didn't understand it. How could a plant talk? It didn't have a mouth, or ears and eyes for that matter.

"How did you end up a plant?" he asked suddenly.

Thaddeus abruptly stopped laughing. "In twenty years you've never asked."

"It's none of my business, and I try to curb my curiosity when it's needed."

"Ah, well as it happens, it relates to your situation, so I'll tell you."

Doc waited patiently. He was in no hurry to go to sleep.

"I was working on my energy signature device," Thaddeus began. "But Jefferson also wanted me to figure out a way to measure the power of creatures. A rating system, if you will. A great deal of power, we would assign a ten. So for instance, you would probably rate a seven or an eight, Ana a six, Bennie a two, and so on and so forth. But that's much too arbitrary, and it's also based on non-scientific elements like your individual personalities. Your power alone doesn't make you a seven. It's you. Who you are, you understand?"

Doc wasn't sure that he did, but he nodded anyway.

"We wanted to be able to accurately measure it, and in my travels to collect... specimens, I met a native woman who was a very powerful shaman. In fact, if I were to rate her, I would give her a fifteen, that is how powerful she was. I tried to convince her to come with me, to help me with my device, for the benefit of all the others, you understand, but she was too clever for that. She knew better than to trust the word of an invading white man."

Thaddeus sighed. "I really believed I'd be helping

mankind and the others. I believed in the end, Jefferson's plan would serve everyone. The end often justifies the means, you know. But I was wrong."

Doc raised an eyebrow. He'd never heard Thaddeus admit he was wrong, even if he was.

"A year or two later, some hunters brought me what they thought was a witch. She wasn't. She was a shaman, but they didn't know the difference. In power, she was perhaps a three. A disappointment, but what chance did a mere human have of procuring anyone over a certain power range? This thought spurred me. I began to think the others would overwhelm us or conquer us if we did not conquer them first."

Thaddeus did not speak for a very long time. Finally he said, "I am not proud of what I did. I deserved to die, horribly. Somehow the powerful shaman became aware of my actions, and she visited me. Her fury was like nothing I'd ever seen, but oddly enough, she didn't lay a finger on me.

"She looked me over once and said 'You will watch, and you will learn to feel pain.' Light began to glow all around her, and the next thing I remember was waking up without my human form. At first I thought I was a ghost, but as time passed, I became aware that I was a plant, a living, thinking plant; and I was sitting on the edge of Jefferson's desk.

"The absurdity did not escape me," Thaddeus murmured. "Were I to reveal my presence, Jefferson would hand me over to his scientists, who would poke and prod at me, cut off my leaves and test them under the microscope, freeze me or expose me to a concentrated sunbeam just to see how I would react. In the end... Well, I suppose it was a fitting punishment."

Thaddeus fell silent, and Doc didn't say a word. If he'd been there, he'd have killed Thaddeus without a moment's thought. He certainly wouldn't have turned him into a plant.

On the other hand, perhaps Thaddeus had changed. For all the good it did him.

"If you wish, you can push me off the deck ledge," Thaddeus murmured.

"Tempting," Doc replied. "But I have other things to do tonight, and I can't be certain it would kill you."

He opened his last bottle of whiskey and quickly drank most of the bottle before dumping the rest of it into Thaddeus's pot.

"I deserved that," Thaddeus sighed.

Doc slowly stripped, trying to gird himself for what was to come. He climbed into his bed and closed his eyes, allowing every moment of pleasure he'd ever experienced to run through his mind.

There were a lot. Some stood out more than others, but most of them blurred together into a reel of his greatest hits. Women moaning and shrieking in pleasure. Women screaming his name. Women collapsing to the bed, totally spent and boneless.

"Silbu," he whispered. "Come to me." He cupped breast after breast, enjoying every shape and texture, applying just the right amount of pressure to bring pleasure. "Silbu," he sighed, imagining her pale form and clear blue eyes.

He drove deep inside each of them, stroking their insides, lighting fire to their rapture, carrying them over the edge into the deep ocean of bliss and endless pleasure.

"Holliday." His name whispered over his skin like fingernails, and he knew she'd come. "It's dangerous for you to be here," she breathed, her form becoming solid. She was naked, clothed only in the darkness of dreams, and her pale form was pressed against his, arousing him fully.

Her tongue gently traced his ear, while her hand caressed

his length. "What do you want?" she murmured, claws scraping gently down his chest.

"You."

"And you shall have me, but if you please me, what is it you want in return?"

"A favor," he managed to say.

"You are worth a favor," she purred, her hair falling around his face like a curtain. "Please me, and you may have whatever you ask."

So he did. Several times. He lost count of how many times, but she still moaned for more. He had one last trick up his sleeve; if it didn't win the hand, he was lost.

"Lay still," he ordered. Then he licked his way down her limber body until he reached the center of her heat, and he used his tongue, hoping his luck would hold.

She began to writhe beneath him, crying out words he didn't understand until finally she screamed so loudly the sound pulsed through the dreaming on all sides.

Doc didn't stop. Not until she'd stopped moving and ceased her moaning. Then he collapsed beside her, feeling completely and utterly spent. He hadn't felt this horrible since... since he'd died.

For a while neither of them spoke. When she finally did speak, her voice was wholly satisfied. "My, my," she purred silkily. "I dare say that was even better than last time."

He couldn't even summon the strength to laugh.

She wrapped herself around him, her form much more liquid than a human, and ran her fingertips down the center of his chest. "Stay with me," she murmured.

Now he did laugh. "As much pleasure as I find in your arms, I wouldn't last another minute with you. You know that."

"Perhaps." She kissed him, and he struggled not to fight her. Too much more, and he'd be dead. For real and for true this time.

"What is it you desire?" she whispered softly.

"I'm looking for someone," he replied. "A woman. She can travel dreams."

"Interesting."

"I was hoping you could help me find her."

"Perhaps. You must tell me everything you know, and I will look."

Doc sighed in weary relief. If Silbu somehow found Sofia, the way he felt right now might actually be worth it.

When Doc woke, he felt old and decrepit. Which was not a feeling he was used to. At least not anymore. His throat was so dry he could barely swallow, and his head was actually throbbing. If this was what it felt like to be mortal, he was glad that he wasn't.

"I'm asking you to give away your mortality," he remembered Señora Teodora saying. "It's not something to be given away without thought. You will die before the sun sets, but if you agree to this, you may never die. Not unless someone takes great pains to kill you."

"I rather like the sound of that," Doc croaked.

"Your friends will die around you. You will never age. Your seeds will not grow. You will be all alone."

Said like that it didn't sound so wonderful. But still... He stared out the hotel window at the gently falling snow. He'd like to swim in the ocean again. He'd like to make love to a woman without his lungs crying out in pain. He'd like to walk an entire city block without needing a shot of whiskey to keep going.

"I'll do it," he said.

"Hangover?" Thaddeus asked, interrupting Doc's thoughts.

"Don't talk so damn loud," Doc snarled.

"I wasn't," Thaddeus whispered.

"Sorry. My head. It aches. I haven't felt this way... since the last time." He shuddered. He hoped he never saw Silbu again, except of course when she told him where Sofia was. He needed that.

"I need a snack," he muttered, pushing up from the bed.

"And soon," Thaddeus murmured. "To put it kindly, you look like hell."

Doc stumbled over to the mirror and studied himself. So this is what it would look like to be a hundred. He was lucky Silbu hadn't asked for anything more. If she had, he'd be dead right now.

"Mental note," he said, grimacing at himself in the mirror. "Stay away from Silbu."

He laughed softly. It seemed he was wrong. Even after all this time, he wasn't quite ready to die. He could lie to himself and say it was because he still had a list of favors to repay, but the truth was he enjoyed living.

He wasn't sure he could wait for Bennie to scare up a criminal. The longer he waited, the weaker he would get and the less control he'd have; and then he might do something he would regret, like kill his plant-watering maid.

He needed a meal, and he needed one fast.

"Is there anyone staying in the hotel that society would be better off without?" he texted Jervis.

"Certainly, sir. Two floors beneath you, in room 304, there is a gentleman who is rough with the ladies. Try to make it look like an accident."

He could do that. He quickly pulled on a pair of trousers

and a shirt, buttoning it as he walked towards the door. He didn't bother with shoes. He wasn't sure he had the energy to both bend over and stand back up.

He rode the elevator down to the third floor. His luck prevailed, as it so often did, because both the elevator and the hallway were empty. He staggered to the right room and knocked on the door.

After a moment a large Scandinavian looking man, with a broad forehead and bulging muscles opened the door.

"This might be harder than I expected," Doc muttered. "Do you happen to have a drink?" he drawled.

"A drink? Who are you?"

"Holliday. John Holliday. I just wanted to stop by, check on your accommodations, make sure everything is to your liking."

"You are the owner?"

"Indeed."

"The room is fine, but the women, eeh; perhaps you can point me in the direction of someone a little more... how do you say... rich."

"Hum." Doc leaned on the doorway, wishing he'd grabbed at least one knife, and pretended to ponder. "I have a few names I could share," he finally said. "I'll write them down for you if you'll get me a pen."

"Where are your shoes?" the man suddenly asked.

"Ah... It's a spiritual journey. For a year, I must go everywhere without shoes."

"Strange. Come in."

Doc stepped inside the room, breathing a sigh of relief when he heard the door close behind him. He was barely standing at this point. He swayed, grabbing hold of the nearby lampstand to keep himself steady. He felt the cold metal under his hand and wrapped his fingers around the shaft, lifting it from the floor and waiting until the man bent over the desk in search of a pen.

"I know it's here somewhere," the man said just as Doc swung the top of the lamp down on his head. The man grunted, but didn't fall, instead he turned with a surprised expression and demanded, "What was that for?"

"There was a fly," Doc said, subtly shifting the lamp in his hand to block the attack he knew would be coming.

"I'll squash it," the man said, standing up straight and popping his knuckles menacingly.

"Oh hell," Doc muttered.

The man rushed towards him, and Doc ducked to the side, but he was a little too slow. The man's fist caught the edge of Doc's head, and he fell backwards, landing on the floor with a crash.

He wasn't used to moving so slow; in fact, he hadn't had to work this hard in decades. If he didn't play his cards right, he'd be meeting up with Death sooner rather than later.

He swung the lamp up like a javelin just in time to stop the man from crushing him against the floor. The man rammed into the lamp shaft, uttering a word Doc didn't recognize but completely understood; and Doc shoved with all his might, thrusting the man away, and scrambled to his feet. If only he had a knife this would already be over.

He blocked a wild punch and another, but he knew he needed to end it before he was too weak to even hold the lamp. He quickly glanced behind him, taking stock of the room, then moved two steps to the right.

"Come and get me," he taunted.

The man roared angrily and rushed toward Doc, arms extended to trap him. Doc waited until the last second before stepping quickly to the side and bringing the lamp down on the man's back. The man stumbled, then fell, bashing his head on the end table. Doc didn't wait to see if he was dead, just jumped on his back and wrapped his arms around the man's neck, choking him out. The man didn't fight; he was already unconscious, but he wasn't quite dead.

Doc knew when he was dead because that was the moment his tattoo began to heat up. He sighed in relief as the man's considerable life force rushed into the tattoo and out into Doc's body, revitalizing him, making him new once more.

"Ahh," he sighed, letting it fully soak into his bones. "So much better."

He stood, stretching as he did, feeling relief when his bones didn't creak. Then he surveyed the room with a frown. "Uh-huh," he muttered. "Jervis is not going to like this."

# 8

"Enjoy your breakfast?" Thaddeus asked as Doc reentered the bedroom.

"Not particularly. Jervis failed to mention that the man was twice my size, and since he asked me to make it look like an accident, I didn't take any knives. You would think I would know better by now, and if you start laughing again, I'll kick you off the deck into traffic."

"I wouldn't dream of it," Thaddeus murmured, amusement coloring his voice.

"Of course you wouldn't," Doc snorted.

"Room 304 needs a very thorough cleaning," Doc texted Jervis.

"So it doesn't appear to be an accident?" Jervis texted back.

"Only if there's a rhino on the rampage."

"I'll take care of it, sir."

"I don't know what I'd do without you," Doc said.

"You wouldn't," Jervis replied.

Lady Luck had definitely been riding Doc's coattails the day he had stumbled onto Jervis. Doc simply couldn't imagine life without him. It was a damn good thing vampires were immortal; and fortunately, Jervis was one of the few vampires who could remain in the norm world without anyone taking notice of him because he was also a shapeshifter.

Jervis didn't change into another creature like some cryptids; he just changed. In fact, he could change his face and form by the minute if he wanted to. So every fifteen years or so, Jervis changed faces and names, and no one even noticed.

Norms were terribly unobservant, which was why Doc was also able to stay in the norm world. On paper, he was James Logan the third. He'd also been James Logan Junior and James Logan Senior. Quite the family resemblance.

Doc chuckled at the thought before calling the kitchen and ordering a full breakfast. Señora Teodora hadn't specified whether or not he needed actual food, maybe she hadn't known. He didn't usually feel mortal hunger; but, regardless, he sometimes ate just for the pleasure of it.

While he was waiting for his food to arrive, he showered and shaved. He rather missed Ana's daily administrations. She could handle a straight razor better than any barber he'd ever met. It didn't hurt that if she "accidently" cut him, she always licked the wound clean.

When his breakfast arrived, he poured the coffee and took a sip, allowing it to sit on his tongue for a moment before swallowing it. He'd had better. He smiled as a memory swelled in his mind.

"Burnt biscuits!" Andrew exclaimed, spewing coffee all over the campfire. "You're trying to kill me! I swear, if you make the coffee one more time, Charlie, I'm gonna..."Andrew trailed off, and Doc noticed that Charlie's eyebrow was raised in question. "Nothing," Andrew mumbled.

Doc chuckled softly as he took a sip of his own coffee. It tasted all right to him. He studied the four other men over the fire, watching them interact. He didn't understand their dynamic at all, and it was rare when he didn't understand something.

Andrew acted as if he was... not scared, but concerned of what Charlie might do, which didn't make sense. Although he was the youngest, Andrew was clearly their leader, and he practically oozed power. The others were obviously dangerous; in fact, Doc would probably go out of his way not to pick a fight with them, but compared to Andrew... The man literally reeked of... Doc wasn't sure. But it made the others pale in comparison.

"It's not like it's not a rule," Andrew said irritably. "Pecos said it was a rule, so it's a rule."

Charlie shrugged.

"Doyle, make me some damn coffee," Andrew ordered.

The memory faded as Doc took another sip of his modern coffee. He had to admit that Andrew was right. Doyle's coffee was like no other coffee known to man. It made Charlie's coffee taste like water, but right now he'd settle for Charlie's. Modern coffee was... It just lacked something. Most food did.

But Doc made a conscious effort not to think about it. If he focused on all the things he didn't like about modernity, he'd go insane; so he didn't. In the end, coffee was coffee, and a steak was a steak. Being able to breathe without hacking up a handful of blood was worth it.

He took a bite of pancake and tried to steer his thoughts in another direction, but Andrew's voice was still fresh in his mind. It had been nearly sixty years since he'd seen Andrew, and he was suddenly gripped with a desire to visit him and have an existential conversation, but he knew he couldn't. Not only would the Andrew who lived in this time not know him, but Doc would very likely screw up everything. And it was imperative he not screw up anything.

Time was messy. Too messy. If Doc went around talking to people he wasn't supposed to talk to, who knew what would happen. He certainly didn't want to find out. Besides, he needed to focus.

"Sofia, Sofia," he muttered. "Where are you?" She could be his plant-watering maid or a stranger he passed on the street, and he would never know. He'd give Silbu two days to find her, and then he'd move onto other avenues.

Jury wouldn't appreciate being considered an avenue. And furthermore, since he was still mad at Doc, he wasn't likely to help unless Doc had something to offer in return. Something besides women, whiskey, and money.

"So what kind of things do witches covet?" Doc asked lazily.

"I'm not a witch," Thaddeus grumbled.

"But apparently you studied them for your power meter thingy."

"I studied them for science, not for gift giving!" Thaddeus snapped. "Why don't you ask one of your witch friends?"

Doc shook his head with a shudder. "I don't think I'm up to it yet."

"Silbu really took it out of you, didn't she?"

"If you say that name again, I'll give you a whole bottle of whiskey."

"What name? Silbu?"

"I warned you," Doc growled as he stood.

"You're out of whiskey. Remember?"

"Hell. I need some air."

Within the hour, Doc was strolling along the carefully trimmed hedges of the Denver Botanic Gardens. He wasn't a nature man, per se, but he appreciated beauty in all its forms; and sometimes being out in the air helped him think.

He checked the date on his phone, and an anxious chill ran down his spine. In four days, Sofia would be gone. He didn't know if that meant she was dead or just unreachable for some unknown reason. He definitely should not have indulged in that last year with Ana.

If he'd found Sofia sooner, he could have hidden her away and then lost himself to wild gambling and sex. There was a reason he hadn't though. There was a reason he'd waited.

Time was chaos, and there was a part of him that had worried that if he hid her away he would inadvertently cause whatever happened to her. If he waited until the last minute, however, he could be sure he'd saved her, not doomed her. At least that was his theory. It was a little muddled in his mind.

As far as he was concerned, speaking to someone in the dreaming from the future and then setting someone on a path to change that future was the equivalent of time travel, or at the very least, time meddling; and he'd only known two people who had any actual knowledge, not just theoretical knowledge, about how time worked. And no matter what they said, he still wasn't convinced that his actions wouldn't cause the event he was trying to prevent. So he'd stayed away. Until the very last minute. He just hoped he hadn't stayed away too long.

He had a sudden craving for a cigarette, which was strange. He'd smoked his last cigarette a week before he'd "died", and he'd coughed so hard afterwards that he'd really believed he was going to die right then and there. But he hadn't.

He hadn't died because Señora Teodora had come, and she'd saved him. Her face swam in his mind, crystal clear, and he watched her lips move as she tried to warn him of what was to come.

"Your time is nearly at an end," Señora Teodora had said. "I must put you into a death sleep so everyone will believe you have died. Once they have buried you, I will retrieve you and revive you."

"You're going to let them bury me?" Doc coughed, feeling his first hint of unease.

"It is the only way. Drink this."

She held a leather wineskin to his lips, and he studied her over it. As far as he could tell she was telling the truth, and even if she wasn't, what did he have to lose?

He carefully began to sip, stopping every few seconds to cough. When the bag was empty, she smiled gently and said, "Rest now. I will see you soon."

Everything started to grow hazy. Señora Teodora was gone, and Kate was sitting by his side, weeping. He tried to speak to her, tried to say it was all right, but his lips wouldn't move. His eyelids slowly slid closed, and everything was darkness.

Doc blinked, allowing the memory to slip away and forcing his eyes to focus on the carefully trimmed evergreen tree in front of him. He had to find Sofia. He'd give Silbu one night, and then he'd visit Jury again.

He briefly considered perusing the high-end shops within the Hidden and looking for an item to bribe Jury with, but he was certain it would be a waste of time. Jury had plenty of money; if he wanted something that was so obviously available, he'd buy it himself. So Doc needed to find something that wasn't available.

I'm getting a little tired of texting Bennie, he thought as he pulled out his phone.

"I need a list of meal options, and also, do you have a line on any items of magical significance that I might be able to acquire within the next twenty-four hours?"

"My rate for quick deals is double," Bennie replied.

"Fine."

"I'll send you a list."

It was a good damn thing Doc was rich, because if he wasn't, Bennie's fees would soon drive him into the poorhouse. He chuckled softly, imagining Bennie in his worm form guarding his mound of treasure like a dragon of old.

Too bad all the dragons had been slaughtered by pious sheep. He would have really liked to see one. When this was over, maybe he would take a little trip to Asia. If dragons still existed somewhere, it would probably be there. Of course, they'd most likely be hiding in the mountains somewhere, and that wasn't really his motif. But, if he could convince Jury to go with him... One thing at a time.

He wandered through the prairie section while he waited for Bennie's response, pausing when he saw a young woman ahead of him on the path, avidly reading each of the signs she passed.

"Rather silly, isn't it?" he asked her in an undertone.

"What is?" she responded, meeting his gaze and holding it.

"To go through all the trouble of cultivating a prairie section."

His lips twitched upwards, and she returned his grin, but asked, "Why's that?"

"Just drive ten miles or so east, and you'll find all the prairie you can stand."

Her grin widened, and she leaned in and whispered, "Yes, but do they have the handy little signs identifying the species?"

"You've got me there," he chuckled. "I've never seen a handy little sign in the wild. Someone should fix that." She finally laughed. Maybe he wasn't as worn out as he'd thought he was.

"Which part of the garden do you prefer?" she asked.

"The part with the flowers," he replied. She laughed again, and he inquired, "What about you?"

"I'm studying the high plains ecosystem, so the prairie."

"So you actually come here to look at the signs?"

"Mostly. It helps me work out problems sometimes," she said with a wide smile.

He wanted to touch her causally, just to see how her skin felt, but he could tell from her manner, no matter how friendly, that she wouldn't appreciate it. She had an imaginary boundary surrounding her, warning everyone to steer clear.

She wasn't like Ferny, good for an easy relaxed tumble. She was a forever woman; the kind of woman you fought for, and once you won, you didn't let her go. Too bad. He would have really liked to know if his guess about her hidden skin color was correct.

He smiled genially. "Today, my favorite part of the garden is right here." He gave her a slight bow and turned to leave. She didn't call him back. He'd known she wouldn't. She wasn't that kind of woman.

His phone beeped, and he glanced at it. Good old Bennie. A five-course meal and three different magical items that might be obtainable if the right sort of leverage was applied. He'd start with the first one.

I should've worked backwards, Doc thought as he stared at the strange, haphazard house in front of him. It was hidden at the back of an old church building, which he thought was rather amusing since it most likely belonged to a witch.

Most of the Hidden didn't put stock in the idea of god or religion, and he didn't blame them. He didn't either. How could you have faith in something that ignored your very existence? The Bible, for instance, was very cut and dried. People, animals, plants, and some very, very bad people who cavorted with the devil to gain special powers.

What about the vampires, who were born not made, and neither good nor evil? What about the shapeshifters, like Bennie, who belonged to both the clan of man and the clan of Worms? What about Silbu, who existed only in the dreaming? What about him?

He much preferred Señora Teodora's version of things, although he'd often wondered if he was keeping all the people he'd killed from returning to the earth. It didn't bother him if he was. He was probably doing the earth a favor keeping all those corrupted souls locked up tight, but still he wondered.

There were other theories about death and the afterlife, but he'd talked to so few people who had actually died, that he couldn't prove anything one way or the other. And so he leaned towards Señora Teodora's point of view because he liked it the best and it lined up with Janey Rufus's theories about the mother.

None of which had anything to do with the task at hand. He needed something to bribe Jury with, and that something was possibly inside this... interesting domicile.

He walked towards it, ignoring the way the windows watched him. And they were watching him. He'd seen them narrow suspiciously at his approach, just like human eyes. If a plant could be sentient, why couldn't a house be?

He knocked on the door and waited. He could easily just walk inside, but he had enough enemies as it was, and he wasn't interested in making more. Furthermore, he'd learned a long time ago it was far better to make friends with a witch than enemies.

No one came, but the door opened, even though it had been tightly closed when he'd knocked.

"Thank you?" Doc murmured, not really sure if he was grateful or not. He stared down the darkened hallway. He did not like this. Not one little bit.

"Anyone home?" he called out. No response.

He slid one foot into the hallway, holding his breath. He'd once gone into Jury's house without permission, and it had not gone well for him. He slid the other foot in and closed his eyes with a cringe, waiting. Nothing happened. He stepped fully into the hallway, and the door snapped closed behind him.

He chuckled softly. He could tell this was one of those days. The days when his luck had deserted him, taken a vacation, a hiatus, a holiday. It'd be back tomorrow. If he was still here to come back to.

# 9

Doc walked slowly along the dark hallway, whistling softly. The lights suddenly turned on, illuminating his path, and a shiver ran down his spine. He was not a fan of magic.

The hallway was cluttered with strange paintings that moved in the light and shelves full of slowly twirling curios. If Doc was certain that one of the moving objects would strike Jury's fancy, he'd be inclined to grab one and run. But in his experience, people, especially witches, did not put their valuables on display.

There was a large stain on the hallway rug, but Doc didn't bother to examine it. He'd killed enough men to know it was blood, even if it wasn't bright red anymore. The question was whose blood was it?

He entered the first room he came to. It was a circular sitting room filled with cozy chairs and tables of many heights. Books were stacked haphazardly on every surface. Some were so old the covers were crumbling; others had thin backs made of glossy paper. He picked up one with a naked woman on its cover and read the title. *A Love that Binds.* Romances? This was getting stranger by the second.

He entered room after room. Each room boasted a different set of curiosities, but no witch. After he'd searched the entire first and second floor, he stood at the foot of the stairs leading up to the attic. He was quite certain the witch was gone. He was also certain that she had not left of her own free will.

Taking a deep breath, he started up the narrow stairway. The door at the top of the staircase opened on its own, and Doc stepped into the room. The large, damp stains on the rough floor told him that at least three people had died in this room. Recently.

And the fact that the bodies were gone told him that whoever had come had more than four men to spare. The witch was gone. Someone had taken her. Someone even a witch and a sentient house couldn't stop.

He frowned, wondering who might have taken her and why, but he stopped himself from following the thought. He didn't have time to get wrapped up in something else right now. After he found Sofia he could get as wrapped up as he wanted, but until then, he needed to keep his mind focused and clear.

He turned on his heel and headed towards the door. It slammed closed. "Very funny," he muttered. "I came; I saw; I'm leaving now." He tried the doorknob. It was locked. He twisted his hand to break the lock, but it held.

"I'll kick it down if I have to. Let me out!" The door remained closed. "This is a fine state of affairs," Doc grumbled. "Locked in a room with no whiskey and no women. I may as well be dead."

He chuckled softly, imagining exactly which women he'd prefer to be locked in a room with. After a moment of indulgence, he turned to survey the room more carefully.

In contrast to the rooms downstairs, this room was empty except for a bed in the very center, standing right smack on top of a large painted symbol on the floor. Doc pushed the bed to the side and took a photo of the symbol with his phone so he could ask Jury what it meant.

This room was completely at odds with the personality of the rest of the house, but Doc had a feeling it was the most important area in the entire house. Maybe that was because the bed was covered in luxurious blankets and fluffy pillows. Doc ran his hand over the rumpled bedspread. It was nearly as soft as a woman's skin.

He'd like to meet this witch, whoever she was. She seemed... intriguing. But without her in the room with him, he wasn't interested in staying.

The small gable window was shuttered so he punched out the wood and looked out onto the church's parking lot. He could climb down, but he'd rather not. There had to be an easier way.

He walked back to the door. Still locked. "What is it you want me to see?" he finally asked. Nothing. Apparently sentient houses didn't talk.

He combed the room again. This time he ran his hands over the walls and tapped on the paneling. He checked under the window ledge. He searched the floor for vents. Nothing. Eventually, he stood in the center of the room and thought, if this were my room, where would I hide something?

His eyes quickly assessed the room once more, halting on the bed. It was an old cast-iron bed, probably older than he was, and he remembered lying naked in a very similar bed once. Kate's bed. He also remembered that the tubing had been hollow, and Kate had hidden a locket that her mother had given her inside one of the rails.

He pushed the mattress to the floor and studied the frame. There were plenty of rails to hide something in, but the question was, how did you access what was hidden? He looked under the four corner post caps, but found nothing.

No one ever made it easy, did they? He ripped the bed apart, rail by rail, shaking each piece and looking inside. Finally, on the very last rail, he found what he was looking for. A small bag had been fastened inside, and he wiggled his fingers into the rail and pulled it out.

"What are you?" he whispered, opening the bag and dumping the contents into his hand. Irritation filled him. It was a rock. A plain and ugly rock at that.

That's it. He was breaking down the door and getting out of here. He shoved the rock into his pocket and turned to the door. It was already open. Apparently the house was done with him.

After exiting the living house, Doc climbed into his car and considered his options. He could go lose himself in cards for an hour or two just to clear his head. He could lose himself in a woman for an hour or two, better make it three, to really clear his head. He could go see Jury empty handed, or he could look for the next item on his list and hope it was better than this one.

In less than four days, Sofia would be lost to him.

He shifted into first gear and headed towards the second address on his list. Hopefully this witch was home and could be persuaded by large sums of money or, if she was a she, extremely personalized attention.

The address was in the middle of a suburban norm neighborhood, and Doc sat in his car for a moment, studying the house's outer facade. It looked totally normal. Which bothered him. He felt like there should be at least one gargoyle guarding the door.

He meandered up the sidewalk, watching the windows and feeling a hint of disappointment when they didn't move. It was just a normal house, in a normal neighborhood. Why would a witch subject themselves to living in such normality?

Just as he was studying the very precise length of the grass, the front door burst open and a small red-haired girl tore wildly down the sidewalk, shrieking, "I won't eat it! You can't make me!"

"I can too!" an older girl yelled back, charging after her.

Doc waited until the little girl was nearly past him, then reached out a hand and caught her by the back of her pink unicorn shirt.

"Looking for this?" he asked.

"Who the hell are you?" the older girl demanded, yanking the small child from his hold and backing towards the door.

Doc bowed slightly and grinned his most charming grin. "John Holliday. I was hoping to speak with Mister or Missus Baker? Do they happen to be home?"

"No!" she snapped. "Now go away. I'm busy."

"Ah, yes. Your little screaming banshee." He glanced around discreetly. "I do hope it's no one we know."

The girl's lips curled slightly before she managed to control them. "Banshees aren't real," she said firmly.

"That's not true at all. I know a very lovely one named Aine."

"Do you really?" she gasped.

"Certainly. She runs a casino in the Hidden called The House of Banshee, but I don't suppose I should have told you that, should I have? After all, you're just a norm."

"How do you know?" she gasped, eyes huge and frightened.

"I'm terribly good at reading people."

"Do the Bakers know?"

"I couldn't possibly say."

"I knew this would happen," she moaned. "I just knew it. But the pay is fantastic, and, for the most part, I manage to keep the kids under control. I swear."

"Like now," Doc chuckled, gesturing towards the levitating welcome mat.

"Addison!" the girl gasped. "Put that down right this instant!"

The mat dropped to the porch, and the red-headed girl began to wail.

"I have to go," the babysitter said hurriedly.

"I can help," Doc said, walking three steps closer.

"I'm sorry. I don't know you, and I have to get Addison to eat, then take her nap. Johnny and Jules need to finish their homework. I just... I need you to go."

"I'm excellent at homework," he confided, stepping another three steps forward.

Addison wailed even louder, and Doc tapped her nose and said, "Look here, I'll show you a card trick. Better yet, a coin trick." She continued to cry, but her sharp blue eyes were pinned on Doc now.

"Look at my hands. There's nothing in them, but look!" He clenched his fists and opened them revealing a shiny silver dollar. "Ta-da!"

"Magic!" Addison exclaimed, tears ceasing and lips turning up into a grin.

"Sleight of hand," Doc said gently.

"Again! Again!"

Doc performed the trick one more time, and then he knew he had them. Addison loved him, and the girl wasn't guarding the door against him anymore. Just one more bit of sleight of hand, and he'd be in.

"So what is it you're supposed to be eating?" he asked.

"Casserole," Addison said, nose tilted up in disgust.

"Oh. I wouldn't want to eat that either. Do you know what they put in there?" She shook her head sharply. "Unicorn breath! Disgusting, isn't it?"

"Unicorn breath?" she breathed.

"Rainbows and all," Doc said, shaking his head.

She was suddenly holding his hand and pulling him into the house.

"No, Addison!" the girl called out behind them. "Stranger, danger!"

Addison ignored her, and Doc followed her cheerfully into the kitchen where she pointed at her plate of gooey casserole and said, "Does this one have unicorn breath?"

He pretended to study it carefully before saying, "Loads of it. Can't you see it? Rainbows are practically falling out of it."

"Yummy," Addison said happily as she heaped up a forkful and shoved it into her mouth.

Doc turned to smile at the babysitter. "See, I'm rather handy to have around. I never did catch your name?"

"Frankie," she said shortly. "Now would you please leave?"

"It's imperative I speak to your employers."

She paled. "You're not going to tell them I'm a norm, are you? I can handle the kids, honest I can!"

He was a terrible man. He knew he was, but he'd given his word to Señora Teodora, and he'd never promised Frankie anything.

"The thing is," he said carefully, "I need an item of magical significance. I'm rather in a hurry, so I need it now.

I'm certain I could be persuaded to keep my mouth shut if you could just point me in the right direction."

"You... you want me to steal from them?" she stuttered.

"They're probably not even using it, and I'd owe them one, which, if we're honest, is probably worth more than some magical trinket anyway."

"Just give it to him," a voice said from behind Frankie.

Doc leaned around her to see a pair of red-headed twins, presumably Johnny and Jules.

"We'll just say we were playing with it..." one of the twins started to say.

"And lost it," the other twin finished.

"But..." Frankie stuttered.

"It's okay," Jules said. "We lose stuff all the time."

"Besides," Johnny said, "Don't you know who he is? He's the legendary Doc Holliday! Dr. Feyrer wrote an entire book about him. According to Dr. Feyrer, he's the only mortal immortal."

Doc raised an eyebrow. Mortal immortal? And who the hell was Dr. Feyrer? And why was Dr. Feyrer writing books about him?

"Doc Holliday?" Frankie choked. "Like THE Doc Holliday?!"

"Yep," Jules said, grinning up at Doc.

"And furthermore," Johnny said, "Dr. Feyrer said that Doc Holliday always honors his debts, so he'll owe us one."

That wasn't precisely what Doc had said, but since they were willing to take the blame, he'd let it go. He made a mental note to look up Dr. Feyrer at some point though, to see how he was getting his information.

"I'll run get it," Johnny said.

Doc smiled at Frankie. "That wasn't so hard, was it? Your

secret is safe with me, I get what I need, and you and the twins here have a favor to be called upon whenever it suits you."

"THE Doc Holliday?" she repeated.

"In the flesh," he laughed, taking her hand and bowing over it.

"But you're dead!"

"Not really."

"I've seen your grave."

"I was only in there for an hour or so," he shrugged.

"Oh my god," she whispered.

"Sit down," Jules said, tugging on Frankie's hand. "I don't want you to pass out again." She turned to Doc and said softly, "This is all a little new to her."

Doc winked. "I understand."

"Here you go," Johnny suddenly said, handing Doc a supremely uninteresting silver ring.

"This is it?" Doc asked suspiciously.

"Yep."

"You're sure?"

"Absolutely. Can't you tell?"

"Not even a little. But you can?"

"Yep."

"And you're a witch?"

"Yep."

"Alright," Doc said with a shrug. Bennie hadn't given him any descriptions, so he'd just have to trust the boy. "If this isn't it though," he said evenly. "No favor."

Jules laughed. "I don't know why you want it if you can't even recognize it."

Maybe he did still get headaches. He felt like he had one right now. Or maybe it was just time for a snack.

## 10

It took Doc another hour to extradite himself from the Baker children's clutches. As he climbed into his car, he was certain his head was aching for real. It was time for course number one of his five course meal.

On his way back to his hotel, Doc stopped by Mr. Sam Whittaker's opulent house. Mr. Whittaker was involved in a sex trafficking ring, but the police could never make anything stick. Mostly because Whittaker's lawyer, course number two, had a way of always getting the evidence thrown out of court.

Doc punched a random code into Whittaker's gate control, grinned as the gate opened, and drove his car up the driveway, parking right in front of the house. It looked like his luck was back. If he was really lucky, Whittaker would have a guard or two that Doc would have to fight to get to the man himself.

He knocked on the door and waited, leaning on the door frame and rolling a silver coin over his knuckles.

A young man wearing a tight polo shirt and black cargo pants opened the door. "Who are you?" he questioned. "How did you get up here?"

"I've an appointment with Mr. Whittaker," Doc said easily. "He's expecting me. You might want to check your perimeter," he added confidentially. "As I was coming up the street, I saw someone scaling the wall. Probably just a thrill seeker, but you can never be too careful these days."

The man was flustered now and not sure what to do. "I... I'll..." He looked between Doc and the wall.

Doc put on a charming grin. "I can see myself to Mr. Whittaker if you want to check your security."

"Yes, I suppose..."

Doc took a gamble. "He's in his study, I presume?"

That sealed it. "Yes. Go on back. I'd better see what's going on." The man took a radio from his belt and said, "Evan and Ryan, report to me at the front door."

Doc gave the man a slight nod, then walked quickly down the hallway. He had no idea where the study was, but usually, although not always, whatever he was looking for was behind the first door he opened.

He pushed open a random door, startling the man sitting behind the desk. "Who are you?" the man demanded. "Who let you in?"

"We have an appointment, don't you remember? You wanted to see a doctor about your heart condition."

"What're you talking about?"

"Your black, filthy heart," Doc replied cheerfully. "I'm sorry. Just looking at you, I can say you're a lost cause."

Whittaker's face turned bright red. "Who are you?"

"Doc Holliday, at your service." He bowed theatrically, then started to walk leisurely towards Whittaker.

Whittaker picked up his phone and barked, "Emmet! Get your ass down here and teach this piece of shit some manners!"

Doc didn't hear the reply, but he assumed it was some variation of "right away, boss". He loved it when his luck was good. "Thank you for calling your men," he said. "Unfortunately, they won't get here in time to help you."

Doc was a mere five feet away now, and since he knew Emmet was coming, he didn't bother dragging it out any longer. He palmed one of his knives and flicked it forward, watching with satisfaction as it buried itself to the hilt in Whittaker's neck. "Buh-bye," Doc whispered, giving Whittaker a small wave as he slumped forward onto his desk.

Doc's tattoo had just finished draining Whittaker's energy when the door slammed open behind Doc. He turned with a grin. The door man was there, along with two others.

"This day just gets better and better," Doc chuckled.

"What did you do to Mr. Whittaker?" the door man, supposedly Emmet, exclaimed.

"Just took a little nibble." Emmet drew his gun and pointed it at Doc's chest. "Are you going to pull the trigger," Doc drawled, "or just stand there pointing it at me all day?"

"Get him!" Emmet hissed.

The other two men rushed towards Doc, but he easily ducked their swinging arms, moving to the side so they crashed into each other. Doc threw a knife towards Emmet, knocking the gun from his hand, then turned back to the two bumbling men and started hitting.

He didn't punch with his knuckles. He never used his knuckles. The first thing his brother had taught him was not to punch knuckles out. Instead he used his hands like hammers, bashing his fists into faces, necks, chests, anything that caught his eye.

He moved so swiftly the men could barely follow him, let alone land a return hit. Doc struck one man's neck, and the man dropped gasping to the floor, then Doc spun on his toes and elbowed the other man square in the nose before landing a strike to his neck as well.

They were both on the floor now, so he turned to Emmet. "What are you?" Emmet stuttered.

"I don't know," Doc shrugged. "A wraith, a ghoul, a soul-sucking vampire. There aren't words to describe me. But I know what you are. Dead."

Emmet was too astonished to put up a proper fight; in seconds he was dead. Doc waited until his tattoo began to cool before finishing off the other men, one by one.

Once they were drained, Doc stretched his arms wide and spun in a little circle. "I feel good!" he exclaimed, shivering as the last thrum of power soaked into his veins. "I take back everything I said. This is an excellent day!"

It only got better, because when Doc entered his suite, there was a box of whiskey waiting for him. A suck-up gift from Bennie. The note said, "As a thanks for your frequent flier miles."

Doc laughed heartily and took a sip straight from one of the bottles. If his luck held, Silbu would have news for him tonight, and he would be able to collect Sofia.

He stared out his window at the flowing traffic beneath him and tried to ignore the cloud of depression that lurked in the back of his mind.

A good gambler knew how to ride the high tides of luck. Just as a good gambler knew that a low tide usually followed on its heels.

Silbu didn't come that night. Not that he'd entirely expected her to. He didn't understand the dreaming any more than he understood magic, but he knew enough to know it was massive. Sure, only certain people could travel through it, but that was pretty much canceled out by the fact that all people who could travel it, all throughout time, could all be inside it at once.

He frowned at the mirror on his ceiling, trying to shake the sleepy cobwebs from his mind. He wasn't sure that made sense. He wasn't sure anything about the dreaming made sense. He only knew that if he were a dreamer, he could go to sleep and have a conversation with Señora Teodora if she was asleep somewhere as well.

He wouldn't deny that that would be handy right now. He could ask her to ask Sofia where she was. But which Señora Teodora would he meet? The one after Sofia had disappeared or the one before? And for that matter why couldn't Señora Teodora talk to Sofia before she disappeared and warn her?

He squeezed his temples. For a man who didn't have headaches, he was sure having a lot of them lately.

He only had three days. He didn't have time for Silbu to find her. He needed to find Sofia now. Before it was too late.

Doc studied the gargoyles on either side of Jury's door. He didn't mind a good fight. In fact, he rather enjoyed a good fight, but there was no point in fighting gargoyles. They were just stone and magic. He couldn't draw any power from defeating them, which is why he'd rather not waste his time or energy. The gargoyles didn't appear to be on the alert though, so he stepped between them and knocked. He waited for a full minute, but Jury didn't answer the door, so Doc knocked again.

"I know you're in there!" he called out.

"I'm not!" Jury called back.

"See, that's called a tell," Doc responded. "Now I really know you're in there."

"I don't like you," Jury snapped.

"The feeling isn't mutual. I rather enjoy you," Doc chuckled.

"You didn't give me back my tooth."

"Ah, but you didn't bother to check."

"I shouldn't have had to check," Jury grumbled as he opened the door. "Why are you here? You said one question, and I answered it. Furthermore, I don't accept more than one favor at a time."

"Of course not. This time I come bearing gifts."

"Gifts, huh? This ought to be good."

"Coffee?" Doc asked. "I don't suppose you could conjure some up from the eighteen hundreds?"

"I don't suppose," Jury muttered.

"So you can't?"

"No! I'm a witch, Doc! Learn the damn difference!"

"So no time travel?" Doc asked curiously.

"Exactly! Time is part of the ether; I'm stuck firmly in the earth. I can't wiggle about."

"That must be so frustrating for you," Doc chuckled.

"It is. If I could time travel, I would visit myself in 1925 and tell myself NOT to go on a gambling binge."

"Curious. If I could travel through time, I'd revisit this one night when I stumbled into a town full of sex-starved women—"

"Why are you here?" Jury interrupted.

"I can't find Sofia."

"And?"

"I only have three days before she's gone."

"What avenues have you attempted?"

"The Graves have been looking for her for the last six

years. Virgil can't even find a trace of the family line after 1994. They assured me that they thoroughly combed the Hidden, but they were looking for a witch, not a shaman. Tessa was a... little strained when I mentioned shamans, so I fired them, to keep them from alerting the Bureau."

"Smart," Jury said. "What else?"

"Um... I may have asked Silbu to look for her."

"Silbu?"

"She's a succubus," Doc said softly.

"That's... brilliant!" Jury exclaimed. "Who better to find a dreamer than someone who lives in the dreaming!"

"That's what I thought. But I'm running out of time."

Jury frowned and looked Doc over. "How exactly did you manage to bribe a succubus?"

"The old-fashioned way," Doc grinned.

"And you're still alive?" Jury asked incredulously.

"It was a near thing," Doc murmured.

"Why's this so important to you?"

"I gave my word."

For a moment he was lost again to the past. So lost that he could feel the horrendous ache in his chest.

Señora Teodora stared earnestly into his eyes and said, "If you agree to protect Sofia from whatever has harmed her, I will give you immortality."

Doc laughed painfully. "I'm already dying, Señora, why torture me with fairy tales?"

"It's not a fairy tale. I'm offering you immortality, should you choose to take it."

"And if I don't?"

"I must look for another."

He didn't like the sound of that. He wasn't that easy to replace. She'd chosen him for a reason. A cough racked his frame, and for a second he truly wished he could die, just to be free of the pain.

"Why me?" he whispered.

For the first time since she'd entered his room, Señora Teodora smiled. "Because I know that if you give me your word, nothing but death will stop you."

"How could you possibly know that?" he managed. It was getting difficult to breathe and even more difficult to talk, but he couldn't just give his word. He'd done that too many times.

"My grandson told me what you did."

He should have known. That explained why she had forgiven him.

"You and your word," Jury sneered as he placed a cup of coffee on the table in front of Doc, pulling Doc back to the moment at hand. "She's dead, you know. The woman you made your promise to."

"But I'm not," Doc stated evenly. "Will you help me?"

Jury sighed, and Doc knew he'd won. "You said something about a gift?" Jury muttered.

"Here." Doc handed him the ring. "It doesn't look like much to me, but the boy I got it from said it was what I needed. If he lied to me, I can always go back and eat him," Doc said with a chuckle.

"Not bad," Jury said with a shrug.

"Not bad?"

"It's an item of small significance."

He was going to kill them. He'd performed the same sleight of hand trick twenty-five times for Addison. He'd helped solve two dozen math problems. And he owed them a favor. All for an item of small significance.

"Maybe you'd rather have this," Doc huffed, tossing the rock onto the table.

Jury's face went ashen. "Where did you get this?" he whispered.

"It's a rock," Doc said.

"Where?"

"Well, I suppose a house gave it to me."

"What do you mean?" Jury demanded.

"I asked Bennie for a list of magic things that I might be able to acquire. Anyway, the first one on the list was this... rock. The house was alive, but the witch was gone. Someone took her."

"What do you mean someone took her?"

"There was blood. Recent blood, but she wasn't there. The house wanted me to find the rock though. What is it? I mean, besides a rock?"

"This is the Stone of Alarius," Jury said reverently.

"So it's a rock."

"No! I mean yes, it is a rock, but the point is it increases the bearer's power exponentially. Assuming the bearer is a magic wielder," Jury added.

"Obviously. I had it in my pocket all day, and I didn't notice the women flocking to me anymore than normal."

"It doesn't... Never mind. You said the witch was gone?"

"Yes."

"Who was she?"

"Bennie didn't give me a name, but here, this was in the room with the rock."

"Stone of Alarius," Jury corrected.

"Right." Doc held out his phone to Jury with the photograph of the symbol on the floor. If Doc had thought Jury's face was pale before, he was wrong.

"She was gone?" Jury stammered.

"Yes."

"I recognize this symbol. It's used to focus all one's energy into one specific task or spell."

"So?"

"For the last hundred years or so, there haven't been any successful attempts because it requires more power than even a band of witches could possess."

Jury was speaking, but Doc wasn't quite following. "And?" he asked, hoping Jury would clarify.

"There's a rumor of someone who might be powerful enough to control it, especially if she was in possession of the Stone of Alarius."

"But?" Doc prodded.

"She's not a witch."

# 11

"But you just said..." Doc began. "You said it only worked for witches."

"Sorry. I should've clarified," Jury admitted. "It works for witches... and shamans."

Oh hell. This was not good.

"What exactly are you saying?" Doc asked slowly.

The tide was ebbing out. He could feel it.

"Bluegrass Goodhunt is a rather powerful shaman."

Doc absorbed that, then said, "I thought you didn't know any shamans."

"I don't. I know of a shaman. There's a big difference."

Doc stared into his empty coffee cup. Pieces were falling into place, like cards in a hand of gin rummy.

"Correct me if I've got this wrong," he said slowly. "I'm looking for Sofia, who is a shaman, who I know for a fact goes missing or dies in three days; and, in a seemingly random coincidence, the most powerful shaman around has also recently gone missing. Does that sound about right?"

"More or less."

"I need whiskey."

"That's the least of your problems."

"Can you help me find her?"

"I don't know. Do you have anything that could help me?"

"I have a coin Señora Teodora gave me."

"On you?"

"Yes."

He always carried it. It reminded him of the debt he owed. A debt he was intent on paying. He fished the silver coin out of his vest pocket and tossed it to Jury.

"I don't know if it'll work," Jury said. "I need time."

"You can have a day," Doc said.

"Wow, a whole day? I don't know how to thank you."

Doc sighed. "Look, I need you."

"I'll do my best," Jury grumped.

"Use the rock."

"Are you kidding?! Do you have any idea what using that thing would do to me?!"

"Increase your powers exponentially?"

"For a moment or two. I doubt if I'm powerful enough to keep it in check. I could burn out, completely. And then... well..."

Doc grinned. "Some other time, then?"

Jury shuddered. "I don't think so."

"Let me know when you find something," Doc said. "And maybe next time I come by, you could have some whiskey."

"Doubtful," Jury snapped.

"Doesn't hurt to ask."

Before long, Doc was pulling the bell pull at Graves, Graves, and Graves. Magnus opened the door, and in lieu of speaking, just grunted and pointed towards Virgil's office.

"Thank you, Magnus," Doc murmured. "I do so enjoy our conversations. In fact, I think this is the most stimulating conversation I've had all day," he added as he walked down the hallway.

"Talking to yourself?" Virgil asked when Doc stepped into his office.

"Sometimes," Doc chuckled.

"I was under the impression you had dismissed us from your employ."

"I have," Doc agreed. "This is regarding something else entirely."

"Totally disconnected?" Virgil asked.

"Completely. No connection whatsoever. If someone were to ask."

"Sounds interesting, and I have some free time. What's on your mind?"

Doc glanced around Virgil's office. Virgil was very, very good at what he did. In fact, the Graves family had been in the business of bridging the gap between the norms and the Hidden for nearly two hundred years. They were the best in the business. But even the best sometimes lost.

"I have a sudden yearn for a stroll," Doc said conversationally. "Would you care to join me?"

Virgil didn't even hesitate. "Certainly. I'll get my cane."

As soon as they were outside, Doc glanced behind them.

"Do you think I'm under surveillance?" Virgil asked.

"I've no idea."

"What's going on, Doc?"

"I think I'm about to walk into a gigantic mess. Have there been reports lately of missing shamans?"

"By shaman I take it you mean the sort who use spiritual elements?" Virgil clarified.

"Yes."

They walked in silence for a moment. Finally Virgil said, "You and I are old friends, so please don't take this the wrong way. I think you're getting in over your head."

"I don't have a choice," Doc said.

"There's always a choice."

"Not for me."

Virgil sighed. "You're not involved in the politics, so you don't understand how dirty these things can get."

"I don't care. Tell me what you know."

"If it gets out that I talked to you..."

"Damn it, Virgil!" Doc snapped, feeling an unfamiliar surge of anger. "I get you're trying to protect yourself here, but people are in danger. You can label it, you can say it's about politics or protecting humanity, you can wrap it in a box and put a bow on it, but the fact remains, someone is hurting people and I'm going to put a stop to it!"

"I was afraid you'd say that," Virgil grumbled. He glanced behind them, then motioned for Doc to turn down a side street. "About seven years ago, a man named Hieronymus Bosch took over the BCA."

"Like the painter?" Doc asked.

"Yes, but not the painter."

"You're sure?"

"Pretty sure. By all accounts Bosch is a norm. I've only met him once, and I can't say I cared for him. He seemed like a cold fish, if you catch my meaning."

They both nodded to a group of women strolling along the shop fronts. The women twittered and waved.

Virgil turned down another street before he continued speaking. "At first it was business as usual. Then reports starting cropping up about certain cryp species going missing.

The Magistratus investigated, but it was strange. There wasn't any trace. Nothing. The witch sweepers couldn't even find anything."

Now that was strange. Witch sweepers were a team of witches who could supposedly read a scene if they arrived within a set time frame. If they weren't able to find anything, it meant something was blocking them.

"After a year or two," Virgil continued, "the reports began to ebb off, but they also became more focused. For a while only vampires went missing. Then a few banshees. Lately, it's been witches with access to the spiritual realm, or shamans. The Magistratus still haven't found anything, which some people think is a little suspicious.

"The whole situation has created a sort of panic. Last year cryps started trying to leave the Hidden for the normal world, and that's when things got nasty. Travel visas were revoked, sight was redacted, whole groups of cryps were rounded up and put away for unlawful disclosure to norms."

Doc couldn't believe it. There was no way all this had been going on right under his nose without his even noticing or catching wind of it. Then he remembered. He'd been in a vampire induced sex coma for five years. He was beginning to regret it; although Ana was a talented and experimental lover, so maybe he didn't regret it.

"Then," Virgil said, voice low as they passed a business man, "last year, Bosch moved the BCA headquarters to Denver."

"That's a little strange, isn't it?"

"The headquarters have always been in Washington, DC, close to the action," Virgil confirmed.

"So what's going on?" Doc asked thoughtfully.

"I have no idea. Anyone who asks questions or looks into it disappears."

"So you haven't asked questions."

"I'm not in the business of saving people, Doc."

Doc didn't blame him. Most people were just content to live their lives and let things happen around them. But Doc wasn't one of those people. He never had been.

Doc went to the House of Banshee next. Not because it would help him find Sofia, but because he desperately needed to be around something familiar for a moment or two. He needed to lose himself to the sounds of chips clanking and cards whispering. He needed the smell of half-drunken despair.

He sat down at a busy poker table, took a hand, and evaluated the other players. One of them was playing too deep, with money he didn't have. Doc could tell by how his leg was twitching nervously. One of the players was playing to win, but he didn't need the money. The other three players were just having fun.

Doc set his mind to win. He had no sympathy for people who gambled when they shouldn't. Play continued for nearly an hour until it was just Doc and the other man who wanted to win.

The other man was very good. He kept his expressions under perfect control, and all of his movements were part of a measured cadence. He had practically no tells whatsoever. Except one.

He was a Takaheni, a creature generally categorized by norms as a sasquatch. It was true that Takaheni were generally humanoid in shape, quite tall, and rather hairy; however, they didn't reek like norms insisted they did. And furthermore, they were usually considered quite brilliant. This Takaheni was no exception. Not only was he an excellent dresser, he was also an incredible card player. But the very tip of his furry ear tended to twitch when he got a good card. Just a tiny twitch, but a twitch nonetheless, and it hadn't twitched at all this round.

"All in?" Doc asked casually.

The Takaheni studied him for a moment before saying, "Fold."

Doc took the pot, and they played another hand. The Takaheni's ear twitched once, but Doc was certain his own cards would win the hand, and they did.

They were down to the final few hands; Doc could feel it. A familiar rush of excitement zipped down his spine. This was why he wasn't ready to die yet. There were still too many games to be played. Too many opponents to study and discover their minuscule tells. Too many games to win.

They played for three more hands before the Takaheni would go all in. His ear had twitched twice, with the first round and the fourth. Doc had done some figuring in his head, and he had a fair guess what the Takaheni's cards were, but there was only one way to find out.

"Call," the Takaheni said, pushing his chips into the center and revealing his two cards.

Just as Doc had suspected. A full house. Doc grinned slightly as he flipped his own cards. A four of a kind.

"Good game," the Takaheni said solemnly.

"Indeed."

"You're Doc Holliday?"

"In the flesh."

"Just glad I held out as long as I did."

Doc laughed. "A rather high compliment."

"The name's Simon. Simon Redgrove," he said, holding out his furry hand.

Doc shook it enthusiastically. "THE Simon Redgrove?" he asked. Simon shrugged modestly. "Then the honor is all mine," Doc chuckled. "You own half the Hidden, but more importantly, you're a damn good poker player."

"Numbers make sense to me," Simon laughed.

That was the difference. Numbers were just numbers. Doc understood them, but it was people he truly understood. He wasn't playing the cards. He was playing the people.

"If you ever want a rematch," Doc said, handing Simon his card, "I'm happy to oblige."

"That sounds like a very pleasant way to lose money."

Doc laughed. "I don't always win."

"That's not what I hear."

Doc shrugged modestly. "I'm afraid I have an unfair advantage." He leaned towards Simon and whispered, "Lady Luck adores me."

"I'll keep that in mind," Simon said with a chuckle.

Doc grinned and went to greet Aine.

"Did you lose?" Aine asked.

"Do I ever?"

"Sometimes."

He grinned. "Not since Bennie got me a pack of Banshee cards."

"He didn't!" Aine exclaimed, fury making her eyes seem to glow.

"Of course not. Bennie knows better than to cross you," Doc chuckled.

"If I find out he did..."

"I know. You'll string us both up by our man bits."

"That'll be the least of your worries," she snarled.

"I lost my taste for cheating about a hundred years ago. Give or take." Jury would know the exact date, not that Doc was planning to ask him. "Is there somewhere we can speak... in private?" he asked softly.

Her eyes narrowed. "What for?"

"Something to do with... something," he said, glancing around the room. "There could be ears anywhere." Bennie could be curled around a nearby lamppost for all Doc knew.

"I need to check an order on the dock," she said, turning on her heel and striding towards an "employees only" sign.

Doc followed her, waiting until they were fully outside and he could see that no one was nearby before asking, "Do you know anything about the Bureau kidnapping cryptids?"

Aine's skin didn't have any color, so she didn't visibly pale, but her eyes widened briefly before she remembered to control herself.

"No."

"I can tell you're lying, Aine."

"You don't want to get into this," she whispered. "Bosch is..." she shuddered. "Norms call us monsters, but he's a monster. Through and through. He... He's dangerous, Doc. You can't... I can't..."

"Chances are I'm going to meet up with Bosch sooner or later," he pointed out. "I can either do it with your help or without."

"Why do you do this to me?" She chewed her lip for a second before saying, "I can't talk now. I'll come by your place after closing, okay?"

"I look forward to it," he drawled.

"Doc," she chastised.

"Sorry," he laughed. "Thank you."

He didn't go back inside with her, just headed home from the alleyway. This whole mess was getting out of hand. Anytime the Bureau was mentioned, people started shaking in their boots. It wasn't like Aine to be anxious or scared. He didn't know Tessa well, but it wasn't like Virgil to be quite so evasive. Jury had flat out said he didn't want his name mentioned. Ms. Goodhunt was missing, and who knew how many other shamans and cryptids; and Sofia would be gone in three days. He glanced at his pocket watch. Two days.

# 12

Doc opened his suite door with a long sigh. Ever since he'd sent Ana away, he'd accomplished exactly nothing. He could just hunt down Bosch and be done with it, but since he didn't know exactly what was going on, he wasn't entirely certain that killing Bosch would save Sofia. And if he didn't go to sleep at some point, he'd never know if Silbu had found her.

"Pleasant day?" Thaddeus asked dryly.

"Didn't kill anyone, didn't make love, did win a game of cards though."

"Sounds absolutely tragic. My day was a tad slow, thank you for asking." Doc rolled his eyes. Here they went again. "You did remember to open the curtains, so at least I had some sunlight. Of course, you forgot to move me, so I spent the entire morning staring at your rumpled sheets. Fortunately," Thaddeus droned on, "Rosa came to clean and moved me to the sitting room, where you now see me."

"Sorry, Thaddy, old boy," Doc said earnestly.

"Would it be too much trouble to find me a companion of some sort?"

"Like a dog?"

"Good god, no! Do you have any idea what dogs do to plants?"

"A vague one," Doc chuckled. "Would you like a plant girlfriend?"

"You're being quite insensitive. Can you imagine spending your day stuck in a pot of dirt?"

Doc couldn't. But he could imagine being buried alive. Because he had been. His eyes might have been closed, but his senses had still been alert. He'd known when they had closed the lid and nailed it shut. He'd felt the coffin settle to the ground. He'd heard each shovelful of frozen dirt land on top of him, sealing him in. And he'd felt dread. Dread that Señora Teodora wouldn't come back for him.

He hadn't been able to move, to speak, to open his eyes; and when he'd finally heard the shovels digging through the loose earth, he would have wept with relief if he could have.

Arms pulled him from the casket, laid him inside a wagon bed, and covered him with a rough blanket. Then the shovels went to work again. Filling Dr. John Henry Holliday's grave.

The wagon rattled along frozen, muddy tracks. Doc didn't know what time it was, but he assumed it was night. The cold was seeping into his motionless form, and he began to worry that he might never move again.

His body was lifted and carried someplace new. This time inside. He could feel the heat of the fire, and he wished he could turn his face towards it. He wished the heat could drive away the coldness that lived deep inside him.

"Drink," Señora Teodora commanded, holding something to his lips. He couldn't move; how could he drink? She poured liquid into his mouth, and he tried to force himself to swallow. Some of the liquid leaked down his throat, but most of it dribbled out his mouth.

She tried again. And again. And again. Finally he managed to swallow. Finally he could open his eyes. He wasn't dead. Not yet.

"I must complete the enchantment," she said. "You haven't much time."

Doc didn't have the strength to nod. He just lay there while she quickly opened his shirt, exposing his pale, emaciated chest.

"This will hurt," she apologized.

She held a cup in one hand and a bone needle in the other. "Lay still," she said as she dipped the needle into the cup, then pushed it into the skin of his chest. Doc didn't even flinch. It hurt, but he'd been in worse pain.

He wasn't so sure an hour later. Or an hour after that. The symbol she was painstakingly tattooing onto his chest was huge, and by his estimation, she wasn't even half finished.

He swallowed carefully, trying not to trigger a coughing fit. "Give him more cough root," Señora Teodora ordered her daughter. More liquid trickled down his throat, calming his lungs, but not removing the pain.

The sun began to come through the window, and still she wasn't done. "I need more blood," she said, holding the cup out to her daughter.

Doc's muddled, pain-soaked mind tried to process that. She was tattooing him with blood? Whose blood? And why blood?

He drifted in and out of consciousness. He dreamed he was dead, and this was his hell. In his dream, she looked like a horned demon. He woke and saw the sun glowing behind her head. She was beautiful. He'd never realized how beautiful she was. Wasn't she old? He drifted out of consciousness again.

He stood in the center of a clearing, the moon high above him, and the forest all around him was alive. White wisps formed like women danced past him. Trees tore their roots from the ground and sang to the night sky. It was strange and beautiful at the same time.

Fingers entwined with his, and he glanced over to see Señora Teodora smiling at the moon. Her face was glowing, and her hair swirled around her head like a river of silk. He'd never seen anyone more beautiful. She was magnificent.

The singing faded, the sky went dark, and he was all alone. Cold and small and lonely. "Mother?" he called out. She didn't answer. She was dead. He knew she was dead, but he thought if he could just find her, he could bring her back. He'd never be able to find her though. Not here. It was too black. He was lost, and she was lost with him. The darkness crushed him, and he was nothing.

When he finally woke, his chest was on fire, but Señora Teodora was finished.

"It's done," she said, smiling slightly. "Only one more thing to complete the change."

He hoped it wasn't painful. He'd nearly had all the pain he could stand.

She pointed towards a shadow in the corner of the room. "This man killed his brother so he could have his wife. She does not want him; he does not care. Kill him, and his life is yours."

He was too tired to kill anyone. He couldn't even move his head.

"If you do not kill him, you will die."

He hadn't gone through all that pain for nothing. "Knife,"

he croaked. The daughter pressed a cold knife handle into his hand, and he forced his fingers to close around it. He closed his eyes for a moment, trying to remember what it felt like to be warm, to be whole, to walk without pain, talk without pain, but he couldn't. He could do this. He'd been doing it for years.

He rolled over and pushed slowly to his knees. Everything hurt. He forced himself to stand. He wobbled, and Señora Teodora steadied him. He took a shallow breath. Only five steps and he'd be there.

One. A cough crawled its way up his throat, and for a moment it was all he could do to keep his feet. Two. His legs wobbled. Three. His strength left him, and he dropped to his knees. Never mind. He would crawl.

The man was just in front of Doc now. Eyes wide, mouth bound with a rag. His hands were lashed together in front of him, and Doc could see from the wrapping on the man's wrist where Señora Teodora had gotten her blood.

Darkness clawed at him, but he was nearly there. All he needed was the strength to lift his arm. "I'm not done," he whispered, pushing everything he had into his hand and rolling forward far enough to shove the knife into the man's throat.

Doc fell to the floor, exhaustion pulling him towards the darkness. He was dying. Señora Teodora had lied. He was going to die.

"Are you even listening to me?" Thaddeus snapped, ripping Doc from his remembrances.

"Sorry, old boy," Doc murmured. "I heard you. You'd like a cat."

Thaddeus sputtered for a moment. Finally he said, "No. I would not like a cat. I don't want a pet, you rakehell. I want a companion."

Doc sighed. It was so like Thaddeus to pick today to throw a snit. "If I happen to run across another talking plant, I will be sure to bring it home."

Thaddeus started complaining immediately, but Doc had more important things to deal with so he left Thaddeus alone, grabbed a bottle of whiskey, and strolled into his bedroom. He tossed back a shot, then stripped and draped his clothes carefully across the back of his leather wingback chair.

He sat on his bed for a moment, drinking another swallow or two. "I need you, Silbu," he muttered.

He set the whiskey bottle on his dresser and climbed into bed, stretching out beneath his fine linen sheets. He wished he had a woman beside him, but it was better he didn't. Silbu wasn't the type to enjoy competition.

He dreamed of Señora Teodora. Only it was Sofia with Señora Teodora's face. She was pale. Dead. Drained of blood in a ditch. He had failed. He wept until the world went dark around him.

"Holliday," Silbu purred. "My favorite human lover."

He didn't point out that most men could never love her more than once. Making love to a succubus was like riding a horse over the edge of a cliff. There was a thrilling edge of excitement for a moment right before you realized you were going to die.

"Please me again," she whispered, dragging her long claws over his sensitive skin.

"I can't tonight," he murmured. "Did you find her?"

"Perhaps."

For once he didn't have time for games. Not to mention it was incredibly difficult to read a succubus, unless he was in the midst of making love to her. When making love, all women, human or not, were easy to read.

"What do you want?" he asked.

"You."

"I gave you pleasure. Nineteen times if I counted correctly."

"I crave more," she whispered, body curling into his. It's not that he wasn't able. He was. He just didn't want to, but he'd do it for Sofia.

"Will you tell me if I pleasure you once, not twice, not three times, not four, just once more?"

"I will tell you everything I know."

"Will it help me?"

"Perhaps. I am not a mortal. I do not know what mortals look for."

It was a chance he'd just have to take.

He ran his hands up her silky form, feathering his fingers, listening for her sighs. He kissed her ice-cold lips, warming them with his life, feeding her with his pleasure and hers.

He took his time, making every stroke and touch count. He felt her tremble beneath him, and he pushed her further. When she began to moan helplessly, he gave her everything he had, committing his entire essence to pleasing her, and he did. He pleased her very well.

"Holliday," she finally sighed. "Promise me you'll seek me out again someday."

"When I'm ready to die, Silbu, I'll come to you."

She laughed softly. "To be a mortal must be very strange. I do not remember not being. I feel like I have always been."

"Perhaps you have." He was trembling slightly and sweating. Pleasing an immortal being who fed off sexual pleasure was no small task. He needed a snack. He needed a genuine nap.

"I cannot see the girl myself; I sent an incubus."

For some reason that bothered Doc, but he couldn't say

why. He'd never even met Sofia. What did he care if she had dream sex with an incubus? He was better. Silbu proved that because she could have sex with all the incubi she wanted, but she wanted him. He chuckled, feeling rather silly. He wanted to save Sofia, not make love to her.

"She is hiding," Silbu said. "But she is not in the place you call Hidden. She is somewhere else."

"That certainly narrows it down," Doc muttered. He'd already guessed as much as that.

"Patience, Holliday, I am not yet done." She ran her fingers through his hair and kissed his lips gently. Some of his warmth was still upon her.

"Lemus says she is someplace dark and cold. A little old, but not very old. He said the air feels stale. She is not alone, but she is frightened. That is all I know."

Doc closed his eyes and tried not to let the tide drag him under. Even if the luck was bad, the game could still be won.

# 13

Someone was screaming, and it wasn't him. Doc knew it wasn't him because he didn't scream like a little girl. But Thaddeus did.

Something was wrong. He needed to wake up. Doc tried to shake off the silky webs of Silbu's embrace, but everything was hazy and lust filled. Something crashed to the floor, and Doc jerked awake. If that was Thaddeus's pot he'd never hear the end of it.

"Wake up, you self-indulgent idiot!" Thaddeus screamed.

Doc sat up in bed. His room was dark; it was still night. But someone was bumbling around in the dark in his sitting room. None of his friends would sneak up on him. They knew better. So this wasn't a friend.

Doc rolled out of bed. His knives were on the chair with his clothes on the other side of the room, but he didn't need knives to kill. He picked up the whiskey bottle from his dresser and padded silently towards the bedroom door.

He heard the bedroom doorknob turn and flattened against the wall. Four large, shadowy figures entered his room, knives silhouetted in their hands. Whoever had sent them obviously didn't know Doc very well.

Doc waited until they were well inside the room before slipping behind them and softly closing the door.

"Did you hear that?" one hissed.

"Shut up, shit face!" another one whispered. "Do you want 'im to wake up?"

"Too late," Doc drawled.

"Where is he?" one gasped as they spun around looking for him.

"Right here." Doc swung the whiskey bottle down with enough force to shatter it over the first man's head. The man dropped like a rock.

Doc's tattoo started to glow, but Doc ignored it and dodged a knife thrust from another man. He swung the broken bottle up and into the bottom of the man's jaw, shoving it so deep that it stuck. His tattoo was on fire now.

The third man lunged at Doc, but he turned the man's knife against him, using it to slice his throat from ear to ear. The last man tried to stab Doc in the back, but Doc sensed his approach and slid easily to the side, grabbing the man's arm as he did and yanking him forward so he crashed face first onto the floor.

Doc stood still for a moment, enjoying the power that flowed into him from the men he'd killed. Then he stepped over their bodies and flipped on the light. Just as he'd planned, the last man was still alive, and when the man woke up, he was trussed tightly to Doc's wingback chair.

"I don't appreciate being attacked in my own bedroom," Doc drawled slowly as he buttoned his shirt. "And I can't think of anyone I know stupid enough to try it. So who are you working for?"

The man didn't say a word.

"I figured you'd say that," Doc said with a shrug. "You may not know this, but I'm a trained dental surgeon. Which means I know how to hurt a man," he added as he picked up a shard of glass.

The man began to sweat, but he still didn't say anything.

"The way I figure it," Doc said, "you're probably a little scared of your boss, but I suggest you forget about him and focus on me. I'm not going to lie to you. You're a dead man. You were dead the second you stepped foot into my home. The only question now is how quickly do you want to die?"

Doc gently and quickly made a little zig-zag cut down the man's cheek. "I once met a fellow who tortured the man who raped and killed his wife for three months. When the rapist lost too much blood, he'd patch him up, wait until he healed, and start all over again." The man was trembling now, which was just what Doc wanted.

"Now, I don't have that kind of time, and I want information, not soul-wrenching suffering. So I will do this as quickly and painfully as possible to achieve maximum results."

"I don't know anything—" the man began to say, but Doc interrupted him.

"You're probably thinking you can lie to me, but I have my ways of knowing if someone's lying. I've also already taken a picture of you. If you lie, I'll find out who you are and hunt down everyone even remotely related to you and kill them just as painfully as I kill you."

Doc bent so he could look directly into the man's terrified eyes. "Have I made myself clear?" Doc asked.

"But I don't—" The man trailed off with a scream as Doc used the glass to peel a strip of skin from his arm. He could scream as loud as he wanted too. The walls and floor were soundproofed; no one would hear him.

"Do I make myself clear?" Doc asked again. The man nodded shakily. "So tell me, who's your boss?"

"Lance Merrick," the man stuttered.

"He works for the Bureau?" Doc demanded.

"Yes."

"Called it," Doc murmured. "Too bad I didn't bet anything. Did he send you here to kill me?"

The man nodded.

"Why?"

"You asked questions."

"What do you know about the cryptids the Bureau's been kidnapping?"

"I don't know nothing, I swear!"

Doc measured that and decided it was true. "Who told the Bureau I was asking questions?"

"I don't know," the man sobbed.

"Then how did they find out?"

"An informant. Someone overheard you at that Banshee place."

If someone had overheard him that meant... Aine. Doc drew his knife and shoved it into the man's heart. He didn't have time for more questions. He had to get to Aine.

Glad that he'd taken the time to dress and don his knives before the man woke, he rushed for the door, leaping over Thaddeus's broken pot.

"Doc!" Thaddeus cried out.

"Later, old boy!"

The elevator was for leisure. Doc took the stairs, leaping down them three or four at a time. If Aine died because he'd asked the wrong questions... He refused to let that happen.

He crashed through the alley exit and sprinted up the sidewalk towards the House of Banshee. There was no point taking his car. By the time he got it out of the garage he could have run there.

It was late enough that only a few people were still out, but Doc didn't pay them any attention. He dashed barefoot up the sidewalk, pushing all his strength into his legs, and hoped he was wrong.

The House of Banshee was still running. It didn't close down until four in the morning when the fashionable crowd was ready for bed. Doc pushed past the doormen and down the hallway, searching frantically for Aine, but he didn't see her silver-white hair anywhere.

"Where's Aine?!" he demanded, grabbing her manager's suit jacket. "Where is she?"

"She went to her office," the man stuttered. "She had a meeting."

"At three in the morning?" Doc snarled, tossing the man to the side and tearing across the room towards the employees only sign. He crashed through the doors and sped down the hallway. His lungs were beginning to burn from the effort, but he just pushed harder.

He slammed into Aine's door, crashing into her office and surprising the man strangling her. Doc roared furiously, and a knife streaked from his hand and tore through the man's eye socket. He fell dead to the floor, taking Aine with him.

Doc's chest burned, but he wasn't done. He tackled another man, dropping him onto the desk and breaking his neck over the edge of it. He felt the cold slice of a knife across his back and turned with a growl. The remaining two men backed away from him, knives still in hand, measuring their attack.

They shouldn't have waited though, because Doc's knives had already left his hands. Before they could rush forward, the knives slammed into their hearts, killing them instantly.

"Hell," Doc grumbled. "I meant to leave one alive."

He stepped over their bodies and lifted Aine from the floor. Her pale skin was covered in bruises, but she was breathing. A flash of guilt filled him, but he didn't bother to indulge it. He hadn't done this to her. He'd asked the questions, but Lance Merrick had sent the kill order, and he would pay for it. Doc would make sure of it.

# 14

Doc took Aine to Reginald Butler, a norm doctor he'd almost eaten once. Reggie was on a short list of people who actually owed Doc a favor, and it was one of the few places Doc could be sure she'd be safe.

"Call me when she wakes up," Doc said as he left.

"Sure thing, Doc. I'll take good care of her."

Doc nodded and walked to his car. He needed to see Jury right away, but first, he needed to warn Virgil. "The Bureau didn't like my line of questioning; make sure you and Tessa are safe," he texted.

Virgil quickly responded. "Already taken care of."

Doc texted Jervis next. "There's a rather large mess in my room."

"I'll take care of it, sir."

"Also, get Thaddeus a new pot. A bigger one. Maybe blue? And make sure no one steps on him."

"Certainly, sir."

That done, Doc checked the time. It was only five o'clock. Jury wasn't exactly at his best early in the morning, but Doc couldn't wait any longer. He only hoped Jury didn't shoot him on sight.

Jury's guard gargoyles ignored him, which Doc hoped was a good sign. He stepped carefully between them and knocked on the door; Jury opened it immediately.

"I'd like to note how much I resent you dragging me into this!" he snapped.

"Dragging you into what?" Doc asked innocently.

"Goddamn it, Doc. When other people see a hornet nest lying on the ground, they walk around it. They don't goddamn kick it!"

"You're in a fine mood this morning. Coffee?"

"Coffee?! As if I've had time to make coffee," Jury grumbled.

"I'll make it," Doc offered. "You tell me what you've found."

"I've found a whole hell of a lot of trouble!"

"Don't keep me in suspense," Doc said.

"I started poking around after you left, not literally of course, just a few spells here and there, but I kept hitting walls."

"What do you mean?"

"Imagine that a spell is a dice roll," Jury explained. "But halfway down the table there's an imaginary barrier that keeps stopping the dice so they can't reach the wall."

"That's bad," Doc said.

"Exactly. I tried to cast a location spell using the coin. Nothing. I tried to cast a listening spell on the BCA's breakroom. Nothing. Of course that didn't surprise me terribly much. Only a complete idiot wouldn't have installed protections against listening. But there's a coffee shop nearby that a few of the BCA crypts use. Benedict Arnolds, all of them," he spat. "I tried listening in there, but it was also blocked, and that's a tad extreme."

He paced back and forth for a moment. "I tried a handful of other spells, but nothing worked. Something's going on. Something big. And you pulled me right into the middle of it."

"I just asked for information," Doc said. "It's not like I expect you to go out looking with me."

"Ha! As if you get to decide!" Jury exclaimed. "I may live outside the Hidden, but these are still my people. If someone's hurting them, it's time they pay."

Doc looked the other way so Jury couldn't see his grin. He loved it when Jury jumped on the bandwagon. It made everything so much more interesting.

"I had a run-in with some meat for hire this morning," Doc said. "Four thugs. Said they worked for a Bureau fellow named Lance Merrick. He also sent some men after Aine."

"Is she alright?" Jury asked.

Doc shrugged. "Reggie said she would be." And he had to believe that Reggie was right. "I got there just in time."

"Smart leaving her with Reggie," Jury said, finally sitting down. "Merrick is Bosch's right-hand man."

"So what do you think they're up to?"

"I have no idea, and that really bothers me. Usually when something's going on, no matter how top secret, there're rumors and speculations. But not this time."

"It's kind of strange though..." Doc started to say. He shook his head, tapping his fingers on the table.

"What?"

"It's probably nothing."

"Just spit it out."

"It's just that Merrick sent eight men after Aine."

"She is a banshee."

"I know that. And that's the thing. They even knew how to kill her. They lost a few before I got there, but they had her. She was done for."

"And besides the obvious, why is this a problem?"

"He only sent four after me, and they were bumbling idiots."

"So you're jealous?"

"No!"

"You still killed more than she did."

"That's not the point," Doc grumbled.

"What is the point?"

"I just... Do you really think he thought four guys would be enough?"

Jury shrugged. "You have been gone for five years. For all you know Bosch thinks you're a ridiculous playboy."

"Huh... Maybe." He stared at Jury's barren wall for a moment, thinking. "Yeah, maybe that's it. Anyway, I still have to find Sofia," he said. "Silbu said she's hiding, scared, and not alone. She said the place isn't in the Hidden, it's oldish, and the air smells stale."

"Well that narrows it down!" Jury declared.

"It does?" Doc asked skeptically.

"Certainly!"

He hated it when Jury didn't make sense. "Explain," he said.

"You're certain she's in Denver?"

"Yes."

"Alright, so we're looking for an old, abandoned building or structure inside Denver."

"Have you looked around lately?" Doc asked with a sigh.

"You're thinking like a norm," Jury chastised. "I got you some whiskey. Help yourself. I need a few minutes." He wandered off into his work space and started moving things around.

Whatever Jury was doing, Doc hoped it paid off. He was down to two days. He glanced at his watch. More like a day and a half. At best.

He walked into the kitchen space and opened random cabinets, looking for the glasses. Eventually he found one, then he stopped in front of the whiskey bottle on the counter.

"What the hell is this?" he demanded.

"Whiskey," Jury said, chuckling loudly.

"Are you sure?"

"Yes."

"It's pink."

"I know. I paid extra."

"Why would you do that?"

"I thought it'd be funny."

"You're a cruel, cruel man, Thomas Jury," Doc said as he filled his glass to the brim.

"That's an eight ounce glass," Jury commented.

"It's pink. I need the extra compensation."

Jury laughed loudly. "Now shut up," he said after a moment. "I need to focus."

Doc shrugged, sat on the couch, and slowly sipped the whiskey. It was terrible, but he didn't have anything else to do. For a moment, he remembered the fear he'd felt when he'd seen Aine pressed against the wall, face turning blue. She'd almost died. If she had died... Doc shook his head. She couldn't die, not yet; not if he had any control over it.

His phone rang, pulling him out of his dark thoughts.

"What?" he answered.

"Mr. Holliday? This is Frankie."

"Ah, the witch babysitter. How are you?"

"I'm fine," she said, irritation making her voice sharp. "Johnny just wanted to know if the ring worked out for you."

"Tell Johnny that it's an item of small significance."

Something crackled over the speaker, like a hand covering it, but Doc still heard her say, "He said it's an item of small significance."

"Really?" Johnny demanded. "Do we still get a favor?"

"I am not asking him that!"

"Do it," Jules said.

"Fine," Frankie ground out. "Johnny would like to know if we still get a favor?"

"Small significance, small favor," Doc drawled.

Her hand covered the phone again, and she said, "He said small significance, small favor."

"That's not fair," Jules burst out. "We're grounded! For three weeks!"

"Jules says—"

"Don't tell him that!" Jules shrieked. "He's Doc Holliday!"

"So what do I tell him?" Frankie hissed.

Doc drank the rest of his whiskey while they tried to figure it out. He could already tell that this particular favor was going to come back to bite him in the ass. He should have just paid them for it.

"I'm sorry," Frankie finally said. "I'm sure you're a busy man, and we're wasting your time. We'll call when we have a small favor to ask for."

"I can't wait," Doc said.

She laughed awkwardly, then the line went dead.

Doc chuckled softly, then laid his head against the back of the couch and fell asleep.

"I've found her!" Jury exclaimed, shaking Doc awake.

"You what?" Doc mumbled.

"Found her."

Doc froze. "You wouldn't mess with me, would you?"

"Well, yeah, but not about this."

Doc jumped to his feet. "Well, what're we waiting for? Let's go get her!"

"Alright, but I get to drive."

Doc deliberated for a moment. He needed Jury, but letting another man drive his car was no different than letting him ride his horse or make love to his girl. It made him cringe just thinking about it.

"I suppose if you'd rather owe me another favor..." Jury shrugged.

"Not so much as a scratch!" Doc snapped. "She's rare."

Jury grinned widely. "The good news is," he said as they walked outside, "we're leaving my house. So if something gets broken, it's bound to be something of yours!"

Doc walked around his shiny McLaren, running his hands gently over its clean lines. "It's not my idea, love. If he hurts you, I'll find a way to make him pay."

"You coming?" Jury asked from inside the car.

"Coming."

Jury took off with a tire squeal, heading straight towards a pedestrian. The man looked up in surprise and jumped out of the way. "Sorry!" Jury yelled out the window as they passed.

"Are you trying to get me arrested?" Doc growled.

"You know that's not going to happen."

"I'm not so sure right now."

In general, the Hidden world was very similar to the norm world. The most startling difference was that some of the Hidden residents were not humanoid, or, even if they were, the ones like Simon would have a difficult time living among humans.

There were other differences, plenty of them, but the governmental side of things was not that different at all. There was plumbing and electricity. There were building codes. There were laws. If the laws were broken, there was a police force, the Magistratus, to enforce the rules; and there was a judicial system to dole out punishments. That being said, a cryp wasn't likely to get arrested in the norm world. Even if they'd done something really, really bad.

If a norm police officer entered a cryp's identification number into the norm system, they received a warning that basically told them to describe the nature of the problem in the box on the screen, submit the form, release the offender, and forget they'd ever seen anything. The information entered went directly to the Magistratus, and it was up to them to continue the investigation.

Some cryps had both norm and cryp identification. Doc, for instance. He couldn't operate in the norm world without norm paperwork, and he couldn't partake in the Hidden world without cryp paperwork.

He found the whole structure needlessly overcomplicated. Some of the old ones argued that modernity was the issue, but Doc insisted that apart from technology, modernity, in the way they meant it, had always existed.

Even thousands of years ago there were laws and people enforcing them. There were landowners, and there were renters. There were the elite and the working class. Really, not that much had changed, just the platform it functioned on.

Jury squealed around a corner, and Doc swallowed a surge of irritation. "Where're we going?" he asked.

"Church."

"What?!"

"Don't worry. I'm pretty sure the old stories about demons

burning if they enter a church aren't true. You should be fine."

"But what about you?" Doc laughed.

"Nah, the church never could figure out how to identify a proper witch. For the most part, they just burned people they didn't like. And furthermore, fire's an earthly element. If a bunch of idiots tied me to a stake and tried to burn me, I can guarantee you it wouldn't be successful."

"Doesn't that just prove the point?"

"Hadn't thought of that," Jury said with a laugh. "I suppose they'd eventually find a way to kill me, huh?"

Jury drove onto a college campus and parked in one of their lots. "You'd better pay the piper," he said, gesturing towards a meter in the center of the lot. "Norms are vicious about their parking fees."

Doc stepped from the car, examining the paint as he walked past it. There weren't any scratches. Yet.

He stopped in front of the meter and read the instructions. "Five dollars an hour! For parking?!" Doc exclaimed. "That's highway robbery!" He'd once bought a horse for five dollars. It hadn't been a good horse, but still.

He shoved his credit card into the machine and payed for five hours. He had no idea where they were going. Jury hadn't exactly spelled it out.

He followed Jury as he headed out across the campus towards one of the churches. "It's a little ironic, really," Jury said. "For a witch to hide inside a church. You'd be surprised at how many witches hide right under the church's nose by being part of it," Jury went on. "My great-great-grandfather was a minister. I read one of his sermons once; it was incredible. His tongue would've given you a run for your money."

Perhaps he preferred Jury when he was taciturn and angry. "If you want to get together and play cards, knock back some whiskey, and chat, I'm game," Doc said. "But right now, could we focus on the task at hand?"

"This is certainly a twist," Jury laughed. "You asking me to take it seriously."

Doc shrugged. Most things he didn't take seriously, and he could find amusement in nearly every situation, but this was a payment he needed to make. He needed to save Sofia. If he didn't...

He hadn't ever failed before. He'd lost plenty of games, but he'd never not delivered on a favor or a promise. Señora Teodora had given him life; if he failed in this, then he didn't deserve all those years she'd given him. All those moments of joy, of love making, of whiskey, of breathing the air.

"I'm pretty sure she's in here," Jury said as he started up the stone steps of an ornate church building. Doc's heart began to pound. If she was here... He would have won. Maybe. Assuming his getting to her now protected her from whatever happened if he didn't protect her. Damn Andrew and his confusing time rants.

Jury tried the door and found it locked. "You or me?" he asked.

Doc glanced behind him, then gave the door a light kick, tearing the lock from the door frame. They stepped inside and closed the door behind them.

The church was empty, but light filtered through the stained glass windows making the dusty light sparkle.

For a moment, Doc's mind wandered. He watched himself as a child bowing between pews, bony knees digging into the kneeler. He watched himself beg. He begged God to save his mother, for hours and hours. He begged; he made promises;

he gave all his money to the poor. But if God did exist, he hadn't bothered to notice young John's pleas. His mother had died in a sweaty bed, coughing up blood until she couldn't cough any longer.

No one had begged for Doc's life, but witchcraft and murder had saved it. He'd never kneel again. He'd never beg. If he wanted something done, he'd do it himself.

They walked through the nave, glancing along the empty, dust-covered pews. There was no one here. Doc couldn't even see a spot where the dust had been disturbed.

"She's not here," he said, frustration filling him.

"Goddamn, Doc, since when do you give up so easily? This is just one room."

They carefully searched the entire church. Doc opened every cabinet and looked inside, but he already knew she wasn't here. Their own tracks had smeared the dust on the dull wooden floor. No one had been here in years.

"We're dealing with a shaman," Jury said as he studied the nave once more. "Nothing is necessarily as it seems." He stood behind the pulpit for a moment, gazing out at the pews. "It's been a long time since I've been to a church, but I feel like I'm forgetting something," he mumbled. "Something to do with wine."

"Wine?" Doc asked.

"Yeah, churches love wine; don't you remember? Especially old churches."

"So? Oh," Doc said. "Wine."

"Yeah. Wine equals wine cellar; so where is it?"

Doc started looking at the floor. "It wouldn't be here," he said. "Not in the nave. Maybe in the back?"

"Why didn't we see it?"

"You just said why! A shaman."

Doc rushed through the nave to the back of the church where the reverend's study was located. There were still books on the shelves, abandoned sermons and books of theology. A desk dominated the center of the room, and a plush leather desk chair lay sideways on the floor behind it, a spiderweb covering its wooden limbs.

"If I was touting a fire-breathing, remote deity, I'd want my wine close at hand," Doc drawled.

Jury's hands glowed blue for just a second, and then the blue magic spiked into the air and zipped around the room before settling on the floor in a two by two square.

Jury grinned at Doc. "After you."

"Beauty before age," Doc chuckled.

"I believe the saying is age before beauty. You go ahead."

"Prima donna," Doc muttered. He felt the floor for a latch, wiggled his fingers beneath it, and pulled the hidden door open, staring down into the darkness for a moment.

"How powerful do you think she is, anyway?" Doc asked.

"I honestly don't know."

"Would you say that a shaman who knew she was in danger would be inclined to set traps?"

"I definitely would."

"Can you see them?"

"Afraid not. I can scan an area for witch spells, but shaman spells are an entirely different thing. I'm not even sure if I would see them."

"I was hoping you wouldn't say that," Doc sighed. "The direct approach is probably best then."

"Assuming she finds your face trustworthy."

"Most women do."

"Since she's possibly the last shaman running free in Denver, I'd guess she's a good deal smarter than that."

Doc couldn't help it; he laughed. "Here's to hoping she's not," he chuckled as he stepped into the hole. "Señorita Sofia?" he called out. "My name is Doc Holliday. Your grandmother, Señora Teodora, sent me to help you."

He descended two more steps. "I don't mean you harm. I'm here to help you. I swear to it. So if you have any traps set up, I would very much appreciate it if you removed them before I step into them."

He reached the bottom of the staircase. So far, so good, but his instinct told him he'd reached the end of the line. "Señorita, are you here? If you can't trust me, trust my friend Jury."

"He uses the term friend rather loosely," Jury put in.

"Not helping," Doc muttered. He took a deep sigh and readied his foot to step forward. "I'm taking another step," he said. "It's now or never." He lifted his foot and began to move it slowly forward.

"Stop!" a woman cried out. "Don't move. Why should I trust you? You could easily have found out about Lita, but can you prove it?"

"You can prove it, can't you?" Jury hissed.

Doc wasn't sure. That entirely depended on what Señora Teodora had told Sofia before today. "I know you met Señora Teodora in your dreams."

"Lucky guess," she scoffed.

He hadn't come this far, gotten this close, to fold at the end. He had to find a way to convince her. He flipped through his memories, trying to find something she might know.

"Did she tell you about Petra?" he finally asked.

"What about her?"

"Petra was her granddaughter."

"Great-great-granddaughter," Sofia corrected.

That didn't surprise him. Señora Teodora hadn't looked a day over forty, but witches aged much slower than humans. Unlike vampires, they did still age, they just aged very, very, very slowly.

"Anyway," Doc continued. "I once spent some time in Pueblo, and while I was there I met a young man named Balam. He lost rather badly in a round of faro trying to make a big win," Doc tried to explain.

"Do you have a point here?" Jury whispered.

"Patience; I'm getting there."

"I hope so."

"Anyway, he thought that if he made a fortune, he might be able to convince his great-uncle twice removed, I'm a little sketchy on the details, to dissolve his daughter's engagement to a rich man. The two were distant cousins but very much in love."

"What's your point?" Sofia snapped.

"I'm getting there! If you don't want all the details, long story short, on Petra's wedding day she was found in an extremely compromising position with yours truly. Sadly, the wedding was cancelled, and her father was only too happy to let Balam take his soiled daughter off his hands."

He shrugged slightly. "It was a happy ending for most involved, although Señora Teodora did have a rather stern word with me."

"That's your proof?" Jury whispered.

Sofia was silent for a long time, and Doc waited patiently, staring into the dark. Finally she demanded, "What did Lita do to you?"

"Isn't my story proof enough? Who else would know those details?" he asked.

"What did she do to you?"

He sighed. "She showed up in my bedroom one night and nearly ripped off my manhood." Behind him Jury started laughing, and Doc resisted the urge to elbow him in the balls. "But later Balam must have told her that I did it to help them," Doc added. "Not that I minded. Petra was gorgeous."

"You're disgusting!" Sofia snapped.

"I appreciate a fine woman," he drawled. "Now, have I proven myself? Can I step into the room without something terrible happening to me?"

"I suppose," she said, and suddenly the cellar was filled with green light. Doc blinked, allowing his eyes to adjust before surveying the room. Silbu was right. Sofia was definitely not alone.

# 15

"I can honestly say I have never seen this many gargoyles in one place," Jury said softly.

Doc could only agree. The cellar was packed full of them. Like sardines in a tin can. And Sofia was in the middle, sitting on the largest one's shoulder.

He stared at her. She wasn't at all like he'd imagined her. He'd thought she'd look like Señora Teodora, majestic and foreboding, but she didn't. In fact, she was nothing like Señora Teodora.

If Doc was pressed to describe her, he'd say Sofia looked like a pixie hooker from Vegas. Disappointment coursed through him, and he tried not to analyze it. Sometimes the purse turned out not to be as good as he'd expected. It was still a purse though, and that's what he needed to remember.

Jury pushed past him, walking boldly through the menacing gargoyles and stopping in front of Sofia. "We didn't really get a proper introduction," he said. "My name's Jury, Thomas Jury."

"I've heard of you," she said, ignoring his outstretched hand.

"Really? Good things, I hope."

She shrugged; and Doc grinned, his discontentment of a moment ago forgotten.

"Why're you here?" Doc asked.

"Someone's trying to find me," she replied, dropping to the floor and moving through the gargoyles until she was facing him.

"The Bureau?"

"The FBI?" she asked, brow wrinkled. "I don't know."

That was interesting. "Do you live in the Hidden?" Doc asked.

"The hidden?"

Very interesting. "How long have you been hiding?"

"A month," she replied. "Ever since the border went up."

"The border?" Jury broke in. "What border?"

"There's a border around the city. Can't you see it?"

"No." Jury looked at Doc in question, and Doc shrugged. He had no idea what she was talking about.

"How do you know they're looking for you?" Doc asked.

"The gargoyles told me."

Doc cast a sideways glance at Jury, and Jury shook his head. "I'm a tad confused," Doc admitted. "You aren't part of the Hidden, you don't know what the Bureau is, but you think someone is searching for you because the gargoyles told you. Did I cover all the important parts?"

"I dunno," she said.

"How did you find so many gargoyles?" Jury asked.

"I didn't find them," she said. "I made them."

"You made them?" he repeated, eyes wide with shock.

"Yes."

"Is that a big deal?" Doc asked Jury

"Yeah," Jury said, but didn't explain.

"If you have different magic," Doc said, "how come you both have gargoyles?"

"They aren't the same," Jury stated, like it was somehow obvious. Doc left that alone. Even if Jury explained the difference, he probably wouldn't understand.

"Wait, if you don't know about the Hidden, how have you heard of Jury?" Doc demanded.

"He has a vlog I follow."

"Excuse me?" Doc asked.

"A vlog. On modern witchcraft," she said.

Doc covered his mouth with his hand, trying to hide his grin. "I'm sorry," he suddenly laughed. "I need to really savor this moment. Can you repeat that one more time?"

"What?" Sofia asked in confusion.

"The part about Jury and the vlog," Doc laughed.

Jury punched him in the arm. "This isn't really the time," he snapped. "Besides, it's a legitimate advertising forum. You can't just list 'witch' in the damn yellow pages!"

"You're wealthy," Doc gasped, trying to control his laughter. "You don't need to work."

"It's a way to fill the hours," Jury ground out. "It's better than screwing and gambling all the time!"

Doc was laughing so hard that he had to lean on the wall just to hold himself up. "Thomas Jury," he laughed. "Witch vlogger. Oh hell, I have to look you up!"

He pulled out his phone, but Jury snatched it from his hand. "You can make fun of me later; right now..." he gestured towards Sofia.

"Sorry," Doc chuckled. "It just... surprised me; that's all. Does your mother know?"

"No!" Jury snapped. "And if you tell her..."

"You'll what?" Doc demanded.

"I'll bring my parents over to your place the next time they come to berate me."

Doc shuddered. "Your secret's safe with me," he said sincerely. "Now where were we? Right. You." He pointed at Sofia. "We need to get you someplace safe."

"What's wrong with here?" she asked.

"We found you."

"Point taken." She turned to the gargoyles, closed her eyes, and suddenly the gargoyles began to glow a strange green color. They grew brighter and brighter, then all at once they began to fade, and the green glow rushed across the cellar and into Sofia's chest.

"Can you do that?" Doc hissed. Jury didn't respond, just glared at him, and Doc took that to mean no.

"That was... impressive," Doc said.

"Is it?" she asked with a slight shrug. "I've been doing it since I was little."

He was definitely in way over his head.

"Did you really know Lita?" she asked, brown eyes narrow with mistrust.

"If by Lita, you mean Señora Teodora, then yes."

"How?" she whispered, gently touching his face. "You're young."

There was so much she didn't know.

"I'm... immortal," Doc said carefully.

She burst out laughing. "Immortal! That's not a thing!"

Doc cast a sideways glance at Jury. He wasn't sure how much to tell her and how fast he should do it.

"Next, you'll tell me you're a vampire or something," she giggled.

"There are some similarities—" Jury began, but Doc stopped him by stomping on his foot.

"I think it'd be best if we talk about this later. Let's focus on getting out of here," Doc said, turning and starting back up the stairs.

"So, Sofia, why don't you like me?" Jury asked as they entered the church proper.

"I didn't say that," she hedged.

"It was implied, wasn't it, Doc?"

"It was," Doc agreed.

They quickly crossed the nave, and Doc took a quick peek out the front door to make sure there was no one who looked out of place before he stepped back out into the sunlight.

"Come on," he urged, hurrying them towards the car.

"So?" Jury asked.

"So what?" Doc replied.

"I wasn't talking to you. I was talking to Sofia. Why don't you like me?"

"Is this really the time?" she muttered.

"It's not like we're doing anything else."

Doc rolled his eyes, unlocked his car, slid into the driver's seat, motioning for Sofia to follow him.

"What the hell is this thing?" Sofia asked, staring at him. "The driver seat's in the middle!"

"She's a McLaren," Doc said, running his hand over the steering wheel. "She's beauty on wheels."

"But how can you drive from the middle?" Sofia stuttered.

Doc stopped himself from rolling his eyes and smiled at her widely. "I can drive from anywhere. It's one of my many talents."

"Just get in the car," Jury suggested as he sat in the bucket seat on Doc's right. "Otherwise this'll turn into a whole thing."

Sofia finally climbed into the car, closing the door softly behind her. "This is so weird," she muttered.

Jury was silent for a second then he said, "I just don't get it. You watch my vlog."

"That's just it!" Sofia exclaimed. "You're all about witchcraft and this and that, and you talk about the four elements and how to tap into them, and it's just a bunch of shit! None of it works!"

Doc struggled not to laugh as he shifted into reverse and backed out of the parking spot.

"That's because you're not a witch!" Jury snapped, voice hard with annoyance.

"Really? I didn't see you materializing gargoyles. I did that. So there!" Sofia snapped back.

"Children, children," Doc interrupted. "What Jury is so eloquently trying to say is that you are a shaman, or rather that your magic comes from spiritual elements; whereas Jury is a witch. His magic comes from earthy elements. There, all explained. You can be friends now."

Doc pulled onto the road and headed towards Dulcis Requiem. He could think of safer places, especially since he'd already been attacked there, but he wanted to grab a few things before they went into hiding for the next two days.

"What do you mean spiritual elements?" Sofia asked.

"I don't actually know," Doc chuckled. "Jury?"

"It's hard to explain," Jury said. "I haven't spent any time with shamans, so I'm not really all that clear on how your magic works, but for instance, you can walk the dreaming, but I can't. The dreaming is part of the ether."

"There're more people like me?" she whispered.

"Sure, or at least there used to be. They seem to be in short supply right now."

"The Bureau is hunting them down for some reason," Doc put in. "That's who's after you. At least I think it is."

"What bureau?"

"The Bureau of Cryptid Affairs."

"Cryptid Affairs?"

Doc glanced at her and saw she was nearly as pale as Aine. She'd handled things well enough for a minute or two, but it was suddenly dawning on her that she had no idea what was going on. She was probably also realizing that she'd just climbed into a car with two complete strangers.

"Listen, there's apparently a lot you don't know, and I can't explain it right now because someone is following us, and I need to drive."

"Are you sure?" Jury asked glancing out the back window.

"Pretty sure."

He'd probably led them right to her, but he'd be damned if he was the thing to cause her disappearance. Andrew had sworn that he didn't think time worked that way, but honestly, who could really know?

Doc punched the gas and tore around a corner, swerving to avoid a slower car. He flinched when a parking meter tore along the side of his car but didn't slow down. He needed to lose them fast.

"A little help here, Jury?"

Jury turned in his seat and moved his hands. Doc could see Jury's blue light energy magic dust, or whatever the hell it was, floating around Jury's hand, but nothing happened. The car just kept creeping closer and closer to Doc's bumper.

"Seriously?!" Doc snapped.

"They have it shielded," Jury growled. "I'll try something else." Whatever he did didn't work, because the following car just kept following.

Doc was driving in a tight circle, trying to avoid any areas with severe traffic. If they came to a standstill, they'd have to fight it out on the street, and open conflict between cryps among the norms was a severe violation of the rules, not that he cared. Jury probably cared though.

He turned the wheel, and the car skidded around a corner, tail end tapping a parked car. Doc hissed as the metals rubbed together. "I'm sorry, love. It's Jury's fault. If his magic was worth a damn—"

"My magic is fine!" Jury argued. "They've got some kind of damn protection shield. What really burns me is that a witch would've had to create it. You know the world is going to shit when witches turn against their own kind."

"Get off your damn soap box and figure out a way to get them off our tail!" Doc commanded.

"Shouldn't we call the police?" Sofia gasped as Doc hit the gas again.

"And tell them what?" Doc snapped. "That you're a shaman, Jury's a witch, and we're being chased by a governmental agency inside the Hidden?"

"Don't treat me like I'm stupid!" she complained.

"I'm not. You just don't know what's going on."

"Can you materialize other stuff?" Jury asked Sofia.

"What do you mean?"

Doc rolled his eyes. Sofia was crying a little, and he could tell she wasn't going to be any help at all.

"Like a spike strip!" Jury snapped.

"I don't even know what that is!" she exclaimed.

Doc cut in front of a city bus and punched the gas. If he could make it to a crossroads in time, he could lose them. He watched his rearview mirror. The tailing car still hadn't made it around the bus, so Doc turned left and zoomed down the street, bumping into parked cars just to get through. He checked the mirror one last time and grinned. He'd lost them. If he kept zigzagging, they'd be home free. He turned again, then again, heading away from his hotel and towards the interstate.

Jury was yelling at Sofia, and she was crying, but Doc ignored them. He had more important things to do right now than baby a full-grown woman.

He glanced in the rearview and hissed. How the hell had they found him? It didn't make sense. Unless, of course, they were tracking them somehow. He should have thought of that. It's not like this was his first time.

"Jury, did you check the cars for trackers?"

"Um, no. Which kind?"

"Goddamn it! All of them!"

"Right, sorry!" After a minute, Jury exclaimed, "Found it!"

"Get rid of it!" Doc snapped.

"Already did."

"Was it normal or magical?" Doc asked as he skidded through a red light.

"Magical."

"Did you check for normal?"

"Yes."

"You sure?"

"Yes!"

"Alright, instead of a direct magical attack, could you try something more creative?"

"Such as?" Jury snarled.

"I'm a little unclear on how it works..."

"I can affect and utilize what's already there. Wind currents, rocks, metal. And I can cast spells utilizing those elements, but I can't create out of nothing, like some people should be able to."

"Alright, so can you pull down a stop light?" Doc asked, tapping his brakes to avoid eating the backend of a slow-moving car. He wrenched the wheel to the right, bumped up onto the sidewalk, drove slowly down the sidewalk for a second, allowing the pedestrians to jump out of his way, then hopped back down onto the street.

"I can do that," Jury said, grinning like a boy in a toy shop.

"Then do it!" Doc ordered. He sped through a light, watching in his rearview mirror. The tailing car wasn't very far behind them, so if Jury didn't get his timing right, it would be a waste of effort. Fortunately, Jury was good at timing.

The stop light dropped just before the car reached it. The car skidded to a stop but still crashed into the light bar. It didn't stop their pursuers though. They just backed up and drove around the light, and, as far as Doc could tell, the car didn't have a single scratch or dent.

"We're gonna need something bigger," Jury stated, searching the streets. "I've got an idea," he said.

"Better be a good one," Doc muttered. "We're running out of gas."

"Already?"

"It's not like I knew we were going for a high-speed chase."

"Always be prepared," Jury declared. "It's the Jury family motto."

"Say it in Latin then," Doc shot back.

"Semper paratus," Jury said easily.

"Isn't that the Coast Guard's motto?" Doc demanded.

"The Jury family had it first," Jury shrugged.

"Something big," Doc said. "NOW!"

"I've got this," Jury said.

"Don't say you've got it, just do it!"

Doc was at the end of his patience. If they didn't shake them soon, he was going to have to do it the old-fashioned way. One throat at a time.

He careened through another intersection, ripping the wheel violently to avoid being t-boned by another car. Jury was muttering to himself, and behind him Doc could see the cars on the street moving. They were shifting sideways, some even flipping on their sides, and Doc realized Jury was using the cars to create a wall.

He slammed the gas pedal to the floor and turned right the first chance he had. He sped through a residential area, turning erratically as he went, heading nowhere in particular, relieved to see that this time they had definitely lost them.

Without warning, Sofia suddenly grabbed his arm and screamed, "STOP!!!!" Doc didn't see anything though. He didn't even see it when his lovely red McLaren crashed into it going eighty miles an hour.

# 16

Doc blinked slowly, staring in confusion at his broken windshield.

"What the hell was that?" Jury mumbled, stirring slightly beside him.

Doc shrugged, and glass tinkled from his head.

"It's the freaking barrier," Sofia coughed. "Can't you see it?"

Doc still couldn't see it. All he could see was the mashed up front end of his car.

"You killed her," he said flatly. "This is all your fault, Jury. You jinxed me from the outset."

"Sorry," Jury said, not looking the least bit sorry. "We should probably go."

"Without giving her a proper burial?" Doc tore off his seatbelt, unbuckled Sofia, and pushed her out of the car.

"It's a car, Doc. You don't bury a car."

"So you're just going to leave her out here, all torn up, where just anyone can see her?" Doc walked around the backend, moaning slightly when he saw all the dents and scrapes. "I can't believe you did this."

"Technically, the invisible wall did it," Jury retorted.

"And why did I bring you along," Doc growled, "if not to give me a heads up on things like invisible walls?!"

"I probably would have," Jury said, trying to keep his face serious. "If I could see it."

"Why can't you see it?"

"I don't know."

"How come she can see it?" Doc pointed at Sofia.

"I don't know."

"What do you know?!"

"That we should get out of here before they come looking for us."

"What the hell is wrong with you guys?!" Sofia screamed. "We were just in a car wreck! Who cares about the freaking car? I could have a neck fracture or a punctured lung!"

"You don't," Doc said dismissively.

"How the hell do you know?!"

"Don't worry; I'm a doctor. You're fine."

"Oh, the 'I'm a doctor' line," Jury said. "Haven't heard that in a while."

"Women aren't as impressed by it as they used to be," Doc replied with a shrug.

"So now you use the 'I'm a billionaire' line?"

"Hell no!"

"Are you serious right now?" Sofia shrieked.

"She's no fun," Doc said.

"I'll second that."

"You guys are insane! I'm calling the cops!"

"Really?" Jury laughed. "What're you gonna say?"

"I should've stayed in the cellar," she muttered.

"You'll warm up to us," Jury said. "Probably."

Doc placed his hand on the car's side. It was still warm,

but he knew it was dead. "I'm sorry, sweetheart. I should have brought the Lambo."

He turned away from it and said thoughtfully, "Why is this the first we've heard of a border anyway? Seems like that would be all over the Hidden?"

"I'm not sure," Jury said, reaching out his hand to feel it. "That's strange," he muttered. "I don't feel anything."

"And I walked all the way around the car!" Doc exclaimed. "Sofia, walk through the border."

"I can't," she said.

"How do you know?"

"I've tried before."

"So where exactly is the border?" Doc asked.

"It's around the main part of Denver."

"Denver the actual city?"

"What do you mean?"

"Like we can't go out to Thornton or Arvada?"

"No. It's just like right here, around the center."

"Interesting," Doc mused. "I guess I need to start getting safe houses a little closer to home. Oh well, I know a guy. We need to get to Union Station."

It took them nearly an hour to get there. Mostly because Doc refused to use a taxi. He had no idea what they were dealing with. If the Bureau was really behind it and at least some witches were helping them, who knew who else was backing them? The Magistratus could be in their pocket. They could be hooking into the norm police system. For all Doc knew, norm police men were searching the streets for them right now.

So they'd walked, and after walking in a circle for a while, Doc had used his considerable charm and a couple hundred dollar bills to acquire them some different clothes. He wasn't thrilled to be wearing joggers, but he suspected no one would ever look for him in joggers either. And it helped that Jury looked absolutely ridiculous in shorts. Sofia had refused to wear someone else's clothes, and Doc hadn't pushed it. It's not like changing her clothes would change her ridiculous hair.

He was beginning to wonder what Señora Teodora even saw in Sofia, but it didn't really matter. He'd given his word, so no matter how annoying she was, he would protect her until the time had passed.

He accidently glanced down, grimacing when he saw the light grey material swallowing his legs. Thank goodness he'd gotten a backpack to carry their regular clothes in. Just the thought of wearing these loose, unfitted clothes for the next two days made him want to weep. Clothes may not make the man, but they certainly improved him. There's no way he would have gotten as far as he had if he'd worn joggers and t-shirts.

He glanced at Jury. "Plaid looks good on you," he chuckled.

"Stop bringing it up," Jury muttered. "I still think you should've worn the shorts."

"And take off my knife? I don't think so."

"Excuses, excuses."

When they finally reached Union Station, Doc scanned the chairs for Darius. For a moment he didn't think he was there, but then he spotted him at a table near the street playing a game with a teenager.

Doc motioned for them to sit. He wasn't about to interrupt Darius's chess match. That would be nothing short of rude.

"What're we doing?" Sofia complained.

"Waiting," Doc said.

"For what?"

"Don't worry about it." He ignoring her whining and waited patiently until the boy shook Darius's hand and left, then Doc stood and approached the table.

"Darius," he said softly, sitting across from the old man.

Darius glanced up with a smile, then did a confused double take. "Is that really you, Doc? You look..."

"Preposterous?" Doc supplied.

"No... relaxed."

"Not hardly," Doc chuckled. "I've a favor to ask, old friend. I need a place to lay low. I wouldn't ask, because I might be putting you in danger, but I don't have access to my normal hideouts."

"I could stand the company."

"I've two friends with me."

"It'll be a bit tight, but we'll make do."

"Thank you," Doc said. "I knew I could count on you."

Within the hour, they had settled into Darius's small one-bedroom apartment.

"Would you be up to going out to get some food and other necessities?" Doc asked casually once Darius had given them the tour.

"Whatever you need," the old man replied.

"I need whiskey," Doc whispered, handing him a wad of cash. "And lots of it. They'd probably prefer food type items." He glanced back at the table where Sofia was sitting with her head in her hands. Jury was sitting beside her, an irritated look on his face.

"Jury looks a tad peaky," Doc said softly. "Make sure you get some meat and whatever else you want, and don't worry about the cost."

As soon as Darius was gone, Doc turned to Jury and demanded, "Have you done what you can to hide us?"

"Yep."

"You're sure? You thought of everything?"

"I don't know about 'everything'," Jury admitted, "but I covered the usual bases."

Doc sat at the table. "This is a mess," he said.

"What's your plan?"

"To sit here for another day until the danger has passed."

"What makes you think the danger will be passed?" Jury asked.

That's the question, isn't it? Doc thought as his head began to throb. It had always been the question. In fact, he and Andrew had argued the semantics of it for hours.

"Time isn't set," Andrew had once insisted. "It can be changed. Even if something has already happened in one time, a tweak in another time can totally rewrite it. You understand?"

"No," Doc said. He truly didn't. To hear Andrew tell it, time was like taking a hundred decks of cards, removing a hundred random cards, then throwing everything out into a big, messy pile.

"I'm saying that just because Sofia will disappear in one timeline, doesn't mean you can't change the event that caused it in another timeline."

"But what if I am the event?"

"I doubt it," Andrew said. "In the time she disappeared, you were already dead."

"That makes no sense," Doc argued.

Andrew's eyes glowed intently. "See, if I accidently killed my grandpa today, I would cease to exist. Then everything I've ever done would be erased."

"Even though it's already happened?"

"Exactly."

That sounded terrible. He honestly didn't understand how Andrew could live with that hanging over his head. He could sneeze and change the world. Yet here he was, drinking coffee, telling nonsensical jokes, and laughing with his men.

Doc's mind refocused on the problem in front of him. In one time, Sofia disappeared tomorrow. So logically if Doc kept her safe until then, he'd changed time. BUT, it occurred to him now, that she might just disappear the next day or the next. He couldn't stop at changing that one event. He had to remove the threat completely.

"We need to figure out what's going on," he said.

"For once I agree with you," Jury said, wrinkling his brow in disgust.

"Don't take it so hard," Doc laughed. "You can't always be wrong."

"This is why I hate you."

"That can't be true," Doc said sadly. "What about the friendship bracelet you gave me?"

Jury's eyelid twitched. "It's a protection bracelet."

"No, that can't be right," Doc argued. "Look." He held his wrist out next to Jury's. "They match."

Red was creeping up Jury's cheeks now. "They are protection bracelets," he insisted again. "And if you're not careful, I'll take it away."

Doc chuckled softly. "No need. I'll be good. I swear." He winked at Jury, then looked across the table at Sofia.

They definitely needed to figure out what was going on, but he supposed they needed to fill her in on what they knew first. She hadn't said a word since they'd arrived, and she was watching Doc with a worried expression. He wished there was a way to make this easier on her. But there simply wasn't an easy way to say 'the world as you know it is a lie'. He guessed the best thing to do was start with what she did know.

"How did you get to be so proficient at magic?" he asked.

Her troubled eyes caught his, and she didn't speak for a moment. Finally she said, "I really don't know how to do much, just the gargoyles and the dreaming. Which is really pretty useless. Mom tried to teach me how to make plants and stuff grow, but I can't do it."

"Where is she?"

"Dead."

There was sorrow in her voice, sorrow Doc understood. "How long ago?" he asked gently, just to make sure it didn't have to do with the issue at hand.

"Seven years or so. She died in a dream."

Jury leaned forward. "A dream?" he asked.

"Yes. She once told me that for us the dreaming is real. I wasn't with her. I'm not sure what killed her."

Virgil had said that Hieronymus Bosch took over the Bureau seven years ago. Coincidence? Doc wasn't sure.

"So it's just you," Doc stated.

"And the gargoyles." She finally smiled. "They have quite a bit of personality, you know."

"I didn't. In fact I don't think Jury's do."

"What do you know?" Jury snapped.

"Nothing. I was just saying."

"They're... Who am I kidding?" Jury muttered. "They're totally stiff."

Sofia didn't laugh like Doc had thought she might. She just looked between them as if she wasn't quite sure how she had ended up with them. Doc wasn't either.

He glanced at Jury, and Jury shrugged. They both knew that the only real way to get answers was to find Bosch. But Doc had to wait. He had to wait one day. He needed to know that he'd changed it. Then he'd be confident moving forward that he could handle whatever they stumbled into. That gave them a little over twenty-four hours to fill her in on everything she'd been missing.

"Where's Darius and that whiskey?" Doc muttered.

"I can," Jury snapped his fingers with a grin, "bring you the whiskey from my place."

"Absolutely not! It should be illegal for such swill to bear the name whiskey."

"Bennie said it's all the rage right now."

"Bennie's a lying sack."

"That's strange; I even told him it was for you," Jury said, trying to smile innocently.

Doc ignored him and asked Sofia. "Do you play poker?"

"Um... no."

"You'll learn." Doc pulled out his cards and dealt three hands, explaining the rules as he did. They played for a while before the door opened and Darius tottered inside, weighed down with several grocery bags.

Doc got up to help him. "I didn't know what you'd like," Darius apologized, "so I got a little bit of everything."

"I'm sure it'll be perfect," Doc assured him, setting the bags on the counter.

Jury pushed Doc out of the way and grabbed a bunch of bananas, peeling one on the spot.

"What's with you?" Doc laughed.

"Hungry," Jury said around a mouthful.

"You don't say?"

"I'll put this away," Darius said, trying to shoo them both out of the kitchen.

"I'm about to break some rules, Darius," Doc said. "There're things you don't know and aren't supposed to know. Can I trust you to keep my secrets safe? A lot of people depend on it."

Darius chuckled softly. "I'd be a bit of a fool not to know that you're different than other folks. I've known you for twenty years now."

Doc grinned briefly. He'd always liked Darius. Quick wit and a good game. Excellent qualities in a companion. "The things I say can never leave this room," Doc said. "Never. It could put countless lives at risk."

"You've my word, Doc," Darius said seriously. "I'll not betray you. I won't."

Doc believed him. "Good man," he said. "Even better if you remembered the whiskey."

"Whiskey!" Darius exclaimed. "I knew I was forgetting something."

Behind him Jury snickered loudly, and Doc reconsidered the pink whiskey. Nope. He couldn't do it.

"Just yanking your chain," Darius chuckled. "I've got it right here."

"Oh, good. I was worried I'd have to sober up," Doc exclaimed gratefully.

"When was the last time you were sober anyway?" Jury jeered.

"At a guess," Doc mused, "during the early days of prohibition."

"I'm surprised."

"Well, it didn't last long," Doc drawled. "I won an entire liquor store in a card game. That was a good game," he said dreamily.

"I hate to interrupt your trip down memory lane, but do

you think you can finally explain what's going on?" Sofia demanded petulantly.

"Doubtful," Doc said. "But I'll try. What I said to Darius goes double for you. This conversation does not leave this room. Do you understand?"

"Who would I tell?" she snorted.

"No one. That's the point. Should we start at the beginning?"

"No," Jury cut in. "I don't think I could stand it if you gave us a history lesson right now."

"Maybe I should have Jervis bring Thaddeus over."

"Absolutely not! Why don't you just let me take care of it?"

"If you insist," Doc replied with a shrug as he filled his coffee cup with whiskey.

"So you live in what we call the norm world," Jury began.

"Good start," Doc interjected.

"Shut up! There's another world called the Hidden."

Doc leaned back his head and closed his eyes, letting Jury's words wash over him. When he'd first learned about the Hidden, his world had been a little shaken, but it hadn't lasted long. He wasn't a man to let something small, like a hidden world just around the corner, ruin his day. It was just a different type of opportunity. And furthermore, it was a world he fit into rather well.

Some creatures found it too difficult to immigrate to the United States, and some didn't want to; but there were Hidden places everywhere, and Doc had been to many of them. He'd met creatures from all over the world. Banshees from Ireland, gremlins from England, a minotaur from Greece.

He'd played Choko with an African vampire who was more than a thousand years old. He'd made love to a selkie on a beach in Iceland. He'd spent two days playing poker with a tribe of shapeshifting wolves in Germany. He'd killed an evil skinwalker in India, and it hadn't been easy, considering she was a tiger. So yes, his world had been shaken, but in a good way. And he never would have seen any of it if it wasn't for Sofia.

He wished he could tell Señora Teodora that he'd found her. He wished he could tell her how close he was. Just one more day. Just one more day.

Jury's voice faded, and Doc once again remembered the feel of the cold, hard cabin floor beneath him. He had been so tired, so tired, and he was dying. It was about damn time too. He was getting a little weary of holding on so hard. It was amusing that it had come down to killing a man and he'd failed. It was the only thing he was really good at.

A laugh gurgled its way up his throat, and he allowed it to come. If he was going to die, he'd rather die laughing than coughing. He laughed and laughed, waiting for the coughing to follow, but it didn't. And that's when he realized his chest was glowing.

He rolled to his knees and stood up, gazing down at the glowing tattoo in awe. "What is it doing?" he asked.

"Taking his essence and giving it to you," Señora Teodora said, motioning towards the dead man at Doc's feet.

"Ah, is that why I feel so... good?"

She smiled slightly. "You feel good because you are alive."

Doc wasn't sure yet. He took a tentative breath. His lungs moved without hurting. He took a deep breath. He didn't feel the slightest urge to cough. He pressed his hand to his chest, relief filling him when he felt his heart pumping madly.

"I am alive!" Doc laughed. "I'm alive!" He spun around the room, grabbing Señora Teodora's hands and taking her with him. "I'm dancing!" he exclaimed. "I'm alive, and I'm dancing!"

He began to laugh again, and this time she joined him. They spun to a halt in the middle of the room, and Doc said, "Thank you. I can't... Thank you." And he kissed her. Thoroughly and passionately because that's the only way he knew to show his gratitude. And she kissed him back.

It had been a glorious way to start a new life. Absolutely glorious.

"Are you listening?" Jury snapped, tearing Doc back into the moment.

"Sorry!" Doc opened his eyes with a grin. "What did I miss?"

"Everything!"

"I doubt that."

"She doesn't believe me."

"Wait, what?"

"She doesn't believe me."

"About what?"

"Anything!" Jury exclaimed with frustration.

Doc turned to Sofia. "You don't?"

She rolled her eyes. "I don't know what you expect. You come to me, tell me you're Doc Holliday, a man who died like two hundred years ago; and then you say there's a world right beside our own that's full of monsters, and nobody's ever noticed."

"I didn't say monsters," Jury broke in.

"Vampires, sasquatches, brownies, wood sprites, are you serious?!"

"I take offense on behalf of my friends," Doc said. "I've met more human monsters than I ever have Hidden ones."

"Take offense all you want!" she half-screamed. "They're not real!" She dropped her head into her hands and whimpered. "It's not real."

The problem wasn't that she didn't believe them. She did. She just didn't want to believe them.

"You believe us, don't you, Darius?" Doc asked.

Darius hadn't spoken yet, and his eyes were huge. He looked from Doc to Jury, then nodded his head once.

"See, Darius believes us."

Sofia opened her mouth to say something, but closed it.

"There's only one thing for it," Doc yawned. "We'll have to take her in."

"To the Hidden?" Jury hissed. Doc nodded. "Right now?"

"No. We'll wait until tomorrow," Doc decided. "Right now, I could use a nap. We should tie her to a chair though so she doesn't get any bright ideas about running off."

"Are you freaking serious?" Sofia screeched.

"The thing is I don't really trust you."

"You don't trust me?!" she yelled. "I don't trust you! You broke into my cellar, not the other way around."

"Nonetheless."

She jumped to her feet and opened her mouth, but stopped herself. "Fine," she muttered. "You can tie me up if you want, but at least let me use the bathroom first."

"You know where it's at," Doc drawled.

As soon as she had left the room, Jury hissed, "You really want to tie her up?"

"Unless you're going to stay up and watch her."

"Feels kinda... I don't know... Bad guyish."

Doc shrugged. "Can't win them all."

"How about I sleep in front of the door?"

"If you want."

"Want's a strong word," Jury muttered.

"Thanks for helping me find her," Doc said.

"You regretting it?"

"No. She just... I'm sure she'll get better."

Doc sat in Darius's recliner and said, "I suppose she can have the couch."

"You're really going to let me sleep in front of the door?" Jury complained.

"It's either that or tie her up," Doc murmured, eyes already closed.

"I hate you."

"You know that's not true."

# 17

"I'm still not sure this is a good idea," Jury muttered the next morning as Doc drove Darius's car towards a poor district of the Hidden.

"For the most part, unless we start flashing money," Doc argued, "We'll fit right in."

"That's the least of my worries," Jury huffed.

"You're right. She'll cause a fuss. Sofia, you're too showy; do you think you can tone it down a bit?"

"What?" she gasped from the back seat.

"Can't you use your magic to make yourself look more... normal?"

"Goddamn," Jury hissed. "Where's your Southern charm?"

"We don't have all day," Doc responded.

"A damn monkey could have been more tactful."

"You're the one who brought it up."

"I did not!" Jury snapped. "That's not even what I meant."

"Why didn't you say so?"

"I didn't not say so!" He sighed deeply. "You want me to glamour her?"

Doc considered that, then said, "No. It'll be alright. I'll protect her."

"That's ridiculous. I'll protect her." Jury insisted.

"I'm not sure you know how," Doc drawled, enjoying the outraged look on Jury's face.

"I've protected your ass more than once!"

"I let you think you did. It helps your general self-confidence and cheer. You were rather depressed that day."

"Goddamn it," Jury sputtered.

"I can protect myself, thank you," Sofia said icily.

"Excellent," Doc chuckled. "Would you mind keeping an eye on Jury while you're at it? He's a little off his game today."

"I can still kick your ass," Jury growled.

"I could use another tooth."

"Quit bickering," Darius ordered. "It's childish."

"I still don't understand why he's here," Jury ground out.

"He's helping us, and he deserves a little reward for his trouble," Doc explained once again.

"But he's a norm," Jury argued.

"I used to be a norm. I know how it feels."

"Fine, but if we get in trouble for this, I'm blaming it on you."

"I'd expect nothing less."

"Are you guys like enemies or something?" Sofia asked.

"Nah, they're like an old married couple," Darius put in with a chuckle.

Doc cast a sideways glance at Jury. "They just don't get us," he said with a shrug.

"No one does," Jury agreed.

Doc parked the car, and they all climbed out onto the sidewalk. Sofia looked up and down the street, then demanded, "So where is it?"

They were standing in front of two apartment buildings. Jury and Doc could easily see the doorway squished between the buildings, but Sofia and Darius couldn't see a thing. Doc had never been to this particular access point, but he knew from the plaque that it was a doorway to a city, not just a building.

There were several different kinds of Hidden places. The House of Banshee and Bluegrass Goodhunt's house were a single building hidden between or behind norm buildings. This, however, was a Hidden neighborhood, which meant there was an entire city structure behind that tiny door, which made no sense whatsoever. Jury had tried to explain pocket dimensions and hidden spaces, but Doc had never been able to grasp it. All he could say was that on this side it looked like a closet door, but once you passed through the doorway there was an entire city on the other side.

"Come on then," Doc said, taking Darius's arm and leading him towards the door. He could feel Darius's hesitation when they reached it, probably because all Darius could see was a solid wall, but Doc didn't let him stop, just opened the door and walked through it, pulling Darius with him. Beside him, Darius gasped.

They'd entered onto Market Street, and in some respects it greatly resembled the outside world, but in others, it was totally different. For instance, most of the vendors had street carts. The Hidden simply wasn't large enough to accommodate hundreds of store fronts, so most of the sellers sold off the street.

And that was just the beginning. The fashion was different, influenced by a hundred different cultures; the money was different, created by the Hidden for the Hidden; there were no cars, just bicycles and feet. Sometimes lots of feet. Dogs and cats were eaten here, not kept as pets; and pretty much any type of liquor that had ever been invented was available. For a price, of course.

For another thing, with the exception of utilities, the Hidden was caught somewhere between the late 1700s and early 1900s. Everything was a strange mishmash of styles and goods, but the things the norms most heavily coveted would not be found here. As a whole, cryptids approached technology the same way norms approached magic. They didn't seem to mind things like lights, but a lot of the cryps Doc had met had little to do with cell phones or computers or televisions, or any kind of technology really.

Aine had a cell phone, but he'd watched her do her books by hand many times. In fact, there wasn't a single computer in the House of Banshee, and nothing was automated. She didn't even have any of those terrifically annoying pull-bar machines that jangled and tossed out coins if you were lucky enough to hit upon the correct symbols.

"Meat pie!" a vendor yelled. "Only one quarter taliesin! Genuine hamster!"

"But... but..." Sofia stuttered.

"Close your mouth and put on your poker face," Doc suggested gently. "You don't want people noticing you."

"But these aren't people," she whispered.

"They certainly are. They're no different than you; that man just happens to have fur," Doc said, nodding towards a Takaheni.

A family of three walked past them, laughing cheerfully, as the child swung from the parents' hands. "That family looks human," Doc murmured, "but I'd lay money they're shapeshifters of some kind."

He gestured towards the meat pie man. "He's a Nimerigar.

They're known for their volatile tempers and excellent cooking. Last I heard, there's a pretty intense rivalry between them and the Lutin bakers from France."

"He's little," Sofia uttered softly.

"I'd advise you not to point that out to him."

Doc began walking forward, towing an absolutely baffled Darius with him. "I could probably find you a good partner here somewhere."

"They play chess?"

"They're just like you," Doc said once more. "They just look different."

Darius chuckled softly. "Seems like I've heard that line before."

"Then you know what I mean," Doc replied.

He paused beside a vendor selling leather satchels and said, "Do you happen to know a good chess player in the neighborhood?"

"How good?" queried the vendor. He was a rather tall, tree-like man, and when he spoke, his voice rumbled deeply.

"Extremely good."

"Huh," the tree man shook his head slowly. "Seems like I knew someone once, but my memory's a mite hazy." Doc handed him a silver coin, and the man grinned, revealing wooden teeth, and pointed across the street. "That building there, top floor, room four eighteen."

"Thank you," Doc murmured, steering Darius across the cobblestone street. He glanced back to make sure Jury and Sofia were following them and then entered the building.

Cryps didn't like elevators either, but Darius was still spry for an old man, so they were up the stairs in no time at all and were soon knocking on the door of four eighteen.

The door opened, revealing a tall, blue serpent woman.

Darius took a startled step back, and Sofia gasped. Doc swallowed a sigh. They would both make terrible poker players.

"What do you want?" the woman hissed.

"Are you by any chance a chess player?" Doc asked solicitously, smiling a wide, charming smile.

"Why do you ask?"

"It just so happens that my friend Darius has a difficult time finding suitable opponents, and you were recommended. Would you care for a game?"

She moved forward a bit, and her tongue flicked in Darius's direction. "You?" He nodded, eyes wide with apprehension. "You would play me?" she demanded.

"If you're willing," he stuttered.

"Give me a moment to change," she hissed.

The door closed, and Doc grinned at Darius. "You handled that well."

"I... She's... a snake," Darius stuttered.

"I believe they prefer serpent. Has a more intelligent ring," Doc explained. "It's fascinating really. There're shapeshifters, men and women of a tribe who can shift from human to one creature, like a serpent. But there're also people who don't change shape, but their spirit animal, or something to that affect, comes upon them, imbuing them with all its power and strength. Nothing to do with tribes or peoples, just some people are. And then there're skinwalkers, who steal the skin of an animal and wear it to become that animal and use its strength."

Doc shrugged and added, "You don't see many skinwalkers nowadays just because it's not as easy as it once was to find a cougar or a bear and kill it. Nobody wants to be a squirrel, and a zoo creature wouldn't have quite the same... vim and vigor, I don't think. But what do I know?"

"More than me," Darius muttered.

"It's not too much for you, is it?"

"No, I just... I can't believe... I can't believe I'm this old and having a new experience. It's amazing!" Darius's eyes were shiny, and Doc looked away.

Darius was dying. Not right this second, maybe not even this year. But his time was nearly at an end. Doc wasn't sure how he knew; he could just sense it. He sometimes could. That was part of the reason he'd brought Darius along. Why die sitting all alone in your apartment when you could be out living?

The door opened again, and a lovely woman of older years smiled shyly at them. "I don't often have visitors," she said carefully, middle-eastern accent coating her words. "Please come in."

They entered her apartment, and she gestured towards the table where an ornate chessboard was meticulously arranged. "If you please," she said to Darius.

"I think you can handle this, Darius," Doc grinned. "We'll swing back around in a bit to pick you up."

Darius didn't respond; he was too busy studying the chessboard. "This is beautiful!" he exclaimed.

"It was my great-great grandfather's. Please, take white."

She sat, and Darius sat across from her. Doc could tell it was going to be a very good game.

"Let's go," he whispered. Jury and Sofia followed him back out onto the street. "So now do you believe us?" Doc asked. Sofia shrugged, and Doc sighed.

"Stop being so goddamn stubborn!" Jury snapped. "What don't you get, anyway?"

"I don't get anything!" she exclaimed petulantly. "Like why does this Bureau even want me?"

"I don't know," Doc confessed. "We can find out tomorrow."

"Why tomorrow?"

"Señora Teodora told me the exact day she lost contact with you. So by tomorrow morning, we should be past that point."

"What did she say, exactly?" Sofia asked, eyes wide.

"She said you just disappeared and she couldn't find you."

"So I died? Tonight?"

"I don't know."

"What if I died in a dream? Like my mom?"

Doc couldn't answer her questions. He only knew what Señora Teodora had told him. Sofia was there, and then she wasn't.

"But what if you exposed me to them? What if you're the reason I disappear?" she demanded.

"I'm pretty sure it doesn't work like that," Doc replied.

"How could you possibly know?" she snapped. "Next you're going to tell me you're friends with a time-traveling alien!"

"Actually," he murmured, motioning for her to lower her voice. "I am friends with someone who time traveled, and he told me that's not how it works."

"Maybe I'm already dead," she mumbled. "Maybe this is hell."

"Señora Teodora doesn't believe in hell," he said firmly.

"And just because she doesn't, I shouldn't?!"

"Precisely." Doc was beginning to lose his patience. "I get this is a big shock, and I understand it's a lot to process. But Señora Teodora was the most strong-willed, incredible woman I have ever met, and if she saw you right now she'd cuff you upside the head and tell you to straighten up. I can't help you and you can't help me if you're falling apart at the seams. Accept what is, and move on!"

He glared at her, feeling a brief stab of guilt when her eyes filled with tears, but he pushed it away. "No," he said. "No tears. There's no reason for tears. Hours ago you were scared and alone and locked in a cellar with a bunch of gargoyles. Now you're with three loyal friends, and you have a chance. You should be celebrating."

"The gargoyles have better personalities than you," she muttered, brushing the tears from her eyes.

"I'm sure they do," he agreed. "Now, we're in a world you've never seen before." He gazed around the street, taking it all in. "What should we do first?"

Jury gave him a "what the hell" look over the top of Sofia's head, and Doc shrugged. What else were they going to do? It was either have a little fun or go back to Darius's apartment and drink whiskey.

Sofia didn't respond right away, but after a moment she said, "I like to shop."

"Alright, shopping it is."

Jury shook his head in disgust, and Doc shrugged again. He didn't want to go shopping either, but if shopping would get Sofia out of her funk, he'd do it. At least he hoped it was a funk.

"Lead the way," he told Jury.

"I'd rather you did."

"I'm really not that familiar with this area."

"What makes you think I am?"

Doc chose not to answer.

"Fine. I think there's a Lutin bakery this way," Jury grumbled, cupping Sofia's elbow and leading her down the street."

Behind them the meat pie seller yelled, "Lutins bake baby bones into their bread!"

"They don't," Jury assured Sofia.

Doc chuckled softly and trailed after them. He liked it here. There was an ease to these people that norms seemed to lack. Even poor, he'd seen more people smiling here than he usually saw in ten city blocks.

Even so, he knew people, and these people were on edge. It was subtle. A quick glance to the side. A sudden shudder. Something was bothering them, and Doc wondered if their general unease was connected to the missing cryptids.

He heard Sofia laugh cheerfully and grinned. Hopefully she was laughing with Jury and not at him. That would put Jury into a foul mood for days.

He swept the street with his eyes, coming to a stop on a man sitting on a bench and writing in a journal. The man's eyes darted around quickly, noticed Doc, took measure, then dropped back down to his book. His hand moved quickly, presumably writing down exactly what he'd seen.

Whatever was going on, that man would know, but Doc didn't particularly want to know today. Today he had to protect Sofia. Nobody and nothing else mattered. Not until tomorrow.

He approached the man and greeted him. "Afternoon, good man. I've a favor to ask."

"What's in it for me?" the man grunted, dark eyes squinted suspiciously.

"A gold merlin."

This man would be an excellent poker player. Nothing about his expression changed. Not a single thing. His body didn't twitch or lean or... anything.

"Do you play poker?" Doc asked, forgetting his purpose.

"No," the man spat.

"Too bad," Doc sighed.

"You mentioned a merlin."

"Right. One today and one tomorrow after you do the favor I ask from you."

"Well?"

"Meet me at Union Station at, say, nine o'clock."

"That's it?"

"Yes."

"Some sort of trap?"

"No."

His eyes were scanning Doc's face, and Doc had the funny feeling he was reading him. Doc grinned and said cheerfully, "I think I like you."

"Don't. If it's a trap, I'll kill you slowly."

"If it's a trap, I'll let you try," Doc replied.

"Gimme the gold."

"Here you are," Doc said flipping the coin into the air with his thumb.

The man caught it, moving almost without moving, and said "tomorrow then" before turning back to his journal.

Doc swallowed a laugh. Clearly their conversation was finished, so he turned and headed after Jury and Sofia. She seemed to be having fun now. She was carrying a bulging cloth bag, eating a pastry, and laughing.

Doc watched them, feeling just a subtle hint of sadness. He felt foolish for expecting her to be like Señora Teodora, and he felt foolish for still wishing she'd just change and be someone else. He'd helped people he didn't actually like before. It just wasn't as enjoyable as helping someone he did like. But that was ridiculous. He was doing this for Señora Teodora, not Sofia.

He shook off his forlorn mood and snagged the arm of the boy beside him. "You'll need to develop sneakier fingers than that," Doc laughed, pulling the boy towards him.

"Don't know what you're talkin' 'bout," the boy stammered.

"Sure you do. There were five merlins in my pocket. Now there are three. Really a pretty sloppy grab all the way around."

The boy straightened angrily. "It weren't! I only meant to take two!"

"So you did."

The boy's eyes widened as it dawned on him what he'd done, and he swallowed fearfully. "Don't turn me over," he pleaded. "Here, take 'em back." He held the coins out to Doc with a shaking hand.

"Who would I turn you over to?" Doc asked curiously.

"The BCA," the boy whispered.

"Walk with me," Doc said. "We're drawing attention."

He started to walk along the street, leaving his fingers gently wrapped around the back of the boy's neck. "Put those coins away," he advised. "They're yours now."

"But..." the boy stuttered. "But you caught me."

"I have an unfair advantage; you're really quite good. Since when are criminals turned over to the Bureau?"

"I don't know," the boy replied just barely loud enough for Doc to hear.

"Have many people gone missing from here?"

"Momma said no one can talk 'bout it." He was shaking with fear now.

"But why not?" Doc pressed.

"'Cause that's when they take you," he breathed.

Interesting. Doc fished the other merlins from his pocket and handed them to the boy. "Go," he said. He didn't have to offer twice. The boy snatched the coins from Doc's hand with surprising quickness and dashed between two carts. In a mere second Doc couldn't see him anymore.

Something very strange was going on. Something much larger than just Sofia. Something that had all the cryps fearful and on edge. And Doc was going to figure it out. He enjoyed a good puzzle. But he wasn't going to do a damn thing until tomorrow.

# 18

"Let's go," Doc said when he caught up with Jury and Sofia.

"Already?" Sofia asked, eyes bright with excitement.

"I'm glad to see you've managed to adjust," Doc grinned. "But I think we're safer at Darius's. I do need to make a few calls though. Do payphones still exist?"

Sofia started laughing.

"What?" Doc asked.

"Payphones? Don't you have a cellphone?"

"Certainly," Doc said patiently. "But there's a high possibility they might try to use it to track me."

She stopped laughing immediately. "Oh my god. Do you really think so?"

Doc felt his lips twitch, but he stopped himself from smiling. This was new to her; it wasn't her fault she was a bit slow. "It had crossed my mind," he said. "You aren't still using your cell phone, are you?"

"No." Her eyes clouded over, and she added. "I don't have anyone to call."

"When this is all over, you can put Jury on speed dial and myself on reserve," Doc said cheerfully, winking at her.

"Excuse me!" Jury snapped.

Sofia giggled, and Doc wrapped her arm around his. "Let's get you home, shall we?"

Jury elbowed him, but Doc ignored the hint. He was playing the Southern gentleman now. "So what do you think of the Hidden?" he asked as he led her back towards the serpent woman's apartment.

"It's... It's really incredible," she exclaimed. "I honestly can't believe I never knew. I wish I knew if my mom knew. Did Lita know?"

"If she did, she didn't mention it."

"What was she like?"

"Fierce," Doc answered without hesitation. "And loyal." She had also been an incredible lover, but Doc doubted if Sofia was interested in that. "But you should know that," he added.

"I guess I do. She's been visiting me since I was about ten. Sometimes, all three of us would meet. My mom, you know. Usually Lita just says hi, asks me how things are going, kisses me on the forehead, and disappears." She was silent for a moment, then she said, "I didn't realize there were others like me."

"That might be what's kept you safe," Doc said.

As they climbed the staircase, Sofia began to nibble her lip anxiously.

"What's wrong?" Doc asked.

"Nothing... I mean... Well, what if she ate him?"

"Darius?"

"Yes!"

"You're still viewing them as monsters."

"But they are!" she exclaimed. "I mean, literally a vampire is classified as a monster. A sasquatch is a monster. A serpent woman, definitely a monster!"

"I guess that's one way of looking at it," he said. "Another way of looking at it is that there were all these creatures to begin with. All sorts of creatures just like now. But then the man creature, or norms if you will, banded together to create cities and armies and all kinds of things, and, in essence, they took over the world." They were in the hallway now, so Doc pulled her to a stop and turned to face her.

"A norm man in comparison to a vampire or a shapeshifter or a witch is really pretty puny, weak, worthless. But a norm army verses a bunch of individual tribes, well that changes things. And in this scenario, norms hated the cryptids because they had so much more power, so they labeled them monsters and said that every one of them was evil and destructive and needed to die."

He paused and smiled slightly. "Norms are always saying things like that to get rid of things they either don't like or don't understand."

Sofia didn't seem to know how to respond. She opened her mouth, closed it, opened it again, and finally said, "So you don't think she ate him?"

Sometimes he wasn't even sure why he tried. Señora Teodora would not be pleased with Sofia's inability to see past the outer form.

"No, I do not think she ate him."

Doc passed off Sofia to Jury. He would keep her safe, but right now, he was a little disgusted by her blatant incognizance.

He rapped on the door, and the serpent woman, still in her human form, opened it.

"I must apologize for my earlier rudeness," Doc said,

taking her hand and bowing over it. "I was rather distracted and lost track of my good manners. I'm John Holliday, and this is my companion Thomas Jury. And she," he added flatly, "is Sofia. May I have the pleasure of your name?"

"Kaasni," she answered, blushing slightly.

"I trust you two had a good game?"

"It was very good," she said.

"Who won? Don't tell Darius," he whispered, "but I bet on you."

She laughed now, filling the room with a sound like wind chimes. "I did, in fact, win."

"Be still my beating heart," Doc drawled. "I'll be back another day to challenge you."

"I would enjoy that," she smiled.

"But for now, I must steal Darius away. If you ever need a friend," Doc said seriously, "be sure to call me." He handed her a card, brought her fingers to his lips, and turned to leave.

Sofia glared at him when he passed her, but he didn't bother with her. He had no patience for bigots.

"Did you enjoy your game?" he asked Darius as they walked down the stairs together.

"I've never seen anyone play like Kaasni," he replied dreamily. "Thanks," he added.

"Thank you," Doc responded. "I needed a friend, and there you were."


Once they were back inside the norm world, Doc drove a mile or so, then parked near a modern art gallery. "Give me a minute," he said as he exited the car.

He entered the gallery and glanced around, grinning widely when he saw the bohemian-styled young woman behind the small counter.

"Good afternoon," he greeted, using all his Southern drawl. "I'm looking for a piece to hang in my entryway. Is there anything you might suggest?"

Her face brightened, and she hopped to her feet with a cheerful smile. "Certainly, Mr..." She raised her eyebrows in question.

"Holliday," he said, kissing her hand. "But you may call me John."

"John," she twittered. "I'm Alisha."

"A pleasure," he said, tone low and seductive.

"We have quite a few wonderful pieces right now," she gushed. "Any style in particular?"

"How about something nonrepresentational?"

"I have just the thing," she said, guiding him towards one of the walls.

It was a black and white piece called "The Watcher", and Doc rather liked it. It was like gazing out into the night sky while simultaneously being pulled into it.

"I'll take it," Doc said. "Might I use your phone to call my manager and arrange for pickup?"

"Whatever you need," she said, wrapping her hands around his arm and leaning towards him.

He grinned and considered whispering a few things in her ear, but he didn't have time for that right now. He'd have to come back later. He winked at her as he picked up the phone and dialed Jervis's number.

"Jervis here."

"Ah, Jervis, my good man. I trust things are going well?"

"Your room is clean, and Thaddeus is repotted, although he told me to tell you he despises the color blue."

"Good, good," Doc said, nodding for Alisha's benefit. "Make sure you give him a shot of whiskey this evening. It helps him sleep." He covered the mouth piece and said, "My uncle's unwell."

Alisha sighed consolingly and mouthed, "I'm so sorry."

"Anything else I should be aware of?" Doc asked.

"There're a few more pigeons on the roof than normal," Jervis said blandly. Which meant someone was watching the hotel.

"Just leave them be," Doc advised. "I'm sure they'll move on soon. I need you to send a courier downtown to pay for and pick up an art piece. I'm going to hand the phone to Alisha now, and she'll work out the details with you."

"Very good, sir."

"Thank you, Jervis."

Doc placed the phone on the desk and kissed Alisha's hand. "I've a meeting I need to attend. Jervis is on the line. He'll arrange everything. Thank you for your enchanting help."

She looked very disappointed so he added, "Tell him to schedule us for dinner next week when you're available." Her eyes immediately brightened. "Until then," he whispered.

He strolled back out the doors, and as soon as he was out of eyesight, he jogged to the car and quickly drove several blocks away. He had one more phone call to make before they could go back to Darius's and lay low.

He waited until he saw an older woman out walking her dog. Then he parked the car and intercepted her on the sidewalk.

"I hate to bother you, miss," he said. "I lost my phone at the airport, and I'm hopelessly lost. Do you think I could borrow your phone to call my aunt? She must be worried by now."

The worried bit sold it. "Sure," she said with a smile, pulling out her phone and handing it to him.

"You're a lifesaver!" he exclaimed. He dialed Reggie's number and waited impatiently for him to answer. When he finally did, Doc said, "It's John, Aunt Aine; I'm sorry I'm late. I lost my phone and got a bit turned around on the way."

"I've been trying to call you," Reggie humphed. "She's awake."

"I'm fine," Doc said.

"Yes, she's fine. Just banged up a bit. She's chomping at the bit though."

"No, you stay there," Doc said firmly. "I'm on Josephine Street. Just tell me how to get there from here."

"I'll try," Reggie said. "She's not an easy woman."

"Is that Doc?" Aine shrieked in the background. "Give me the phone!"

"Alright, Aunty," Doc chuckled. "We'll go out to dinner when I get there."

Doc disconnected and handed the woman her phone. "I can't tell you how much I appreciate it," he said, taking her hand and smiling at her. "Women like you make the world a better place," he murmured, kissing her fingertips.

She blushed, and he winked at her before returning to Darius's car.


For the remainder of the day, Doc played chess with Darius, and let Jury deal with Sofia. Evening wore into night, and Darius went to bed, leaving Doc, Sofia, and Jury in the living room.

"Keep her awake," Doc ordered. "I don't want her going into a dream and getting killed or something stupid."

"Where're you going?" Sofia demanded.

"Out onto the deck. Call me if you need me," he told Jury.

Jury glared at him and mouthed, "You owe me!"

"Add it to my tab," Doc replied before sliding open the door and stepping out onto the deck.

There wasn't much deck really. It was just big enough for a single chair and a plant box full of green herbs. He leaned on the rail and looked out over the city. Darius's building was on a hill, and Doc could see almost all of Denver from here. There was a full moon high overhead, and he watched it float for a moment, remembering the first full moon he'd seen as an immortal.

He'd been lying on a bed, legs wrapped around Señora Teodora's beautiful form. In his arms, in the wash of moonlight, she had been anything but old. Her face, her form, her energy had been that of a young woman, and Doc had realized that nothing about her had ever been what it seemed.

"I leave in the morning," she said, moonlight turning her black hair gold.

"And what do I do?" he asked. He'd never thought much past whatever moment he was in. There had never been a point.

"Enjoy life," she said simply.

"Can I die?"

"Yes. But not as easy as others."

He twirled her hair around his finger, wondering what he could possibly do with himself for the next hundred and fifty or so years.

"You do not already regret your decision?" she asked.

"Not at all. I'm just... I don't know what to do."

"You will figure it out," she said softly, kissing his neck.

The next morning she was Señora Teodora again. Of middling age and indiscriminate features. Hiding in plain sight.

Once she was gone, he saddled the horse she had given him and rode into the brisk dawn. He was heading east. Not for any particular reason, just because he wanted to feel the sun on his face.

And somehow, he'd ended up riding with Andrew. Doc pulled his playing cards from his pocket and gazed at the worn box, remembering how amazed he'd been to see those lovely pin-up girls. He smiled sadly, suddenly remembering his last round of cards with Charlie.

He wasn't ready to die, and maybe he never would be. But he hated making friends. Hated watching them age. Hated that five years to a mortal was considerably more than a wild night with a vampire.

He sat in Darius's deck chair, bottle of whiskey in his hand, and swam through memories all night. When the light of the sun finally touched his face, he jerked upright in surprise. This was it. The moment of truth.

Had he saved her? Had he fulfilled his promise? Had he given Señora Teodora what she'd asked for? Or had he failed? There was only one way to find out.

# 19

Doc stood and turned to look inside the apartment. For a brief second, his heart stopped beating in his chest, then he saw Sofia at Darius's stove, stirring something, and he grinned.

"I did it," he whispered. "Do you see that, Señora? I did it. You did it."

Sofia was alive and well. And it was the day after the night Señora Teodora had lost her. He had changed time. Changed history. He suddenly grinned. He owed Andrew a dollar.

"What now?" Jury asked as they ate breakfast.

"We find out what's going on," Doc said cheerfully. He hadn't felt this good in years.

"How do we do that?"

"I've a meeting at Union Station at nine," Doc said, glancing at the clock. "We'll start there."

"Do you want me to go with you?" Jury asked.

"Stay here," Doc said. "I'm sure I won't be long."

Doc walked to the station, whistling as he went. When this was over, he was buying a yacht and filling it with succulent women. He grinned at the thought, then laughed outright thinking that if Thaddeus was with him he'd say something doomy and gloomy like "Counting your chickens before they hatch, you reprobate?"

He was. He certainly was. And he'd keep right on counting.

He reached Union at just nine because he could hear the bells of some far-off church ringing dimly. The man from yesterday was already there, sitting in the shadow of the station.

Doc sat across from him with a grin. "I didn't get your name," he said cheerfully.

"You don't need my name."

"Fair enough. I'm Doc Holliday."

"I know who you are."

For once Doc was taken a little aback. "Really?"

"I know a lot. Now what do you want? I don't have all day."

"You're rather like my manager Jervis. Serious and all business. I've rarely seen that man smile. May I call you Jervis?"

"If that'll help you get on with it."

Doc chuckled softly. "Actually, I'll call you Jervis Jr., just to keep things straight."

"It's your party."

"I so wish you played poker. Tell me what you know of Bosch and the Bureau."

"Not for one lousy merlin."

"How much then?"

Jervis Jr. leaned back in his chair and studied Doc warily.

For all Doc could tell, he was a norm. That didn't mean he wasn't a vampire or a shapeshifter or a witch or a hundred other things. Doc just couldn't tell.

"Five hundred merlins," Jervis Jr. finally said.

"For that amount, the information had better be worth it," Doc said evenly.

Jervis Jr. shrugged, and Doc chuckled. "I don't have that amount on me. I can give you an IOU to give to my manager, and he'll give you the funds."

"Why would I trust you?" Jervis Jr. sneered.

"Because you have my word."

"So?"

"I'm Doc Holliday. I always keep my word."

Jervis Jr. processed that and finally nodded.

Doc took out one of his cards and wrote a note on the back to Jervis, signed it, then passed it to Jervis Jr. "There you go. Five hundred merlins as good as yours. Bosch."

"He's experimenting, trying to figure out a way to use cryps' power as his own, maybe even turn norms into cryps; I don't know the exact details. His men come down into the slums every so often and snatch a few people, and nobody ever sees them again."

"Are there any missing shamans?" Doc asked.

"How do you mean?"

He really needed a new word. He wearied of explaining what he meant every single time. "A witch who uses the ether or spiritual elements instead of earthly."

"We had one who lived near Market Junction; she was taken last week or so."

"Was she considered powerful?"

"I couldn't say."

"What other types of cryps have been taken?"

"As far as I know, throughout the Hidden, there's not a race that hasn't been targeted."

"Why haven't the Magistratus done anything?"

"They look, ask questions, search around, but Bosch leaves no trace. He knows the cryps, knows their weaknesses, their blind spots. He uses plastics and synthetics, things the witches can't sense or affect, and he has his own team of witches who sweep along behind him, covering all his tracks."

"Wait," Doc interrupted. "Go back to that plastic bit."

"What about it?"

"What do you mean the witches can't sense it?"

"Plastic and synthetics," Jervis Jr. said slowly. "They're too adulterated and fragmented, too far from the original source. Witches tap into the elements, you understand?"

Doc nodded impatiently.

"Well, there ain't no element in plastic."

"But how could Bosch take advantage of that?"

"Polymer guns, knives made of Kydex, traps devised of synthetic materials. Witches aren't used to people trying to trap them anymore, and they've gotten a bit sloppy."

"So you're saying if I rigged a plastic net outside Jury's door, he'd never see it coming?"

"Not if he's a witch. That's not to say he can't get out of it though. Most witches are pretty quick on their feet."

Doc grinned widely. He couldn't wait to try it out. He could just imagine the look on Jury's face. This isn't the time for pranks, he thought, forcing himself to focus on the issue at hand.

"So Bosch is using their weaknesses against them. But to what end?"

"Your guess is as good as mine," Jervis Jr. replied sullenly.

"Can a shaman sense the plastics?"

"Don't know."

"What else can you tell me?" Doc asked, leaning back in his chair.

Jervis Jr.'s face finally showed an emotion. Pure hate. "I've never met Bosch," Jervis Jr. said, "but his right hand man, Lance Merrick, is a fucker of unmeasurably fuckness. If you happen to kill him, I won't collect on your debt."

Doc grinned rather slowly. "I have every intention of killing him, but don't let that stop you from making a profit. Do you know where I can find them?"

Jervis Jr. shook his head. "Everyone knows where the headquarters is, but I think it's just a front. I've been in there, and it seems completely above board. I can't say for sure though. I didn't have a lot of time to poke around."

"Thank you for your time," Doc said sincerely. "May I suggest you learn to play poker? I would love a chance to win my merlins back someday."

Jervis Jr. actually grinned. "I'll see what I can do."

"So what did you learn?" Jury asked when Doc returned to Darius's.

"Nothing we didn't already know."

"What now?"

"We go to the source." Doc frowned. "But before we go, I should warn you that there's a slight chance this will be the one that gets us killed."

"You always say that, and yet here we are."

"But I'm serious this time. Those other times I was just trying to get rid of you."

Jury laughed. "I'm already in this. What's your plan?"

"Jervis Jr. thinks the Bureau's headquarters is just a front, but there's a possibility it's not, so I think we should go there and check it out."

"I like that plan. In fact, I think it's your best yet."

"I thought it was rather sparse," Doc laughed.

"You don't wanna get bogged down with tiny details," Jury insisted. "Let's do it." His eyes were bright with excitement.

Doc grinned. Next to making love and winning the purse, Doc loved a good fight. The worse the odds the better.

"What do we do with her?" he asked gesturing towards Sofia.

"Her is standing right here!" Sofia snapped. "And her doesn't appreciate you treating her like a child."

"You are a child!" Doc shot back.

She started to say something, then took a deep breath. "Look, I know I disappointed you. You thought I was gonna be like Lita, and I'm not. I... I didn't... I haven't... I'm sorry. I didn't handle any of this well. I'm sorry I called them monsters. You just... It just shocked the hell outta me for a second. That's all. I want to go with you. I can help. If he's using people like me, Jury might not be able to tell. I could see the barrier, but you couldn't."

She had a point. And he had already technically fulfilled his promise, not that he didn't think he could keep her alive.

"Alright," he agreed. "You can come."

"We need a team name," Jury said.

"You sound like Andrew."

"Is that a bad thing?"

"In this case, yes. No name."

"Who made you the leader?"

"I did."

"Shouldn't we take a vote?"

"No. I'm the oldest; I'm the leader," Doc pointed out. "Now let's go."

"I'm never gonna hear the end of that," Jury muttered. "As if fifty years even makes a difference."

Doc didn't really care if they knew he was coming, so this time they took a taxi. The Bureau headquarters weren't that far from Dulcis Requiem, but Doc had never been there before because he'd slept through its construction. It wasn't terribly easy to build new Hidden buildings because there was only so much hidden space. But apparently Bosch knew some people who knew some people.

They stood outside the door for a moment, and finally Doc said, "So I guess I'll go first."

"Age before beauty."

"I'm pretty sure I came out way ahead in the polls last time," Doc drawled. "But if you want, we can have another contest."

"Just go," Jury ordered.

Doc chuckled and opened the door. It looked like a standard norm office building. The paint was a drab and utterly boring tan, there were no windows, the lights were too dim, and the receptionist at the desk looked half-dead.

Doc glanced around the entryway before walking up to the receptionist desk with an easy half smile. "I'm here to see Bosch," he said. "He's expecting me."

"Name?" she asked, voice totally flat.

"Holliday. Dr. John Holliday."

Her expression didn't change. He wasn't sure her expression could change. She just pressed a button and said, "Dr. Holliday to see you, sir."

"Is she alive?" Doc asked Jury in an undertone.

"Yes," Sofia answered. "But something's wrong. Her aura is... strange."

"Strange how?" he asked. He wasn't sure what she meant by aura, but he'd wait until later to ask her.

"I don't know how to describe it. It's... grey? And very flat."

A voice crackled over the intercom. "Send him in."

That was unexpected. Very unexpected.

"Mr. Bosch will see you now," she said. "To the left, end of the hallway."

"I admit," Doc said as they walked down the hallway. "I'm a little confused. Are we walking into a trap?"

"I don't see anything obvious," Jury said.

"Me either," Sofia put in.

"Well, if it's a devilishly clever trap, I've enjoyed every minute."

"Ehh," Jury grunted.

"Really? We stand at the possible door of death, and after all our time together all you have to say is 'ehh'?"

"Ehh."

"Fine. I'm writing you out of my will."

"I'm afraid it's a little late for that," Jury snorted.

They had reached Bosch's office now, and for just the briefest moment, Doc hesitated. Then he reached out, turned the knob, and pushed the door open.

"Ah," the man behind the desk said.

Doc hated him instantly. He had the look of a man in charge, which on its own wasn't offensive, but Doc could see the telltale signs of cruelty around his mouth and eyes. With just a glance he could confidently say that this man was the type to rip the wings from butterflies just to see what would happen.

Bosch was speaking, and Doc forced himself to focus, even though what he most wanted to do was leap over the desk and thrust his knife through one of his scheming eyes.

"Mr. Holliday. What a surprise." Bosch smiled, but it was not an easy smile. It was forced and brittle.

"I doubt that," Doc replied.

"To what do I owe the pleasure?"

"Tell me about the cryptids."

"Cryptids? Surely you know all about cryptids," Bosch said slyly.

He supposed he'd asked for that. "The people you steal," Doc clarified. "What're you doing with them?"

Bosch smiled again, but this time it was condescending. "I do believe you have the wrong idea. This is a government institution, Mr. Holliday. Our sole purpose is to maintain relations between the Hidden and the normals."

"There is no relationship," Doc said flatly.

"But there could be. We're working towards full integration."

Bosch would make a terrible card player. He was lying, and Doc knew it.

"Since you're here," Bosch added, eyes never leaving Sofia, "I'd be happy to give you a tour."

Jury shook his head, but Doc said, "We'd love a tour."

Bosch walked around his desk. His pace was slow and measured, and Doc again had to stop himself from simply driving his knife through one of Bosch's vital organs. On second thought, when the time came to kill him, maybe he'd ask Jury to do it. He wasn't sure he wanted Bosch's life force inside him.

Jury growled when Bosch took Sofia's arm, but Doc laid a hand on his shoulder. "Let's just play along," he mouthed.

"I don't like the way he looks at her," Jury mouthed back.

"We'll make him pay later."

Jury glared at him; Doc glared back, and Jury finally gave a short nod of agreement.

"Bet you're glad we took that lip reading class now," Doc mouthed.

"I hate you."

"I don't believe that."

"When this is over, I'm changing my name and moving to Columbia," Jury mouthed angrily.

"That's what you said last time."

"See, you never listen! It was Bolivia."

"My apologies," Doc mouthed with a grin.

Jury jerked his head towards Bosch, and Doc chuckled softly as he followed Bosch and Sofia out into the dim hallway.

"We have three divisions," Bosch was saying. "One handles relations with the US government, one handles relations with the Hidden government, and the last one is our overseas division. In a way, I suppose you could say we're diplomats." At this he tossed a pleased smile over his shoulder at Doc. "We're outside of the law."

Bosch definitely didn't know him. Doc didn't give a damn about the law. Hidden or otherwise. He never had. But the best way to win the purse when you were playing against an arrogant idiot was to go on letting them think they were going to win.

The building was full of dreary and sterile offices. The people they encountered, norm or otherwise, seemed utterly drained of vitality. They were flat. Or grey, as Sofia had said. Overall, the tour revealed nothing of interest. Not that Doc had thought it would.

"Ms. Baca," Bosch smarmed once they'd reached the entrance again. "You'd do me a great honor if you would consent to join me for dinner tonight."

"No!" Jury exclaimed.

"I don't believe I asked you, Mr. Jury," Bosch said cuttingly.

"I... um..." Sofia glanced at Doc, and he gave her a half shrug, hoping she would get the message. She did.

"I have plans for this evening. Perhaps another night," she said charmingly.

"Excellent. Here's my card, my dear. Call me."

"Thank you," she said, batting her eyes like a moronic debutant.

Bosch didn't seem to mind though. He kissed her hand, leaving a bit of saliva on her knuckles.

As soon as they were outside and away from the entrance, Sofia shuddered and squealed, "Get it off me!"

Jury glanced around, then smiled, and gestured with his hand. A copper hose rose out of the ground behind them, like a cobra from a snake charmer's basket, and Jury used it to sprinkle water onto Sofia's hand.

"Disgusting!" she snapped. "He's... He's not right. He..." She shivered and whispered, "He has no aura." Doc and Jury both stared at her in confusion. "Aura," she said again, moving her hands around her head. "Can you not see it?" she asked.

"No," Doc said. "Can you just explain it to us?"

"I... I'm not sure I can, but I'll try. Can we go somewhere else though? I don't like being this close to him."

"We may as well go to the hotel," Doc said. "He knows we know, but he's mistaken in thinking his status will protect him."

Jury laughed sharply. "He obviously doesn't know you very well."

"That's what I thought," Doc chuckled.

"Or maybe he does, and he's just playing you," Sofia suggested.

Doc considered that before shaking his head. "He's a type. Too full of hubris."

"Seriously?" Sofia demanded.

"What?"

"Hubris?"

"It's a word," he stated.

"I know it's a word!" she snapped. "So you're basically saying he suffers the exact same fault you do?"

"No. I've never suffered hubris, have I, Jury?"

"Not that I know of," Jury replied solemnly.

"I truly am as capable as I say I am," Doc said with a shrug. "Ask anyone."

"I cannot even begin to imagine what Lita was thinking when she picked you," Sofia sneered.

"She was thinking she wanted to win."

# 20

As soon as Doc opened his door, he wished they'd gone to Darius's instead.

"The profligate returns!" Thaddeus snapped from his new, bright blue pot.

"Good to see you as well, Thaddy, old boy. I love your new living arrangement."

"It's your idea of a joke, isn't it? You know I utterly despise blue."

"I didn't, Thaddy, I swear. How can anybody hate blue? It's the most universal color."

"Precisely. It's completely overused!"

"Who's he talking to?" Sofia whispered.

"Don't you have eyes, girl?" Thaddeus demanded. "Can't you see the talking plant?"

"Oh my god, it is the plant!"

"Not it. He, thank you very much," Thaddeus ground out.

"How..." Sofia stuttered. "It's... I mean, he's a plant?"

"He used to be a man," Jury explained softly.

"He crossed the wrong shaman," Doc added. "You might

want to be careful, Thaddy; Sofia here is a shaman as well. You wouldn't want to be an even smaller plant, would you?"

"A shaman?" Thaddeus stuttered. "Powerful?"

"She seems to be."

"Can you turn me back?" he pleaded.

"Turn you back into a man?" Sofia questioned.

"Yes!"

"I... I don't..." she stuttered. "I wouldn't even know where to begin. I don't think I can."

"Never mind," Thaddeus muttered. "I just... Never hurts to ask."

"I'm... I'm very sorry," Sofia apologized, stepping towards him and running a finger over one of his leaves.

"It's not so bad. I have Rosa."

"We'll figure something out, old boy," Doc said consolingly. "Brandy?"

"I just tried to nod," Thaddeus brooded. "You'd think I'd remember by now."

Doc upended a brandy bottle into Thaddeus's pot. He hadn't seen Thaddeus in a depression this deep since he'd first won him. With any luck, the brandy would knock him out for the rest of the day.

"I can't believe you have a talking plant," Sofia whispered.

"I can still hear you," Thaddeus mumbled. "I'm right here. And I'm not technically a plant; I'm a man."

"She meant no offense," Doc said. "Now explain about the auras."

"Everyone has an aura," Sofia said as she sat down on Doc's couch. She glanced at Thaddeus. "Even he has an aura, which just proves he's a man, I suppose. I've never seen a plant with an aura before."

"But Bosch didn't?"

"No. I've never seen anyone without one. I've seen dim ones, like all the other people inside the Bureau had very dim and grey auras. Sick or um... dying? But Bosch didn't have one at all."

"Interesting," Doc said. "What does an aura tell you?"

Sofia shrugged. "I don't really know."

"Your mother didn't know either?"

"She couldn't see them," Sofia explained. "Our magic wasn't exactly the same. We could both walk the dreaming, but my mom couldn't make gargoyles or see auras. She was very good at making things grow and helping people. She could heal people, although she was careful how she did it. They don't still burn witches, but they don't like what they can't understand."

Doc raised an eyebrow.

"Yes!" she snapped. "I'm aware how ridiculous that is. When you took me there I just... I was totally freaked out. I didn't... God, I said I was sorry!"

"He'll remind you about it for another fifty years or so, then he'll probably let it go," Jury chuckled. "How old are you?"

"Me?" Sofia asked.

"Yes."

"Twenty-seven. How old are you?"

"Younger than me," Doc said. "Why weren't your powers the same as your mother's?"

"I don't know," Sofia said. Her eyes clouded over, and she added, "Mom didn't usually have answers to my questions. She'd just say it's how we were, and that I just had to accept it. I never knew there were others like us. Jury's vlog was the first contact I had with anyone different, and I thought he was a fake."

"If you had emailed me," Jury muttered. "I could have explained it to you."

"It's hard for me to... I wouldn't have known what to say. I've never really had a friend," she said softly. "It was always just Mom and me, and she didn't like to stay in one place very long, so we moved a lot."

"Have you moved since she died?" Doc asked, wondering what her mother had been running from.

"No."

"There was a philosopher on our team," Thaddeus said somewhat thickly. "He studied magic more than the rest of us. He had a theory or two, but I don't know how far he got with any of them."

"Go on," Doc encouraged, hoping it didn't turn into a long lecture.

"He postulated that witches, as you call them, Doc, use the elements. Earth, water, fire, air, but that each individual has a strength in one area."

Doc glanced at Jury, and he nodded. "I'm mostly an earth man," Jury said. "I can affect the other elements and use them, but earth is like... my faro."

"I love it when you use gambling terms. So how does this relate to shamans, Thaddy?"

"If you ceased interrupting, I might already be there."

"Apologies," Doc drawled.

"Most people consider the ether or spiritual world to contain just one element. Spirit. But he theorized that it actually contained three."

Doc was in an entirely different conversation for a moment.

"So there's White, Black, and Grey," Andrew said. "I call them shamans; they argue that shaman isn't really the correct term, but..." Andrew trailed off with a shrug.

"Which one is he?" Doc asked.

"Grey."

"I'm not certain I like him."

"No one does, but he grows on you," Andrew admitted. "Although I always kinda shudder when he shows up. He's like an omen of... mischief."

Andrew had gone on to explain the differences between the three shamans, but at the time it hadn't made much sense to Doc. Now he wished he'd listened a little more carefully.

"So what are the three elements of the ether?" Doc asked Thaddeus carefully.

"I thought you'd never ask! Life, death, and the middle."

"The middle? What the hell's that?"

"Everything in between."

"Are you drunk, Thaddy?"

"Not hardly. In fact, just a bit more if you please."

For a plant who couldn't hold his liquor, Thaddeus certainly had a high tolerance for brandy. Doc poured out the rest of the bottle.

"Sofia's mother," Thaddeus continued, "was obviously tapping into the life element, hence her ability to heal."

"What element is Sofia tapping into?" Jury asked.

Doc stared at her, wishing Jury had kept his mouth shut. It was obvious to him which one she tapped into, and that made him wonder if it had been altogether wise to save her.

"Death, obviously," Thaddeus replied.

"What?!" Sofia gasped. "Why death? Why can't it be the middle?"

He sighed heavily. "Must I explain everything? Very well. Allow me to ask you one very simple question. Forgive me, two. Were you near your mother when she died?"

"Yes. I was in the next room."

"And did you experience a power spike?"

Sofia didn't answer. She didn't have to. She was chalk white, and her eyes were wide and moist. "You can't be saying... I don't believe it."

"I don't understand," Jury said. "How can death be tapped into?"

Doc glared at him. "Really? That's what you don't understand? How long have you known me?"

"Is it the same then?" Jury asked. "How can she use that to make gargoyles?"

"Shamans were never well understood," Thaddeus slurred. "There seem to be fewer rules regulating their... magic. The personality of each shaman is the ultimate determining factor, at least that was once a theory..." Thaddeus trailed off, and soon he was snoring.

"Finally," Doc muttered. "He could've carried on all day."

There was something nagging at him, but he was having a hard time focusing on it. It had to do with Jury and magic. He tapped his fingers slowly on the table and sipped his whiskey.

Jury. Magic. Jury. That's right. Plastic. A plastic trap.

"Sofia, would you check your pockets?" Doc asked.

"My pockets," she sputtered. "What for?"

"For anything that wasn't there before."

She stood and started emptying out her pockets. She had seventy-nine cents, a single key, a small wad of cash, a red lipstick, an old crinkled photograph of a young woman, some barrettes, a library card, a bent paperclip, a chocolate bar wrapper, two sticks of gum, an ink pen lid, a wadded up sticky note, a jump drive, and a few small stones.

"Goddamn," Jury muttered. "Is your pocket a goddamn pocket dimension?"

"What's that?" Sofia asked as she started to empty the other one.

"That was just one pocket?!" Jury exclaimed. "Why don't you just carry a purse?"

"Eww. I don't do purses," she retorted.

"You need one," he said as she laid a comb, a contact case, a compact mirror, and a handful of scrunchies onto the table.

"Wait," Doc said, pointing towards a small white disc. "What's that?"

"I dunno," she said, handing it to him.

He rolled it over his fingers. It was definitely plastic. "It's not yours?"

"No."

He held it out to Jury. "What do you sense?"

"Nothing," Jury shrugged. "It's plastic."

"You've been hiding things from me again," Doc chided.

"You didn't need to know."

"I think I did."

"Why? I can't think of any reason why I'd tell you."

"Here's a scenario to try out, 'Hey, Doc, we're probably walking into a trap, but I can't say for sure, because I can't sense plastic junk!'"

"Who would use plastic as a... oh. Well, hell. Maybe I have been keeping things from you."

Someone knocked on the door, and Doc stared at it. "Housekeeping!" a thickly, accented feminine voice called out.

Lies. Jervis was not going to like this. Not one little bit.

"I'll take the door," Doc mouthed. "You cover me."

"I wanted the door," Jury complained.

"Rumor has it they use plastic guns."

"You take the door."

"When I get there," Doc added silently. "Tell them to come on in."

"What the hell are you guys talking about?" Sofia broke in.

"Nothing," Doc said casually. "I was just thinking it's time for more whiskey."

"You drink a lot," she pointed out.

"Thank you."

"Uh, it wasn't a compliment."

"I'll take it as one, nonetheless," Doc said as he stood and moved quietly towards the door.

As soon as Doc was situated along the wall beside the door, Jury called out, "Come on in!"

The door suddenly swung open, and fifteen bulky men rushed into the room. Excellent, Doc thought. At least Bosch was giving him some credit now.

Sofia started screaming, which annoyed him, but he supposed they had been remiss in not letting her know what was happening. Doc hurled a knife at the man closest to Jury and grinned as it sunk deep into the man's neck. One down.

He tripped another man, snapping his neck as he fell. Two. From the corner of his eye, he saw Jury blow a man's brains out. It was a cheap trick really, Jury using his magic to silence the gun.

Doc kicked out a man's knee, thrusting his knife deep into the man's throat as he fell. Three. He suddenly paused and glanced down at his chest. Why wasn't his tattoo hot? He'd definitely killed them.

Something tore through his chest repeatedly, and he turned and glared at the man who'd just shot him. "You'll pay for that," he snarled, flicking a knife with the speed of a snake's tongue. The man's face collapsed under the force. Four.

A raging man with bushy red hair rushed towards him, and Doc ducked the man's swinging arm before coming up underneath it with a solid strike to the side of the man's face. He heard the man's jaw snap just before he finished the job by twisting the man's head and fracturing his neck. Five, but still no burning tattoo.

He threw his last knife into the man about to shoot Jury. Six. There were still five men standing. Doc tossed Jury a smirk across the room. He was winning.

He leaped forward, snatching his lampstand from the floor and breaking off the top before using it to spear one of the men through his chest. "Seven," he hummed as he ripped the stand free and used it to bludgeon another man over the head. "Eight."

He dropped the lamp and grabbed another man by his collar, blocking the man's knife with his arm and ignoring the slash of pain. Then he bashed the man's head into the corner of his coffee table. Nine.

He wiped the blood from his eyes as he stood and surveyed the room. Sofia was still screaming, but all of Bosch's men were dead.

"I won," he said cheerfully.

"Only because you had the advantage," Jury argued.

"I used my hands!" Doc exclaimed. "You used your cheap magic gun."

"My gun is not cheap!" Jury snapped.

"It's a cheap trick, a sloppy sleight of hand!"

"You're a sore winner!"

"You're a sore loser!"

"WHAT THE HELL IS GOING ON?!!!!" Sofia screamed, startling both of them.

"What exactly are you having trouble with?" Doc asked.

"Wrong tack," Jury muttered.

"This!" She gestured wildly around the room. "THIS!"

Doc turned in a circle. It was rather messy. He hoped this wasn't the straw that broke Jervis's back. Which reminded him. He quickly unbuttoned his shirt and stared at his chest with concern. The tattoo was still there. As well as a large amount of blood. He didn't usually bleed for long when he fought people because taking their life force repaired any damage they had done.

"What the hell?" Jury exclaimed. "Why're you bleeding?"

"I have no idea," Doc murmured. His tattoo started spinning, and then the world went black.

# 21

"Goddamn it, Doc," Jury muttered, running his hands over Doc's chest. "What the hell's wrong with you?"

Doc couldn't say. He was drowning in blackness.

"He's been shot," he dimly heard Sofia point out.

"Like I don't goddamn know that!" Jury snapped. "I can't get the fucking bullets out. Fuck Bosch and his plastic shit! Don't you dare do this to me, Doc! You owe me a favor!"

Doc tried to say "I didn't know you cared", but he couldn't move his lips. Everything was numb.

The world was on fire, and Doc was king, sitting on his throne of charred bones, surveying the landscape of fiery orange and red. Phantoms wandered past him, pale voices crying out in anguish.

"What are you doing?" a voice demanded.

Doc laughed lightly. "I think I might actually be dying."

"Why?" Señora Teodora was suddenly standing before him, looking just as she had in his arms, brilliantly beautiful, supremely wise.

"You tell me."

"What happened?" she asked, skimming her warm fingers over his bloody chest.

"I was shot."

"You did not kill them in return?"

"I did," he replied, wrapping his fingers in her hair and pulling her towards his lips. "No one kisses like you," he whispered. At first he'd thought she wasn't really here, but once he tasted her lips he was certain she wasn't a figment of his imagination.

She smiled slightly. "Now is not the best time."

"I'm dying. What better time is there?"

"Do you want to die?"

"Not particularly."

"Will you ever be ready?"

He shrugged. "Who can say."

"What happened after you killed them?"

"Nothing. The tattoo didn't glow."

She was running her fingers along the line of his tattoo, brow wrinkled in confusion and concern. "Why are you still bleeding?"

"Bullets," he coughed, blood spewing from his mouth into his hands. He could think of better ways to die. "Inside," he struggled to say. "Plastic."

"This will hurt," she said softly. She pulled a slim knife from her belt and cut into his chest, digging through his flesh until she found a melted plastic chunk. Doc bit his lip to keep from crying out in pain. Blood was pouring from his chest now, but she kept delving into his flesh, working until she had removed the other five bullets as well.

She held her hand over his chest then, almost as if she was searching for something. Even as he felt his chest pull together and knit closed, he watched her. She was the most beautiful woman he'd ever seen, and yet most of Señora Teodora's beauty came from within and radiated out like a beacon.

He ran a finger down her cheek. "What's your name?" he whispered.

She glanced up briefly, smiling at him. "My real name?" she asked.

"What other name is there?"

"The Christian name they forced upon me as a child."

"No, not that one."

"Tozi," she said softly, kissing him gently. "Now keep still. I'm trying to work."

There was pain again, and he knew she was doing something to the tattoo. Using his own blood no doubt. He closed his eyes and drifted, letting the fire soak into him.

"I am done," she said finally. "But you must wake now. You must feed."

"What happened?" he asked. "Why didn't the tattoo work?"

"I do not know."

"I saved her," he said suddenly.

"I knew you would."

"That makes one of us," Doc said. "She's not like you."

"Of course not."

"I thought she would be."

"Are you very disappointed?" she laughed.

"A little. Can't I stay with you a moment longer?"

"Not if you want to live. Wake." She kissed him, and he wrapped his fingers around her hair, trying to keep her with him, but he couldn't.

"Doc!" Jury exclaimed. "What the devil happened?"

"Not the devil," Doc whispered. "A goddess. I have to feed."

"Why didn't you?"

"I don't know. Something... blocked it."

"How?" Sofia asked. She was sitting on her heels beside him, holding the lumps of plastic in her hands. "They just came out. How?"

"They didn't just come out," Doc coughed. "Señora Teodora dug them out." He didn't use her real name. He was keeping that for himself.

She reached out a shaking hand and touched his tattoo. "What's this?" she asked, eyes wide with fascination.

"Haven't you ever seen a tattoo?" Doc asked weakly.

"It's not just a tattoo," she murmured. "It has power, so much power; I can sense it."

The look in her eyes unsettled him, and he suddenly didn't want to tell her anything about it.

"It's like some kind of soul absorbing tattoo," Jury said.

Doc glared at him, shaking his head sharply.

"Really?" Sofia exclaimed.

"No!" Jury laughed. "I'm just messing with you. He went through this weird hard rock stage, managed to get drunk one night, and that's what he woke up with. And three naked women. Or was it five?"

"Four," Doc muttered, struggling to his feet. "Get your facts straight." He was terribly weak, but not too weak to kill someone. "Get my phone," he mumbled. "Bennie sent me an address."

"Can you last that long?"

"I'm not sure I have a choice."

He stumbled towards the door, stopping when he heard a soft gurgle. Someone was still alive. "One's alive," he said. "Which one?"

Jury looked up from Doc's phone in surprise. "Let me

check." After a second, he pointed to the man on his face near the couch. "He's one of mine."

"Ha," Doc croaked. "Ten." He stepped carefully over the bodies, rolled the man over, and wrapped his fingers around his throat, squeezing. The man's body convulsed, and Doc watched the life fade from his eyes. But still his tattoo did nothing.

"What the hell?" he muttered when he was sure the man was dead. He scanned the room, trying to think. He refused to die. Not after all this time.

His eyes stopped on Sofia. She was standing now, bullets still clutched in her hand, eyes watching him carefully. This should all be extremely overwhelming for her. So why didn't she look pale and peaked? In fact, she was practically glowing.

For a second Doc's mind was back in that conversation with Andrew, the one they'd had about the shamans.

"Every time someone dies a violent death, it feeds her," Andrew said irritably. "Right now, the Black Shaman's sleeping somewhere, growing stronger and stronger with every war." He frowned. "Actually, I never could decide if there was a proximity factor involved, but say she's near a big city, that would be enough to feed anyone."

"Your lips are moving," Doc drawled. "I hear words coming out, but they're meaningless."

"Remind me why I try to tell you anything?" Andrew snorted.

"Because you like me."

"Nobody likes you, Doc. We just put up with you so Charlie has someone to play cards with." Andrew grinned when he said it, and Doc knew better than to take offense.

"You're filching my kills!" Doc exclaimed, stepping towards Sofia.

"What? I don't even know what you mean!" she stuttered.

"What do you mean?" Jury asked.

"She's a death shaman. She ate all these kills, even mine."

"What?! That's insane! I can't do that!" Her color was high now, and Doc studied her. If he wasn't mistaken, she was actually lying.

"Oh," Jury breathed, staring at her. "I think you're right."

"You both stay here," Doc demanded, snatching his phone from Jury's hand. He needed to feed, but he obviously couldn't do it with her around.

"I hate to point this out," Jury said, "but you can barely walk. Let me go with you."

"No. I need you to watch her. Bosch might send more men. Better yet, check your pockets for plastic that shouldn't be there and go to that place you told me you'd never go with me again."

"Ugh. Do I have to?"

Doc cast him a glare, grabbed his knives, and walked unsteadily out the door. "I'll be there soon," he said. He rode the elevator down, vaguely realizing that he should have changed. His shirt was torn, and he was covered in blood, but he needed to eat. Now. He couldn't wait.

He stepped from the elevator and scanned the lobby. "I need your jacket," he texted Jervis as he slid behind a potted tree. "I'm by the main elevator."

In mere seconds, Jervis was beside him. "Here you are, sir."

"Thank you. My suite needs some more housekeeping."

"Wonderful."

"You can sell the bodies to the Worms."

"I always do."

"Double your salary for your trouble."

"I always do."

Doc laughed shortly, leaning slightly on Jervis as he did. He wanted a nap.

"She's rather a shrew, if you don't mind me saying," Jervis said, nodding towards a woman in her mid-thirties who was screeching angrily at her husband.

"Really?"

"Yes. She gave us a terrible review online. Several, actually. Described our service as 'below subpar', and suggested that our chef was a retired prison cook. Pierre nearly walked in front of a bus last night he was so depressed."

"What nerve," Doc hissed, but he wasn't quite convinced. Misleading his potential customers was certainly a crime, but only other shrews would be stupid enough to believe her.

"Her husband's terrified of her," Jervis added. "Although he does try to protect the little ones."

That sealed it.

"Distract the husband," Doc whispered.

"Certainly, sir, but if I may be so bold..." Jervis pulled a handkerchief from his pocket and gently rubbed Doc's face. He frowned and said, "You'll have to forgive me, sir." Then he spat on the handkerchief and tried again. "There. Good as new."

Jervis tucked the bloody handkerchief away, strode across the lobby, and engaged the husband in conversation. As soon as the wife had wandered off a ways, Doc drew all his failing strength and walked towards her.

"Good day, miss," he said charmingly. "I notice your husband is ignoring you, so I hope you don't mind if I offer to buy you a drink?"

"That would be splendid," she gushed. "He's a terrible man.

I wish I could divorce him, you know, but I wouldn't get any of the money. Prenup." She took Doc's offered arm and tried to smile winningly. She looked like a balloon stretched too thin.

"I completely understand," Doc lied. "He looks like a fool."

"Oh, if only you knew. Between you and me, I'm actually considering having him knocked off. This one man said he can make it look like an accident."

"It's easy to do," Doc murmured. It was going to take what was left of his strength, but it was still easy.

Her eyes brightened. "Do you know someone?" she whispered.

"As it happens, I do." He looked around carefully. "Here, come with me." He led her towards one of the employee closets, a special hidden room with just about anything a guest might need; and Doc catered to the rich, so the list was extensive. Everything from toothbrushes to fresh tuxedos and opera glasses. And a few more elicit items.

"To make it look like an accident," Doc whispered as he closed the door behind them, "you just put them somewhere they shouldn't be and have them trip over something and bang their head. Or in your case, fall on a pair of scissors."

"What?" she asked in surprise. "What do you mean my case?"

He had moved them next to a shelf, and he grinned sharply as he shoved a pair of scissors into her heart. Her eyes widened and horror filled her face, turning her even uglier.

"He's better off without you," Doc soothed. "It'll be over soon."

Her lips moved, but nothing came out and before long, his tattoo began to heat, pulling her life out of her and renewing his. "Thank Tozi," he breathed in relief.

He closed his eyes, fully enjoying the rush of power. That was the closest he'd come to dying in a long time, and it made life taste all the sweeter. As the tattoo began to cool, he slowly lowered the dead woman to the floor, positioning her body just so, so it would look like a strange and unfortunate accident.

It was an excellent start, but he needed more if he was going to kill Bosch. Especially if Miss Death Shaman was going to snatch all his kills.

He headed back across the lobby towards the elevator, nodding to Jervis as he did. He'd feel a hundred percent after he donned a fresh pair of clothes, drank a shot or two of whiskey, and had a nice, cozy chat with a lawyer.

The lawyer and his three goons were filling, but Doc was a little leery now. Leery of plastic bullets and death shamans. So he visited the next two people on Bennie's list before heading over to meet Jury at Club Dungeon, a norm dance club on the outskirts of downtown.

"Mr. Holliday," the door man greeted him "Go right in. Mr. Jury is waiting for you in the VIP room."

"Thank you, good man," Doc said cheerfully, handing the man a hundred dollar bill and walking onto the crowded dance floor.

It was no wonder Jury hated it here. There was too much leather, too much skin, and way too many whips. But he was certain it was the role-play Jury really despised. Jury had no sense of humor when it came to pretending. Especially in a place that cast witches as evil, Satan-loving wenches. It was so cliché, but Doc loved cliché. Cliché kept the norms from ever thinking there was anything deeper to life than what the entertainment industry told them.

He weaved his way through the crowds, allowing random women to grab him and kiss him or grope his rear end. He even kissed a few of them back. By the time he reached the VIP room, Jury was steaming with impatience.

"Where have you been?" he demanded. "We've been here for over three hours."

"Sorry," Doc drawled as he sat across from Sofia. "It took me forever to get across the dance floor.

"We're in the middle of something," Jury complained. "You'd think you could at least take it seriously."

"You're just upset because I almost died. You care," Doc said solemnly. He touched his eye, his heart, and then pointed at Jury and held up two fingers.

Jury's eyes flashed and a burst of air hit Doc, pushing him across the room and slamming him into the wall.

"You don't have to say it back," Doc said solemnly. "I just wanted you to know."

"I utterly despise you," Jury snarled.

"You love me."

"We don't have time for this shit," Jury growled. "What the hell happened?"

Doc grinned as he stood and moved his chair back into place. "Bosch slipped a tracker into Sofia's pocket, or a listening device, I'm not sure which. Anyway, he thought he could get the jump on us. He did not, of course. Always underestimating, but since dear Sofia here is a death shaman, she ate my kills, and I nearly died. Sums it up nicely, I think. We'll have to be rather careful going forward, unless we're going to lock her in a room somewhere."

"As if you even could!" Sofia snapped.

"I wasn't serious, darling, just making a point."

"I'm not your darling!"

"Just a figure of speech, love."

Her face turned bright red, and he nearly laughed, but instead said, "Bosch has clearly decided to fully utilize the plastic industry, so you're both pretty much worthless, unless you can sense plastic?" he asked Sofia. She shook her head glumly, and he shrugged.

"So what now?" Jury asked.

"Well, I figure there's only one person who'll know for sure where Bosch's headquarters really are."

"Bennie," he and Jury said together.

"I hate that little worm," Jury sighed.

"But he's so useful."

"And so slimy. For all we know he'll call Bosch as soon as we leave."

"I'd expect nothing less. We'll just have to make sure he doesn't."

He didn't want to take Sofia with them, but he didn't know what else to do with her. She couldn't leave town until the barrier was down, she had no friends, he wasn't sure any of his friends could protect her, and the safest place for her was right by his side.

So as much as it pained him, and it really did pain him, she was going to have to come with them. He just hoped he didn't get shot again. Or stabbed. Or crushed by a building. He grinned widely, feeling a rush of excitement. The stakes had never been higher.

## 22

Bennie wasn't the only informant slash go-to man in the Hidden world, but he was by far the best. Not only was Bennie willing to sell out anyone and everyone for the right amount, he also had a network of spies infiltrating the entire Hidden and norm world. No one really quite knew how Bennie had gotten to be so outrageously informed, but it didn't change the fact that he was.

As a rule, it wasn't easy to physically track Bennie down, but one disadvantage to working with witches was that once they had your scent, or signature as Jury called it, it wasn't very easy to hide from them. Sort of like trying to hide from a wolf.

"Bennie," Doc greeted cheerfully as he slapped his hand down on Bennie's skinny shoulder.

"Doc," Bennie stuttered. "I haven't seen you in... um... well, since the last time."

"You mean the time you sold me out to those Russian bear-shifters looking for some sport?"

"I thought you'd enjoy the meal," Bennie sniveled.

"Oh, I did," Doc lied. He wasn't about to tell Bennie that he could only eat human essences. "But you know, there's a part of me that feels as if we're not quite even."

"What do you want?" Bennie asked, twitching nervously.

Doc turned Bennie around to face him, but didn't let go of his shoulder. Bennie had an unfortunate habit of switching into his worm form just when you were getting what you needed from him. And he was devilishly quick. As a human, he was slow and weak.

"I need info on Bosch," Doc said, staring into Bennie's yellow eyes.

Bennie's eyes widened fearfully, and he shook his head. "I don't owe you that much!"

"Sure you do. What about that time you sold me out to those skin traders?"

"That was an accident!"

"So you say. Name your price, and tell me where Bosch's headquarters are."

"I can't," Bennie whimpered.

Now that was interesting. Doc had never known Bennie to turn down money before.

"Let me put it to you this way, Bennie. Bosch isn't here, but I am. You can protect Bosch all day, but who's going to protect you?"

Bennie licked his lips, and Doc felt the skin beneath his hand shift. He tightened his grip and said, "Jury's right outside the door. He's got this room locked down so tight not even you can worm out of it."

"You can't do this to me," Bennie whined. "What about your meal plan?"

"There are other informants," Doc shrugged.

"What about the whiskey?"

"I'll buy out a distillery."

Bennie was sweating now. "Listen, you're one of my favorite clients, I'll give you three free meal plans on the house." Doc shook his head. "Six!"

"No," Doc said. "I want Bosch." Not only was Bennie turning down money, he was also offering free services. He must be absolutely terrified.

"Not even you can kill him," Bennie moaned. "No one can."

"So he's not really a norm," Doc stated.

"I didn't say that!" Bennie shrieked. "I didn't say anything."

"Look, Bennie," Doc sighed. "I appreciate your fear, I really do, but I don't have all day, and I'd rather not break all your tiny, fragile bones trying to get the information I need. For some reason, I enjoy your sniveling face, and I hate torturing people I like. So don't make me. Tell me about Bosch."

"He'll kill me," Bennie whispered.

"Take a vacation. A sure death now or a possible death later. Take your pick."

"I hate you," Bennie whimpered.

"You know that's not true. I sell you the best bodies. I kill 'em; you eat 'em."

"Rumor has it Bosch isn't a norm," Bennie whispered.

"So what is he?"

"No one knows."

"That's a little vague, Bennie. You're going to have to do better than that."

"I don't know! I swear!" Bennie sobbed. "You have to believe me."

"So where're his headquarters? Where're the people they've stolen?"

"Underneath," Bennie whispered, face white as death now, eyes frantically searching his office as if he expected Bosch to leap out and kill him right that second.

"Underneath what? Oh..." Doc nodded his head. "Underneath."

"Exactly. He's shielded everything with plastics."

"You sure they don't have a second location?" Doc asked, squeezing Bennie's shoulder a little harder.

"I'm sure, Doc. I swear; I wouldn't lie to you about this!"

He would. He definitely would, but Bennie wasn't the best card player, and right now, Doc was fairly certain he was telling the truth.

"What else?" he demanded.

"I don't know anything else!"

Now he was lying. Doc really hated to do this, but he did need answers. Furthermore, Bennie had set Doc up at least ten times, if not more. It was only fair.

Doc kept his right hand on Bennie's shoulder and picked up one of Bennie's beringed fingers with his left. "Your hand has twenty-seven bones," Doc said softly. "How long do you think it would take me to break all of them?" Bennie whimpered, but didn't say anything, so Doc squeezed, easily crushing the tip of Bennie's pinky finger.

Bennie shrieked loudly, writhing beneath Doc's hand. "I can't tell you anything more!" he screamed.

"I think that you can," Doc murmured, crushing the bone in the middle of Bennie's pinky.

Bennie howled in pain, but underneath it, Doc could hear Jury arguing with Sofia outside the door. Apparently, she wanted to know what was going on. For a death shaman, she had an awfully low tolerance for violence.

"Tell me," Doc said evenly. "Or I'll really go to town."

"Just stop!" Bennie gasped. "Please stop. I'll tell you."

"I'll know if you're lying," Doc reminded him.

"He has his plastic defenses," Bennie whimpered, "but he also has a team of witches."

"I knew that already," Doc said.

"Sure. But did you know that they're undead?"

Doc stared at Bennie in shock. He showed no signs of lying; as far as Doc could tell, Bennie was either telling the truth or thought he was telling the truth. "What the hell are you saying?" Doc demanded.

"They're undead. That's all I know."

"As in dead, but not dead?"

"Yeah."

"But still witches?"

"Yeah."

"You have got to be kidding me!"

"I'm not. I swear," he blubbered. "Please, leave me alone now."

"Jury," Doc snapped. "Your turn."

Doc could extort information all day, but he had no idea how to put Bennie into a magical prison so he couldn't just call Bosch as soon as they left.

The door opened, and Jury walked in. He closed one end of a black pair of shackles around one of Bennie's wrists, then pulled the other arm around his back and closed the other shackle.

"That's it?" Doc asked incredulously.

"Sure. Remember the Jury motto? Semper paratus. They'll keep him from moving, talking, and shifting."

"And you just carry these around in your back pocket?"

"No. That would be weird," Jury laughed. "Did you get what you wanted?"

"No."

"He didn't talk?" Jury asked in surprise.

"Oh, he talked. I just didn't like what he had to say." Doc pulled out one of his cards and wrote "IOU a thousand merlins". He signed it and dropped it on the desk in front of Bennie's face. "If we survive, we'll come back around and let you go," he said, patting Bennie on the back. "Wish us luck."

"What's wrong?" Jury asked as they walked back outside.

"Nothing," Doc murmured. "I just need to think for a minute. Maybe sneak in a quick nap."

"A nap?" Jury exclaimed. "I swear you don't even need sleep."

He wasn't sure that he did. But Sofia and Jury probably did, and he needed to think.

"My apartment's shielded; we can probably lay low there for a couple hours," Jury added when Doc didn't respond.

"Fine."

As soon as they were inside Jury's apartment, Doc took the bottle of pink whiskey and sat in a corner facing the wall. He'd never dealt with the undead, but he knew someone who had.

A vivid memory overtook Doc; he was at Andrew's ranch house, sitting across a table from Andrew, winning a round of cards.

"You can't kill 'em," Andrew said intently. He wasn't a bad player, but he couldn't keep his emotions completely under control. His eyes tended to light up when he got a good card or narrow when he got a bad one.

"Everything has a weak spot," Doc argued.

"Sure, if you can generate enough fire to roast them. They're not like movie zombies."

"What's a movie?" Doc asked, throwing in another chip.

"Right; I keep forgetting. They're like moving pictures,"

Andrew explained offhandedly. "Make sure you invest in them when they come along. Sony was big for a while, but I can't think what else."

"Sony?"

"Yeah, just write it down. You also want to get in on Apple and Microsoft."

"Apple? Like to eat."

"No." Andrew rolled his eyes. "It's a computer company."

"Computers?"

"Damn it, Doc! Just write it down!"

"He gets grumpy when he ain't had his coffee," Doyle chuckled, handing Andrew a steaming cup.

"I ain't, damn it, Doyle! I'm NOT grumpy. I just get sick of trying to explain the future. Especially when some people don't take it seriously," Andrew muttered. "How did we get here anyway?"

"You were talking about zombies," Doc reminded him. "Dead people who still walk."

"Right! Anyway, I was just saying they're impossible to kill."

"What about a witch zombie?" Doc asked the empty corner, wishing Andrew was here to ask.

Another memory followed the first one. They were camping by a river one night, not long after Doc had started traveling with them. Doc and Charlie were playing cards, and Andrew was lying next to the fire, eyes closed, listening to the melodic sounds of Joe's harmonica.

"Someone's comin'," Charlie said simply as he laid down his cards, winning the hand.

"How do you know?" Doc asked.

"If Charlie says so..." Andrew said sleepily. "You want I should handle it?"

"And take all the damn fun outta it?" Doyle snapped.

"Let me know if you need me," Andrew said with a shrug.

A short minute later, a group of men surrounded the camp. "Just hand over the gambler," the leader demanded, "and we'll be on our way."

"What's he done?" Doyle asked, teeth glinting in the firelight.

"He cheated."

Andrew started laughing. "Who gives a damn?" he chuckled as he pushed to his feet.

"I do," a brawny man said. "He stole my money."

What a pack of liars, Doc thought as he palmed a knife. He hadn't even played the brawny man.

"Sorry," Andrew said. "One, if you could prove he cheated you'd have handled it right away. Two, if you were above board you wouldn't have followed us three days outside of town. Three, you choose to gamble, you get what you get. Move on."

"There's twenty of us," the brawny man growled. "And only five of you."

Doc wasn't worried, but it still surprised him when Andrew burst out laughing. "Guess I should've worn my brown pants!" he chortled.

Doyle jabbed Andrew with his elbow, and Andrew tried to sober. "Sorry. I take this very seriously. Look, you can all die here, or you can turn around and go home. Those are your two options."

"We ain't goin' nowhere," the brawny man snarled.

"Fine," Andrew said with a shrug. "Sorry, Doyle, I just don't have the patience for this right now."

Doc couldn't exactly say what happened next. There were twenty men surrounding them, guns drawn, and then there weren't. He'd seen Andrew start to move, he'd heard guns fire, he'd even thrown a knife at the brawny man, and he'd watched it tear through the man's throat.

But by the time he had another knife in his hand, all the other men were already dead. "What the hell?" Doc whispered, not even feeling the heat of his tattoo draining the man's life force.

"I hate it when he does that," Doyle muttered. "I only managed to get two."

"Same," Charlie said quietly.

"I didn't even bother," Joe said cheerfully.

"So between us we killed five, but Andrew killed all the rest?" Doc asked slowly.

"Yep."

Andrew was already sitting by the fire, sipping his coffee. "Damn am I glad Jane's not here," he laughed. "I'd hate to have to bury them all."

The fastest, strongest, most ridiculous human being Doc had ever met had said that zombies were nearly impossible to kill. And just normal people zombies not witch zombies. If Andrew said it was impossible, what chance did Doc have?

"So what's the problem?" Jury asked, sitting beside Doc and taking a swig of the pink whiskey. "God, that is terrible!"

"Bosch's witches are zombies."

"Wait... what? You mean like raised from the dead?"

"I guess."

"But they still have their witch power?" Doc nodded. "That's really bad," Jury muttered. "I've never dealt with a zombie, and I've never heard of anyone raising more than one at a time. It's rumored to take considerable power."

"I know. Andrew said they're impossible to kill."

"Andrew said that? Shit; we're totally screwed, aren't we?"

"I don't know. How good are you at fire?"

"Like how do you mean?"

"He said you have to burn them."

"I can do fire, but it depends on the location," Jury mused. "It'd be easier if I had a source."

"Which brings me to problem number two," Doc said. "If Bosch has surrounded the entire complex in plastic, what's that going to do to you?"

Jury paled slightly. "I don't know," he admitted. "It depends on if there're any real things inside the room. Metal, real fabric, water. I mean there should be at least something I can use." He paused then added, "This is the ultimate shit fest, isn't it?"

"Your mother would smack you over the head for talking like that," Doc laughed.

"Fortunately, she's on Necker Island."

"I don't know about this, Jury."

Jury was silent for a long time, finally he said, "Look at it this way, what have we got to lose?"

"I have a date with that gallery girl sometime next week," Doc protested.

"Dime a dozen," Jury said with a dismissive wave of his hand. "It's the pink whiskey. It's depressing you. I'll get you something better."

He stared intently at nothing for a moment, then an odd, wobbly hole opened in front of him. He put his hand into it and after feeling around for a second pulled out a half empty bottle of whiskey. "It's one of yours," he said, handing it to Doc.

"I hate it when you do that, but at least it's for a good cause. This pink stuff is... truly horrific." Doc took a large drink of the good stuff, closing his eyes as it spread through his system.

"What's she doing?" Doc asked.

"Taking a nap."

"I don't want to take her. She's still not... Well, she's not... I don't like her," Doc growled. "Not to mention she apparently makes it impossible for me to eat my kills. She'll just get in the way, but I don't know how else to keep her safe."

"How about the space between here and your sitting room?"

"You mean... put her in the hole?"

"Why not?"

"Can you get her back out?"

Jury shrugged. "Probably. Our chances for success are higher if she's not with us. She's cute, but... she's just..."

"I know. I've been waiting for this moment for over a hundred years, the moment when I saved her, and it's a bit of a letdown."

"In your mind you probably walked in, and she threw herself at you, and you didn't come up for air for a week," Jury teased.

"Something like that," Doc chuckled.

"So let's just shove her into a little rift in space, and get the job done. I heard there's going to be a wet t-shirt contest downtown tomorrow, so, you know..."

"You planning to stay off the stage this time?"

"I have to give the public what they want."

"I'm the public," Doc countered, "and I don't want it."

"You're not the public who matters."

"Isn't that always the way," Doc murmured.

"I've got something for you," Jury said offhandedly. "I was gonna wait until I wanted something from you, but... Well, anyway."

Jury handed him a leather knife harness similar to the one Doc already wore, but with only one knife. Doc turned it over in his hands. Beside the lack of a second knife, the only difference he could see was the strange symbols burned into the leather. Knowing Jury, they could mean anything. Extra protection; extra accuracy, not that he needed it; increased speed. Who knew?

"I worked a little magic on it," Jury said. "Throw the knife."

Doc flicked the knife into Jury's wall.

"I knew I should've been more specific," Jury muttered. "Throw another one."

"What do you mean? There's only..." Doc didn't finish. He didn't finish because there was another knife in the sheath ready to go. "What..?"

"Nice, right?" Jury said excitedly. "I figured out the perfect duplication spell. Throw one; another one appears. Now we're both cheating. I used it on my gun too; I never have to reload," he laughed. "I almost feel sorry for other people, don't you?"

"No," Doc said easily. He studied the wall for a moment, then said, "All we need now are some super charged Molotov cocktails, and we'll be good to go. Although," he added irritably, "they really should be called Holliday cocktails since I'm the one who invented them."

"Sure you did!" Jury laughed. "Just give me a half an hour."

Doc chuckled as Jury jumped to his feet and rushed into the kitchen. They were basically walking into a big plastic rat trap. Their odds of winning this fight were low, even if luck was on their side, but Doc had never walked away in the middle of a game yet, and he wasn't planning to now.

# 23

After forcibly shoving a screaming Sofia into a slight rift in space, Doc and Jury drove to Bosch's headquarters.

"I like it when we hang out," Doc said.

"At least it was your shit that got broken this time."

"Taking turns is only fair. Thanks, Jury."

"Don't thank me yet."

"So you really think the Albuquerque stunt'll work?" Doc asked as he climbed from the car and hoisted one of the five-gallon water bottles onto his shoulder.

"There's a chance they've got an inhibiting spell at the entrance that'll reveal us briefly," Jury said. "Other than that, I stuffed my pockets full of rocks, so I should be able to hold it even when we get into the plastic layer."

"Semper paratus," Doc said cheerfully.

"Semper paratus."

"One of these days, will you explain how your magic works in a way that makes sense?"

"I'll try, but it's like you trying to explain to me how luck works."

"As long as it works," Doc chuckled. "Let's go."

He could see that Jury's magic was in effect because Jury's face wasn't his face and he looked as if he was wearing the uniform of the Hidden's water delivery service. Sometimes Jury was brilliant. Not that he'd ever tell him. His head was already big enough.

They entered the door, and Jury paused for a second to glance at Doc. "Still good," he mouthed.

"I'm sending your aunt a thank you for that lip reading certificate."

"Don't encourage her."

They walked up to the reception desk, and Jury said dully, "Water delivery."

"Go on back," the secretary replied tonelessly, without even glancing up.

Doc hated it when things were easy. It always filled him with a sense of impending doom.

They walked down the hallway toward the breakroom, then casually entered the elevator. There were no buttons for a lower floor, but Bosch had taken them through the upper levels earlier, and they were filled with offices and computer equipment; nothing Doc was interested in.

"Give me a sec," Jury mumbled, staring sharply at the panel.

"What if we just push everywhere there isn't buttons?" Doc suggested.

"I said, gimme a second!" Jury snapped.

Doc rolled his eyes. "No sense in getting testy."

"I can't see anything," Jury finally said. "I think the panel's plastic."

"Allow me." Doc worked the tip of his knife under the edge and ripped off the entire panel, revealing another single button. "Voila!"

"I could've done that."

"But you didn't."

Doc pushed the button, and the elevator began to slowly move downward. "What do you think we'll find?"

"I have no idea," Jury replied. "I'm never good at thinking like the bad guy."

"I came up with a few ideas."

"Of course you did."

"I wrote them down, and left them in the car. You want to bet on it?"

"No."

"Come on. Just fifty merlins."

Jury sighed. "Fine. Fifty merlins you're right."

"You can't... Damn."

"Beat you to it," Jury grinned.

"So you did."

The elevator stopped, and they readied themselves. The doors slid slowly open revealing absolutely nothing. Just an empty room lined with plastic walls and three hallways branching into darkness.

"This is... unexpected," Doc muttered, swinging the water bottle back up onto his shoulder and stepping into the empty room. "Which hallway should we go down?"

"I'm getting a whole labyrinth feel," Jury hissed.

"Here's to hoping there's not a minotaur at the center."

"One is enough for a lifetime," Jury shuddered. "Those bastards are tough."

Doc started walking down the middle hallway. He had a feeling Bosch knew they were coming, but he didn't know what that meant. Would Bosch have cleared everything out? Or would he have just battened down the hatches? If Doc had to lay a bet, he'd say Bosch was waiting for them.

It didn't take them long to realize that the hallway was full of cages. Doc supposed they were really cells, but he'd been locked in a mental institution for a short time, and he knew that a cell was just a cage. It didn't matter if there were bars or walls.

Each cell had a large window into the hallway, for observation Doc supposed, and each cell was occupied. He stared into a window, horror filling him. How could anyone be so cruel, so sick?

A small naked girl was strapped to a table, some sort of apparatus attached to her chest with cables or tubes running out of her and into the ceiling. Doc assumed she was alive, but he couldn't tell. She looked dead.

Suddenly her eyes popped open, and she began to fight. She struggled to transform; her fingers shifted into claws, but the more she fought, the more the machine on her chest pulsed and hummed.

"We have to get her out of there!" Jury hissed.

"Not yet," Doc said, stopping him from messing with the door. "We don't know what that is. If we remove it, we could very well kill her. Bosch first, prisoners second."

"She's in pain," Jury argued.

"I know. Everyone is."

Doc glanced down the long hallway, suddenly quite sure where all the missing cryps had gone. They were here. Caged and imprisoned; cruel machines draining their life away.

They walked slowly down the long hallway, trying not to look, but looking anyway. Cell after cell, prisoner after prisoner.

He couldn't even imagine why anyone would do this. He couldn't imagine being part of it. It was filthy, cruel, evil, completely depraved.

"You're going to lose that bet," Doc muttered as they walked. "I didn't imagine anything like this."

Jury didn't respond, and Doc cast him a quick glance. Jury's jaw was set, and his face was slightly pale. This unnatural place was hurting him, causing him pain, and Doc suddenly wished he'd come alone. He wasn't certain of the outcome of this little venture, and he hated the idea of Jury dying somewhere where he couldn't feel the earth around him. For that matter, he kind of hated the idea of himself dying without the earth around him. However would the earth be able to snatch him up if he was encased in plastic?

There was only one solution. Don't lose.

The hallway ran on for about thirty cells before opening up into a large, open room. Doc didn't need much imagination to know what happened in this room. Hundreds of tubes ran down from the ceiling into a big box covered with gauges and computer panels, and all around the box were more tubes, running into more people, and more tubes running back into the box, and the whole place reeked of death.

But that wasn't the worst of it. The worst was that Bosch was ready for them, just as Doc had known he would be.

"Rather bold, don't you think?" Bosch laughed. "Trying to beard the lion in his own den? I rather think you miscalculated."

Doc hadn't. He'd figured on fifteen or so witches, twenty norm guards, and twenty cryp guards, and at a quick count, he was only off by two.

"What's he done to them?" Jury whispered.

He was talking about the witches. There were thirteen of them, which Doc really should have figured. Normally, if a witch was humanoid, he couldn't tell the difference between a witch and a norm, but these witches were different.

For one, if they had been human, they didn't look human anymore. Their skin was grey; their hair black; their eyes completely gone. They weren't rotting or falling apart, they simply weren't whole, like a wraith he'd once seen on an English moor.

He was beginning to wish he'd just taken Sofia and run. But then all those people would still be locked in cages in the hallways, and he didn't like that. So he was glad he'd come.

He and Jury were standing at the mouth of the hallway, and Doc subtly motioned for Jury to back up. This was going to get messy.

"I hope to hell he does the big villain reveal thing," Doc muttered to Jury under his breath as he slowly put the water bottle on the floor behind him and undid the buttons on his vest. "Because I don't have a clue what's going on."

"You haven't figured it out yet?" Bosch asked, cold smile twisting his lips.

"Figured what out exactly?" Doc asked slipping his cards into his pants pocket and dropping his vest and jacket onto the floor.

"I'm creating a new world order," Bosch exclaimed. "I'm going to remove the weaknesses from all the races and create a new perfect race. Everyone will bow at my feet, and I will rule with complete and total power."

"So when you say race," Doc said slowly, trying to figure out the best plan of attack, "you just mean you."

"Very clever, aren't you? One perfect man can rule the entire world. Ten perfect men and you invite war."

"I see," Doc murmured.

"I'm just missing one tiny piece," Bosch said carelessly. "The conductor piece. The piece that makes all the other pieces work."

Doc had a bad feeling about this.

"Fortunately, you were kind enough to keep my daughter safe for me."

"Daughter?" Doc asked, motioning carefully behind his back, trying to explain his plan to Jury.

"Sofia. She was my very first creation."

Doc froze, trying to process what Bosch had just said. "What?" he asked.

"Sofia. My first successful experiment. Her mother was quite a powerful shaman, as you call them, but her power lay in an unfortunate area. I wanted a death eater, not a life bringer."

"What the hell is he saying?" Jury demanded.

"I think he's saying we just fucked up," Doc said calmly.

"I have plans elsewhere," Bosch said, once again flashing his cold smile. "So I'll let you kids play. I'm afraid this is your last hand, Mr. Holliday. Should've stayed away from the big boys."

Bosch said something to the man at his left before turning on his heels and walking away, three other men right behind him, one of them carrying a rather large leather satchel.

"Now I'm just mad," Doc said irritably because he'd already realized Bosch was going to get away. Typical villain cowardice. Slip away while the heroes fight his little army of twisted creatures. Cliché, really.

"Lance Merrick, I presume?" Doc drawled when the tall, thin man Bosch had spoken to stepped to the front. "I've been asked to kill you."

"Inferior swine," Merrick growled. "I'm going to tear you apart and feed you to the dogs!"

"Did he seriously just call me inferior swine?" Doc asked Jury.

"That's what I heard."

"I think I'm offended," Doc laughed. "I mean it's one thing when Thaddeus does it. It's quite another thing when someone I don't even know does it."

Merrick and his crew of norms and cryps rushed forward, which was exactly what Doc had hoped they would do. Jury was in the hallway behind him, and Doc stepped slightly to the side, placing himself squarely between Jury and Bosch's men. It wasn't a wide hallway, just four feet or so, and given the right tools, he could hold it for as long as it took.

He drew a knife and hurled it at Merrick, hissing in irritation when the knife turned mid-throw and flew right back at him. He hated witches. Generally speaking. He slid sideways, snatched the knife from the air, and waited until Merrick was nearly on top of him before rushing forward to meet him.

Merrick jabbed towards him with a sword Doc could tell was made of some sort of very hard, very sharp plastic. He ducked Merrick's jab and lunged forward, stabbing his knife into Merrick's chest. Or at least attempting to. The force repelling his knife backwards was so great, it hurled Doc five feet down the hallway.

"Feed you to the dogs," Merrick snarled.

Doc landed on his feet and stepped backward another step, taking a quick second to read the situation. So far he was holding the hallway just fine, keeping Merrick's men from reaching Jury. And the witches seemed to be focused on him as well, which was perfect. If he was lucky, everyone would just forget Jury was even here. But Doc's ass was going to get kicked if he couldn't at least kill a few of them as he went.

Merrick grinned cruelly as he strode forward, sword ready

to strike. Since Merrick had hurt Aine, Doc had been planning to take his time killing him, but an army without a leader was always easier to defeat.

Doc dropped his knife and grinned. Merrick swung, and Doc ducked, sweeping his leg out to catch Merrick's. Merrick fell, and Doc wasted no time leaping on top of him and using the lion's hold to break his neck.

Something slashed across his back, but Merrick's life was already flowing into him, healing him. Doc dropped Merrick's body and jumped to his feet, spinning to face the two growling bears blocking the hallway behind him. He hated shapeshifters too. Generally speaking. He honestly didn't mind anyone as long as they weren't trying to kill him.

"Could you move a little faster?" he yelled at Jury as he plowed into the bears, pushing them backwards and falling with them to the floor.

"I'm trying!"

"Try harder!"

Just to check, Doc pulled another knife and jabbed it towards the nearest bear's throat. The knife bounced just before it hit. It was going to take him forever to choke out everyone.

He suddenly grinned. He'd use Bosch's own trick against him. He pushed off the growling bears, taking a hard cuff to the head that knocked him sideways. He hit the wall with a crash, but landed on his feet and dashed backwards, swiping Merrick's plastic sword from the floor.

He'd never liked swords, too long for his taste; but he was adaptable. The bears had gained their feet, and they were rushing towards him again. Doc ducked and made a long, solid slash, opening both their stomachs from side to side. They dropped forward, and he grunted when their dead weight crushed him into the floor.

His tattoo didn't glow. It usually didn't when he killed cryps.

He squirmed out from under the bears, grabbing the ankle of a man trying to climb over the bears in an effort to reach Jury. Doc yanked the man down to the floor, then stood and crushed his head flat with one well-placed stomp.

Four down. Only thirty-eight more to go.

"Are we having fun yet?" he laughed.

"Not really!" Jury snapped. Sweat was rolling down his brow as he worked quickly, pulling small glass bottle after bottle from the inside of the large water jugs and placing them just so. "I'm almost done."

"About time," Doc laughed as he rushed up the dead bears, slicing the sword from side to side, counting each man as they fell at his feet. He gained the top of the bears and fought his way down, pleased to see that the witches were moving closer.

He chopped off a vampire's head, broke a man's knee before stabbing him in the back of his neck, then stepped forward once more. He'd already killed thirteen of them, and he'd suffered very little in return. The high tide was in. He'd better make it count. It was sure to rush out at any second.

He sprinted towards the four guards blocking the hallway in front of him. Their guns were drawn, but he had a plan. As soon as the hallway exploded with gunfire, Doc dropped to the floor, allowing his forward momentum to carry him into their legs, knocking them all to the ground.

He was on his feet in a second, switching his grip on the sword and using it like a knife to slice open their throats. His tattoo burned intensely, but he ignored it. He didn't have time to embrace the feeling.

He stalked forward with a growl, readying the sword to

kill the snarling wolves in front of him. A moment ago, they'd been men, but now they were four legged and rabid. Even after all this time, it took his breath away when a human transformed into an animal or other creature, but he didn't have time to consider that now.

One of the wolves broke from the others and charged down the hall, leaping at the last minute, jaws chomping, greedy for Doc's flesh. Doc speared the sword through its chest, then kicked it back towards the others.

That's when the tide shifted.

One second he was on his feet, and the next second he wasn't. A wall of air had careened into him, knocking him over, and now it was pressing him into the floor. The wolves were moving forward, circling him, and he grunted, trying to move.

He could see the wraithlike witches in the mouth of the hallway. Their clawed hands were linked, and their mouths moved together. He just needed to distract them for a moment so he could break free.

The wolves were right on top of him now, saliva oozing from their jaws onto the floor around him, splashing onto his face. As long as the air was holding him in place, he didn't think the wolves could touch him, but he wasn't sure, and he wasn't going to just lay here and wait for them to attack. He gathered his strength and tried moving again. He could barely wiggle his foot, so he joggled it back and forth, staring at the wolf closest to it, just daring it to try.

At first it just growled, fur raised, but then it leapt forward, snarling angrily, trying to bury its teeth into Doc's foot, and that's when Doc kicked. His foot slammed into the wolf's head, hurling the beast down the hallway right into the line of witches.

The force holding him instantly dissipated, and Doc was free. So were the wolves. They bore down on him quickly, snarling, teeth snapping and tearing at his skin. He ripped them apart with his bare hands, brutally aware that every second he wasted was a second another guard could sneak up behind him and drive a plastic knife into his heart, and he refused to be killed by a lifeless piece of plastic.

He jumped to his feet as he tore the head from the last wolf and checked the hallway. There were seventeen guards left. Under normal circumstances, they'd be easy to kill, but they were tightly flanked by thirteen undead witches.

"You ready?!" he yelled at Jury.

"Just about!"

Doc sighed. He'd just have to kill a few more. He picked up the sword and set his feet, but the guards were just standing there, waiting. Waiting for what?

"Doc!!" Jury yelled.

"What?"

"Didn't you kill the bears?"

"What?"

Doc turned around. The hallway behind him had been filled with death, but now the corpses were shifting and moving.

"What the hell?" he muttered. He dashed forward, dodging between them, scrambling over the writhing bears and sliding down the other side, skidding to a stop just in front of Jury's tower of jars.

"Hurry!" Doc hissed. "They're... Hell, they're zombies! Move your ass!"

"I've got it! This is a terrible idea."

"Just do it!" Doc snarled as he struggled to keep an undead Merrick from attacking Jury. He chopped off

Merrick's arms, but he kept moving forward, towards Jury and the jars. Behind Merrick, the bears were on their feet, moving slowly forward as well, jaws open wide, huge paws raised to strike.

Doc swung his sword forward and down, slicing through Merrick's legs. Merrick fell to the floor and lay there writhing. "I'm not dying in here!" Doc exclaimed. "So push the damn button!"

"There is no button!" Jury snapped.

"It's a metaphor! Stop taking everything so damn literally!"

"It won't work if they're not here!"

"Well, what do you expect me to do with the bears?!"

"I don't know, but whatever you're going to do, get on with it! I'm running out of juice!"

Doc tightened his grip on the sword and rushed forward, slicing like a mad man. Flesh and gore flew through the air, raining down on him, but he kept slicing until the bears were just a puddle of mush on the floor.

"Happy?" he gasped.

"Get them down here," Jury ordered.

"Here witchy, witchy, witchys," Doc taunted.

"Doc!"

"Fine!"

Doc ran down the hallway, slicing everything that stood in his way until he reached what was left of the guards. He killed one of them and moved back two steps. The guards followed him, and the witches followed them. Doc engaged again, killing one, then stepping back again.

By the time he reached Jury, there was only one live guard remaining. The rest were dead or undead or splattered in pieces all over the hallway.

"Alright," Jury said, face drenched in sweat. "Run!"

Doc slid between the bottles and the wall and started running down the hallway. Something cracked behind him, and when he glanced back, the bottles were beginning to glow.

"FASTER!!" Jury yelled.

Doc increased his speed, but he only made it fifteen steps before the hallway exploded behind them, propelling them forward. Doc tumbled onto the floor as the entire building shook, and whole planks of plastic dropped from the ceiling, blocking the hallway behind them.

Doc lay on the floor trying to catch his breath. His ears rang, and he wasn't sure if he still possessed all his limbs. He carefully moved his hands and legs, heaving a sigh of relief.

"That was some Molotov cocktail," he croaked. "I think we should call them Jury cocktails from now on."

"It was pretty cool," Jury coughed. "Do you think it worked?"

"I don't know. If it didn't, we'll use plan b."

"What's that?"

"Slice, dice, and julienne!"

"Disgusting."

"But effective."

"What now?" Jury asked, holding out his hand to help Doc to his feet.

"Let's circle back around and see if we got them."

"I knew you'd say that."

"We'll break that machine, and then maybe we can unhook all those people."

"Do you think they're alright?" Jury asked as they backtracked down the hallway towards the elevator.

Doc glanced into one of the many cells. The man inside was screaming. "I doubt it," he said softly.

They walked down another hallway full of cells back into the large room. It was empty now except for the machine and all the connected people.

"You look at the machine," Doc said. "I'll check on the witches."

As he walked, he picked up an abandoned plastic knife and gun and tucked them into the band of his pants. The hallway had collapsed, and just looking at it, he'd say if there was anything alive inside, they were definitely dead now. But that didn't tell him whether or not the already dead things were truly dead.

"I need your help!" Jury called out.

Doc scanned the rubble one more time before heading back to Jury.

"I can't..." Jury panted. His skin was chalk white, and he was breathing heavily. "This place is making me sick," he muttered. "It's too heavy." He gestured towards the large machine. It was made primarily of plastic. Everything about this place was plastic. Doc had never hated a place so much in all his life.

"When we're finished," Doc said cheerfully, "we'll go to the mountains and just camp out."

"You hate camping," Jury laughed wearily.

"I'm coming around," Doc said, searching for a seam to work from. "No plastic as far as the eye can see."

He ripped off one of the tubes and wiggled his fingers inside the hole. He'd done an awful lot of killing and not as much feeding, so he was feeling just a little under the weather himself, not that he'd admit it.

He took a deep breath and ripped on the panel. It barely moved. He hadn't come this far to fold. He was taking this machine down, one piece at a time if he had to. He braced his foot against the base and jerked again, tearing the panel from the side. Now that it was open, he could easily break the remaining panels. He started tearing them off, while Jury examined the insides.

"I don't understand what this is," Jury said. "It's... It's like some kind of containment unit. Look, these tubes; they go out to the prisoners, I guess, and back into these little glass cubes. Most of the cubes are missing though," he muttered. "What could Bosch possibly be doing?"

"He said something about creating a super race. Is it at all possible that he's bottling their powers?"

"Like extracting it?"

Doc shrugged. He knew how to kill people, make love, and play cards. Those were his things. He spoke Greek, Italian, French, Spanish, and Latin fluently, and on a good day, he could even speak German, but he didn't understand science or magic or the two combined.

Something crashed to the floor behind them, and Doc turned, eyeing the rubble carefully. It was moving. Someone or something was still undead.

"We need to hurry," he urged.

"Just cut all the tubes," Jury ordered. "I'll free these people."

Doc hefted the sword and sliced towards the tubes. The sword bounced like a ball on a concrete floor. "Hate witches," he muttered.

"I heard that!"

"Hate magic, hate Bosch." He pulled out his own knife and tried to slice through a tube, but it didn't even dent it.

He glanced at Jury. He'd released three of the twelve men, and they seemed to be standing on their own. He looked back at the machine. There was a way to finish this, but only if Jury had the strength to pull it off.

A furious roar echoed out from inside the hallway, and Doc rushed to help Jury. In moments, all the men were free.

"Can you walk?" Doc asked one.

"I think." The man was pale and thin, but his eyes were fierce.

"I need you," Doc said earnestly. "I need all of you."

The man who'd spoken straightened. "What do you need?"

Doc handed him the gun he'd picked up. "There are three hallways," Doc said. "Each of them is full of prisoners, and I need you to release them." He handed the knife to another man who looked least likely to collapse.

"Split into two groups. One goes down that hallway." Doc pointed to the left. "And the other goes does that hallway." The men nodded. "Then go down the middle hallway. There's an elevator at the end of the hall. Get everyone the hell out as quickly as you can. This whole place is going to explode."

"It is?" Jury asked.

"Hopefully. Hurry," Doc urged them. "But don't leave anyone behind."

The men nodded as one, then broke off into two groups and scurried down the hallways. Doc hoped they were fast, because if they weren't, they were dead.

"What do you mean it's going to explode?" Jury demanded.

"You're going to bring the whole place down," Doc said.

"What? How?"

The mouth of the hallway suddenly opened as the bulk of the debris fell into the room with a thunderous clap. For a second it was quiet and the hallway seemed empty, but then all thirteen of the witches drifted out into the large room, eye sockets glowing eerily.

Doc picked up the sword. "You can do this," he said to Jury without taking his eyes off the dead witches. "If ever there was a time to use that stupid stone, this is it." He pressed the lighter he'd won off Al Capone into Jury's hand and stepped in front of him, shielding him from the approaching witches. "Make the ultimate Jury cocktail," he said cheerfully.

"Goddamn, Doc. I don't know..."

"Just do it."

It was a terrible plan. They were standing beneath six stories of building and if Jury blew it sky high, they were as good as dead. But the only other option was to run, and Doc had learned a long time ago that he'd rather die than leave the other man standing. Furthermore, he'd be damned if he'd leave anything Bosch could use in one piece.

He steadied his breath, hoping Jury's protection bracelet was super charged as the witches rushed him, claws streaking towards his face. He ducked and stabbed, knowing all he was doing was playing for time.

Claws tore through his clothes, raking his skin. He pushed the pain away, focusing on Jury. He had to protect Jury, no matter what. A witch tried to move past him, and Doc slid towards it, slicing it in half. Or at least trying to.

No matter how deadly his strikes, no matter how fatal his blows, they neither died nor stopped pressing forward. He chopped off claws, but they stayed put. He tore through grey flesh, but the witches didn't crumble or die or cease to be.

The sword was slick in his hands, slick with his own blood, but he refused to let them past. He just needed to hold them off until Jury concocted something that would burn the witches into nothing.

He swung the sword wildly, slicing through several of

them, then froze and glanced down. The knife on his chest was sliding out from its sheath. He grabbed its handle just as it turned on him and forced its point away from his body. Damn witches.

Another knife appeared in his sheath, and he dropped the sword, laughing as this knife slid from the sheath and turned against him as well. He snatched it, holding both knives back with all his strength as the witches converged on him. Another knife appeared, and Doc felt it began to move. He only had two hands. This was it.

Just as the knife turned against Doc, a hand grabbed his collar and yanked him backwards, pulling him down as it did. And then the entire world exploded. A hot, fiery eruption followed the earsplitting boom, and Doc buried his head against his knees, trying to block the terrifying brightness that filled the room around him.

The walls began to fall apart, shaking the floor, but Doc couldn't hear anymore. He was deaf and nearly blind. His skin was on fire; his inner body was numb. This was it. This was how the world ended.

# 24

Doc was shaking, but he didn't know why. For a moment he'd dreamed that the entire world was on fire, burning with such intense rage that nothing was left. But he wasn't hot anymore, and the bright fiery light was gone. So why was he shaking?

"Doc!" Jury yelled in his ear.

Doc jerked upright. "Why the hell are you yelling!" he yelled.

"Oh, thank god," Jury muttered, collapsing to the ground beside Doc. "I thought I'd killed you."

"I'd haunt you if you did," Doc laughed.

"No doubt."

Doc blinked slowly, trying to clear his vision. The ceiling above him was bright blue, which didn't make sense until he realized that the ceiling was gone. The entire building was gone. There was nothing left but a bunch of rubble.

"That was one hell of a cocktail," Doc drawled.

"Yeah."

Doc glanced sideways. Jury looked as if he'd just taken a

lap through hell, but he was smiling. "Did you see it?" he asked.

"Did I see it?" Doc snorted. "I couldn't even look at it."

"We should probably get out of here," Jury advised, trying to stand. "I think I may have broken a law or two."

"Which ones?"

"Oh, you know, the ones about exposing the Hidden world to the norms."

"You think they'll notice?" Doc asked. He ached all over. His ears were ringing, and every time he blinked strange rainbows exploded in his eyes. "I need a snack," he murmured.

"I need some real shit," Jury said. "I need some dirt between my toes, some sun on my face—"

"A woman in your arms and whiskey on your tongue," Doc interrupted.

"I was going to say all the elements but fire. I think I've had enough fire for a while."

Doc laughed softly. "I'm with you on that one. Do you think we killed them?"

"I don't see them moving, do you?"

Doc finally managed to stand and surveyed the wreckage around them. He and Jury were standing on a very small circle of floor, and piled all around them was six stories worth of debris, most of it pitch black and twisted from the heat of the fire. They were standing in the eye of the hurricane, the center of the explosion, ground zero.

They were lucky to be alive.

"See," Doc drawled. "That's how luck works."

"And that's how magic works," Jury grinned.

"How do you plan to get out of here?" Doc asked, gazing up at the enormous mountain of wreckage.

"The same way Bosch left."

"Which way was that?"

"Out the back door."

Doc gave Jury a slanted look. He didn't look deranged. "Back door?"

"Yeah. You were a little focused on the other guys. It's this way." He waved his hand wearily, and the rubble moved just enough that they could squeeze through it. Jury stumbled forward, and Doc followed him. "I can't wait to get out of here," Jury sighed, waving his hand again to move another line of rubbish. "I feel a hundred years old."

"You are a hundred years old."

"But I don't normally feel it."

"I feel two hundred years old," Doc groaned as he bent down to enter the tunnel Jury had uncovered.

"I don't understand why you always have to one up me," Jury complained.

Doc chuckled as they limped up the tunnel together. "I just happen to be older than you and feel worse than you. I was mauled by a bear, for crying out loud. And don't even get me started on your self-replicating knife!"

"Oh please! If I hadn't gone with you, you'd be a hundred kinds of dead!"

"If I hadn't been there to protect you while you took your sweet time setting up your magic, you'd be bear scat."

"This is why I hate doing stuff with you!" Jury snarled as he pushed open the door and stepped out onto the sidewalk. "It's always about you."

"If you hate hanging out with me so much you should just stop!" Doc snapped.

"I think I will!"

He glared at Jury and snarled "fine!" before turning on his

heel and heading the other way. "Wait!" he called out, coming to an abrupt stop. "I forgot about Sofia."

"Sofia," Jury muttered. "I guess we should probably get her out of the pocket."

"If she's still there," Doc muttered.

He'd turned to face Jury now, and at his words, one of Jury's eyebrows shot up. "If she's still there?"

"Bosch had a look."

"Well, let's go then."

Doc smiled cheerfully at the norm who stopped to stare at them. Doc glanced down at his blood and gore soaked clothes, then winked at the norm and said, "I fell down some stairs." The norm's eyes widened, and he rushed past, head tucked towards the ground.

"Do you think the cryps made it out?" Doc asked skeptically, glancing back towards the smoking ruins. "I'm not sure we gave them enough time."

"We did," Jury said, pointing across the street.

A large group of cryptids was huddled together, moving slowly towards the nearest Hidden entrance. Norms were scuttling past, giving them a wide berth like they were infected with a terrible disease, which wasn't all that surprising since most of them were naked and several of them weren't even remotely humanoid. They were all breaking laws today.

Doc watched them with a slight grin. He may not have gotten Bosch, but he'd definitely slowed him down. They had destroyed the Bureau's headquarters, freed the imprisoned cryptids, and saved Sofia. Job well done.

Now he could go home, find a willing woman, get a snack, and drink a whiskey. Maybe not in that exact order. Snack first. Whiskey second. Then a willing woman.

"Let me know if you see anyone society would be better off without," Doc murmured as they walked unsteadily towards Jury's place.

"My downstairs neighbor is annoying."

"Define annoying."

By the time they reached Jury's apartment, Doc was feeling quite a bit better. He'd taken a brief detour down an alley, stopped a rape, and eliminated a rapist from the streets. Jury was feeling better too. Doc could tell because he wasn't shuffling with his shoulders slumped anymore. He was striding. Just being outside away from all that plastic junk had done wonders for his health.

Doc breathed a sigh of relief when he saw that Jury's gargoyles were still in position. Maybe Sofia would be too. Jury pushed open his door, and Doc looked past him to see that everything appeared to be in its proper place. If luck was on his side, Sofia would still be there, screaming her head off, waiting for them to free her.

"Just gimme a second," Jury said as he walked over to the wall and stared at it. The weird wobbly hole opened, and Jury put his head inside and looked around. "Shit," he hissed, pulling his head back out. "She's not there."

"Could she have just wandered off?" Doc asked hopefully.

"Not likely," Jury said. "Besides, Bosch left this." He handed Doc a handwritten note with the words "I win" penned across it.

Doc sighed heavily. She couldn't just stay put like he'd asked her to. She just had to run off with the bad guy. Technically, he had saved her from the fate Señora Teodora had predicted, so he hadn't exactly failed, but this was definitely failure adjacent.

"What now?" Jury asked.

"It would seem," Doc said flatly, "that I'm going to have a pleasant chat with your annoying neighbor; and after that, I guess, we're going to have to save Sofia. Again."

# Ready for another awesome Doc book?
## Check out

## Book 2: COUP D'ÉTAT

## 1

Doc Holliday tipped his whiskey bottle upright and watched as the last of the amber liquid slid down towards his lips, wondering vaguely if he stared hard enough if it would somehow reveal the answer he needed.

"Getting drunk isn't going to help, you know."

"If only," Doc sighed as he tossed the empty bottle towards Jury's trashcan. The can moved at the last second, catching the bottle before it hit the floor. "Nothing but net," Doc chuckled.

"My point. Your aim was way off," Jury snorted.

"Get me another bottle."

"No."

"Come on."

"No. You've already drank seven bottles, and it's getting us nowhere. It's time to get off your ass and get back to it."

"Get back to what?" Doc muttered. "Sofia's gone. Bosch is gone. Sure, given enough time I could probably find them, but to what end?" He shrugged. "I failed, Jury. Failed. Do you have any idea what that feels like?" Doc shook his head in disgust. "What am I saying? Of course you do."

"I'll pretend that's the whiskey talking," Jury said irritably. "Furthermore, it's only been one goddamn week! You searched the Black Forest for that wood sprite for three months!"

"She was gorgeous... and so flexible."

"I know. I saw her," Jury replied, staring off into space for a moment with a lopsided grin. He shook his head and said, "That's not the point; the point is we'll find Sofia, just like you found the wood sprite. But only if we actually leave the building."

"You don't know," Doc muttered. "She could be hiding in the closet. Did you check?"

"Yes, I checked."

"You didn't!"

"I really did."

Doc leaned his head against the couch and closed his eyes.

Jury was right, and he knew it, but he was tired, and he wasn't sure Sofia was worth it. Señora Teodora, Tozi, was worth it. But Sofia? He'd already saved her once, and if she hadn't been such a pantywaist, he might have been able to keep her safe. But she was worthless.

Worthless was perhaps a bit harsh; but it irritated the hell out of him that she'd been born with her power and she didn't even know how to use it or, at the very least, understand it. It had only taken him a couple years to figure out his limitations.

That wasn't all of it though. She was whiney. And self-centered. She dressed oddly. She didn't like Jury. She didn't have any acceptance of other creatures. And she was just all-around annoying.

Not to mention that she probably didn't even want Doc to rescue her because she didn't like the way he did things. She thought he was unnecessarily violent. He laughed harshly. That was half the reason Tozi had picked him.

He could accept his failure in the general scheme of things and move on. He could even accept the loss of Sofia. He'd technically fulfilled his promise, and if Tozi visited him again, that's just what he'd tell her. His problem was Bosch's plan. If Bosch actually had a way to turn himself into some sort of super creature, that would put the Hidden and everyone in it at risk.

So it would seem that his path was obvious. Stop Bosch. But, and this is why he was trying so hard to get drunk, no matter how he figured it, if he started a war with Bosch the people in the Hidden were going to get hurt. If only he knew which way they'd get hurt less. He was beginning to think he was going to have to flip a damn coin and let luck decide.

"Heads up," Jury suddenly hissed. "Someone's coming."

"You going to let them in?"

"May as well. It'd be easier than trying to explain a bloody foyer to the manager."

"You're ridiculous."

"Am not!"

"Are too," Doc retorted. "Don't you own the damn building?"

"Yes, but the manager doesn't know that, does she? And she's a stickler for the rules."

"They're your rules!" Doc exclaimed.

"She doesn't know that! Now shut up! They're at the door."

"I need another bottle," Doc whispered.

"You do not!"

"It'll help me fight."

"You're a goddamn drunk."

"I haven't been drunk in over a hundred years; give or take."

"So you're an alcoholic."

"Now that I can't argue with," Doc chuckled.

Someone was fiddling with the door now, and if Doc could hear them, they weren't very good. Or they were very, very good.

"How many?" he asked.

"Thirty."

"How do you communicate with the gargoyles anyway?"

"It's hard to explain," Jury said.

"And they can count?"

"No," Jury snorted. "They just showed me how many there are. Is this really the time for a gargoyle lesson?"

"I don't know when else we'll have it. What's taking them so damn long with the door anyway?"

"I didn't want it to be too easy for them."

"Oh." Doc glanced around Jury's perfectly clean and arranged loft space and started laughing.

"What the hell're you laughing for?"

"Say goodbye to your apartment."

"I hate you."

"You always say that, yet here we are. What is this, like our five hundredth date?"

"I hope you get shot."

"I hope they don't have some kind of plastic Gatling guns."

"Why do you say shit like that?"

"It just popped into my head."

"Well pop it the hell out!"

The door finally cracked open, and Doc and Jury ducked behind the couch. "You should've gotten the red couch," Doc mouthed.

"I should've moved to Alaska," Jury mouthed back.

After a moment, the door clicked closed, and Doc winked at Jury before leaping upright and tossing a knife towards one of the intruders. These men didn't have witches to guard them, so when Doc's knife slammed into the leader's forehead, it tore right through it, leaving a gaping bloody hole.

Doc didn't pause to enjoy the energy pulsing through his tattoo because the room was suddenly filled with the sounds of gunfire. A bullet tore through his arm, but Doc didn't move, just released four more knives before pulling the couch over the top of them both as he dropped onto the floor.

"Next time," he snapped, "get an apartment with rooms."

"I like open spaces," Jury replied, wiping a smear of blood from his smoking gun.

Doc took a deep breath. "Ready?"

"Ready," Jury replied.

Doc stood again, this time tossing the couch with full force towards the bulk of the men. Plaster rained from the ceiling as stray bullets streaked all over the room. The momentum of the couch carried the intruders across the room and into the wall, and Doc and Jury used the distraction to eliminate the seven men who had already circled around to the sides.

Ever since the witch incident, Doc had been a little wary of his self-replicating knife. But it turned out that it really did make killing people even easier because as soon as one knife left his fingers, another knife was ready to pull.

"Don't forget to keep one alive!" Doc ordered as he jumped onto the couch and started slashing the throats of the men pinned between the couch and the wall.

"You don't forget to keep one alive!" Jury yelled back.

"I'm the one who said it!"

Doc grabbed one man by his throat and slammed him into the wall, squeezing so hard that his fingers punctured the man's flesh. A bullet tore across Doc's cheek, and another ripped through his chest, and he turned with a growl.

"This is my favorite vest," he snarled, ripping the gun from the shooter's hand and bludgeoning him to death with it.

There were a few men caught between the couch and the floor, so Doc threw the couch off of them, tossing knives as he did. One of the men kicked at Doc's leg and hurled a knife at his face, but Doc caught it easily, tossed it over his shoulder, then leaned down and pulled the man's head up by his hair.

"STOP!" Jury yelled just as Doc moved to bash the man's head into the floor.

Doc froze. "What?!"

"He's the last one!"

"Really?" Doc glanced around the room. The walls were splattered with blood, anything that could be broken was, and there were dead bodies everywhere. "That was quick," Doc muttered. "Did you count yet?"

"You're so immature; I'm not counting."

"So you lost?"

"Let's just get on with this!" Jury snapped.

Something sliced at Doc's throat, and he popped the man's head lightly onto the floor, knocking him out. "You're going to regret that," Doc muttered as he wiped the blood from his neck; he could already feel the wound closing beneath his fingertips. He loved being him.

He broke the plastic knife the man had used in two, just because he could and because he was getting really sick of plastic, then he hauled the man to his feet and shoved him into one of Jury's dining room chairs.

He removed a belt from one of the corpses and used it to cinch the unconscious man in place. Then Doc slapped him, but he didn't wake up.

"Shouldn't have hit him so hard," Jury commented.

"I didn't. He's just a weakling," Doc said, slapping the man again.

The man's eyelids crinkled as he struggled to wake, but just as he was opening his mouth to say something, someone knocked on Jury's door. Doc slapped his hand over the man's mouth and sat on his legs to keep him from moving.

"You're covered in blood," he mouthed to Jury.

"Just a minute," Jury called out. He tore off his shirt and used it to wipe his face clean, but he'd been shot at least three times, and blood was slowly oozing down his arm and chest.

"That didn't help," Doc hissed.

"I'll just use a glamour," Jury said. Suddenly he was wearing clothes again, clean clothes, and there wasn't a speck of blood on him. At least that's how it appeared.

Jury cracked the door open. "Sami," he said easily. "What's up?"

"Mr. Jury, it sounds like a warzone up here," a feminine voice replied pointedly. "Is everything okay?"

"It's fine."

"I definitely heard something. You know you can't have parties without prior approval from the owner?"

"I'm aware of that regulation."

"Well?"

"I'm sorry, Sami. I didn't hear anything. You must have the wrong floor."

Doc heard Sami, who he assumed was Jury's bulldog manager, hiss in irritation. "I already checked the other floors, Mr. Jury."

"Then it must be outside."

"Can I take a quick peek inside?" she asked determinedly.

"Um..." Jury glanced back towards Doc.

Doc tightened his grip on his struggling prisoner and shook his head vehemently.

"Mr. Jury, please; just to put my mind at ease."

"Knock him out again," Jury mouthed.

"Seriously?" Doc mouthed back.

"Yes!"

Doc shifted his hands, applying a full choke to the man's neck. He held it just until he felt the man go slack, then let go and stood.

Jury closed his eyes, struggle making his face tight for a moment, and then the entire apartment looked normal again.

So long as no one moved and tripped over one of the invisible bodies on the floor.

Jury swung the door wide open and gestured inside. "See? Right as rain."

Sami stepped into the doorway and glanced around the room, cheeks turning bright red when her eyes landed on Doc. "Mr. Holliday, I didn't know you were here."

Doc frowned. He had an excellent memory for names and faces, and he was sure he'd never met her before. He would have definitely remembered meeting those hips.

"I'm sorry," he said slowly. "Have we met?"

"Oh... No, I mean, I'm sorry; I just know who you are." Her hands fluttered nervously. "I... I... I better go. Thank you, Mr. Jury." She turned on her heels and rushed across the small foyer to the elevator.

Jury closed the door with a sigh of relief, letting the glamour fade. "I need a drink. And a sandwich."

Doc studied him with a frown. He could tell the glamour had drained Jury, and worry filled Doc for a moment; he'd never noticed Jury tire so easily before. There'd been this one time in China when they'd used glamour for three days straight. He pushed that thought away; he had other things to deal with right now.

Doc slapped the unconscious man again, grinning when the man's eyes popped open immediately. "Let's get this done with, shall we?" Doc pulled his knife from its sheath and ran it slowly down the man's cheek, drawing a thin line of blood. "You're going to die. How you die, is up to you. Tell me about Bosch."

"I'm not gonna tell you a thing, you corrupted piece of shit flesh," the man snarled.

"That was a splendid, if slightly confusing, insult," Doc

chuckled. "Felt a bit forced though, not something someone would normally say. Why corrupted?"

The man spit at Doc just barely missing his cheek, and Doc's eyes narrowed. "Why corrupted?" he repeated, slicing his knife gently across the tops of the man's fingers.

He flinched, but didn't speak.

"I know all about the human body, you know," Doc drawled. "I can drag this on for hours. I'm going to start with your manhood though, just to see if we can hurry things up."

The man's eyes widened with horror.

"You'll be dead," Doc said carelessly. "So it's not like you'll be needing it."

"All cryptids are corrupted," the man spat. "Mutated forms of humanity. Abominations."

"That's not the way I heard it," Doc said conversationally. "My favorite version of the story is that the mother birthed all the races. Cryptids and humans alike."

"What mother?" the man sputtered. "God created man. Man! Everything else is demon spawn!"

"That old song and dance?" Doc sighed. "I thought we'd moved past that."

The man's eyes grew bright with passion. "Bosch will remove all the filth from our streets, all the abominations, all the half-breeds. When he's done, we will be clean once more."

"Huh. That's definitely not the way I heard it," Doc murmured, remembering the look on Bosch's face when he'd talked about becoming super human.

Doc drove his knife through the man's wrist, severing the joint. The man howled in pain, and Doc clamped his hand over his mouth to muffle the sound.

"There's more where that came from," Doc said when the man settled down to a whimper. "Tell me more about Bosch."

"You'll burn in hell," he sniveled.

"Perhaps," Doc agreed. "Tell me." He moved his knife deliberately towards the man's crotch.

"You'll be punished," he wavered, face tightening in fear.

"It's funny, isn't it?" Doc chuckled. "You broke into my house—"

"Excuse me?!" Jury snapped.

"Sorry, Jury's house, you endeavor to kill us, quite vigorously, thirty to two no less, and I'll pay? I'm the injured party here." He moved the knife closer. He really wasn't keen to start chopping into the man's giblets, but he didn't have all day either, and he was proving to be stubborn.

"Your existence alone demands punishment!"

"So in your mind, I should be punished just because I'm alive?"

"You and the witch will both burn. You deserve to burn!"

Doc had had enough. He flicked the knife down, slicing through the man's pants and whatever else happened to be there, allowing the man to scream and howl in pain.

"Tell me about Bosch," Doc growled.

"I'll be rewarded for my loyalty," the man sobbed.

"No one's here to reward you," Doc scoffed. "When you die, I'll eat your soul and that will be that. No pearly gates, no crown, no angels feeding you grapes. Dead. Done."

True fear entered the man's eyes. "No," he whispered.

"Yes." Doc smiled, then added, "But if you're a very good boy, I'll let Jury kill you."

"I don't know anything," the man stuttered, tears trailing down his cheeks. "We just got a message telling us where to go and who to kill."

"Not good enough," Doc said. "Was the message from Bosch; is he your leader?"

"Yes."

The fingers on the man's functional hand twitched, and Doc knew he was hiding something. "But?"

"But what?"

"Bosch sent the message, but..." The man's lips tightened. "Who's your leader?" Doc demanded, shoving his knife into the man's severed wrist and twisting it.

"I don't know!" the man screamed.

"So not Bosch?"

He shook his head and glared at Doc with such a fierce hate that it reminded Doc of someone else he'd once met. Someone possessed with such religious fervor that it had quite gotten him killed.

"Oh hell," Doc whispered. "You're an Acolyte, aren't you?"

Disbelief crossed the man's face, and he began screaming, "Forgive me, Appointed One, forgive me!"

Doc snapped the man's neck with one motion, feeling no joy when his life powered Doc's tattoo. He stared at the Acolyte's dead body, feeling a horrible sense of foreboding. Sometimes luck was a bitch.

# BUY NOW AT AMAZON.COM

# Want to see how Doc's friend Andrew Rufus became a LEGEND?

The entire seven book series **THE LEGEND OF ANDREW RUFUS** is available on Amazon.com under M.M. Crumley or THE LEGEND OF ANDREW RUFUS. That being said, here's the very first chapter of book one, DARK AWAKENING, to wet your palate.

# 1

Worst summer ever, Andrew Rufus thought sullenly as he tossed his baseball towards the ceiling for the fifteen hundredth time. He was bored. So bored that he might actually consider reading one of the books his mom had brought back from the library.

He glanced at the stack of books and shuddered. He didn't give a crap about leprechauns or the secrets of Middle-earth. If only his mom would bend on the no television in his room rule. After all, it's not like he could help the fact that he had a broken leg.

He tossed the ball again, but he wasn't paying attention so it slipped from his glove and rolled onto the floor. "I guess that's that," he muttered.

He counted the neon stars on his ceiling, but he already knew there were a hundred and six of them. He'd known that since yesterday morning.

"You need anything, baby?" his mom hollered up the stairs.

"How 'bout a TV?" Andrew yelled back.

"Anything you can actually have?"

"No," he grumbled.

"Alright. My online meeting's about to start. I'll check on you when it's done."

"Whatever."

"I heard that!"

"Whatever," Andrew mouthed sulkily.

If he didn't do something soon he was going to scream, so he grabbed a book from the pile at random and read the title. *American Folklore: Pecos Bill and Others*. Gag me, Andrew thought, but it had to be better than a book about how to trap leprechauns. And if it wasn't, he'd hobble to the window and hurl himself to his death.

He flipped to the beginning of the story and started reading. He rolled his eyes after a line or two and stifled a yawn. Boring, he thought as he scanned the page. Exactly how long were these cowboy dudes going to keep riding into the sunset? A car chase would definitely be more exciting.

The sun blinded him for just a minute, and he closed his eyes, rubbing them with the back of his hand. He squinted at the page, trying to see the words clearly, but they kept blurring into a mess of brown. Maybe the pain pills were finally taking affect.

He read another line but abruptly coughed as dust swept down his throat, choking him. He reached blindly for his cup of water. His fingers grazed the smooth glass, then he heard it shatter on the floor. Another cough racked his frame, and he dropped the book and struggled to his feet.

The earth suddenly shifted beneath him, and he flung his arms out to the sides, trying to grab hold of his dresser, but there was nothing there, and he started to fall.

"No," he whispered fearfully. He didn't want to fall. What if he hurt his leg?

He flexed his legs in fear, gasping in relief when he didn't hit the floor. But then he lurched forward and backward and forward again. What the hell was going on? Was he having a seizure?

He blinked frantically, trying to clear the dust from his eyes so he could see again. He squinted and realized he actually could see, but all he could see was dust. It didn't make sense. Nothing was making sense.

He glanced down, wondering where the floor was. "Holy crap!" he gasped. There was no floor. There was no floor because he was sitting on a horse. A horse. Not just sitting. Riding. That's why he was lurching back and forth. He grabbed hold of the saddle thingy and held tightly, then stared at his hands in utter dismay. Those weren't his hands, but how could they not be his hands? He released the saddle with one hand and felt his face.

"Oh hell," he whispered. It wasn't his face. He knew it wasn't because it was rough and full of angles. It wasn't his nose or his hand or his body. Those weren't his legs. What the hell kind of medicine were they giving him anyway? This had to be a hallucination. It just had to be.

The horse suddenly leaped into the air, and Andrew jerked in terror, grasping the saddle tightly. The horse landed easily, but Andrew didn't. "Crap!" he hissed as he slid precariously to the side. He flung his arms around the horse's neck, hugging it for dear life and desperately hoping it would stop soon.

Then he heard it. An angry voice, gruff and gravely, yelling, yelling very loudly, INSIDE Andrew's head.

*WHAT THE HELL'S GOIN' ON?!*

Andrew couldn't help it. He screamed; he screamed at the top of his lungs. But the more he screamed, the more the voice inside his head yelled.

*WHAT THE HELL YOU DOIN'?! STOP THAT SISSY CRYIN'! RIGHT NOW!!!*

Andrew's mind raced, trying to figure out what was going on, but he simply couldn't think. The voice in his head was too loud. Why was there a voice in his head? Where was his body? Where was he? What was happening?

*Who are you?!* the voice snapped. *You some kinda witch?*

"Witch? What? No," Andrew stuttered, eyes widening when he heard his own voice. It didn't sound right at all. It was deep and menacing, like the voice inside his head. He stared at his hands again. They moved when he moved them, but they just weren't his hands. The wide, red gash from his fall wasn't there. These hands had thin, white scars across the knuckles; they were callused, sun-browned, and huge.

He squeezed his eyes shut. He must have fallen asleep reading that stupid book, and now he was dreaming. That was it. He was dreaming. All he had to do was wake up. He pinched himself. It hurt, but he didn't wake. He slapped himself. Tears welled in his eyes it stung so badly, but he still didn't wake up.

*What the hell you doin'?!*

"Trying to wake up," Andrew mumbled, weirded out that he was having a conversation with someone he couldn't see. Like he was talking to himself, but he wasn't. It felt like madness.

*Wake up?*

"I'm asleep; that's the only explanation."

*Asleep? I ain't asleep. GET THE HELL OUTTA MY BODY!! NOW!*

"I don't know how."

*Try!* the voice snapped.

"How? I don't know how I got in here." Andrew was trying to remember if he'd ever had a conversation in a dream before, but the voice just wouldn't shut up.

*GET OUT!!!*

"I already told you, I can't!"

*Do it anyway!*

"How?"

*Just do!*

Andrew rolled his eyes and glanced around. This was surely the most vivid dream he'd ever had. It was so vivid he could feel the heat and taste the dirt. Maybe he should back off the painkillers.

"It's just a dream, you know," Andrew said. "I'm sure I'll wake up soon, and then you'll have your body back." What a dorky thing to say. When he woke up, the dream would be gone.

He relaxed his stranglehold on the horse and sat up straighter in the saddle. He wasn't so scared now that he realized he was in a dream. He was certain he could ride a horse in a dream, and if he fell, he'd just wake up. Besides, the horse wasn't actually moving anymore. Surely he could sit on a horse without falling.

*When I get my hands on you, I'm gonna tie you in a knot.*

"A knot?" Andrew laughed. "Is that really the best you've got?"

*You laughin' at me?*

"A little. Be pretty hard to tie someone into a knot. Beat me up, sure. Tie into a knot? I don't know."

*Who the hell are you?!*

This was bizarre, but his mom hated it when he was rude, so Andrew sighed and said, "Andrew Rufus; and you?"

*Pecos Bill.*

Andrew burst out laughing. Now he knew it was a dream. He felt stupid for not realizing it right away; everything had just felt so real. The sun was burning down on his back. He could feel sweat beading on his skin; he could feel the roughness of the horse's hair beneath his hands; he could feel the grainy dust in his eyes. He'd never had such an intense dream before. It was so real, so vibrant. It had to be the drugs.

*What's so funny?* Pecos snapped.

"Nothing, it's just… I really am dreaming."

*What the hell you talkin' 'bout?! Ain't no dream! What'd you say your name was?* Andrew, Andrew Rufus, Andrew thought, wondering if he needed to speak out loud for Pecos to hear him. *Ain't never heard of you,* Pecos growled back. Course not. You're not real. I'm real. I'm dreaming, so I've heard of you 'cause you're in that dumb book I was reading before I fell asleep. *What?!*

Andrew sighed. Dreams weren't usually so complicated. When he woke up, he was tossing the pills in the trash. Listen, I'm not really here. You're not really here. This is all just a dream. *Ain't no damn dream!* Pecos sputtered. *Get out of my body right this minute…*

Pecos went on and on, but Andrew wasn't listening because he'd just noticed three other riders heading towards him. They were already fairly close, and Andrew could just make out their faces. He was suddenly very glad he was dreaming because he didn't know how to make the horse move again, and if this were real life, he'd be riding the other way. He'd never seen such scary-looking dudes.

They had serious expressions on their faces and guns on their hips. Lots and lots of guns. And knives. They were riding into the sun, so their faces were shining, and a shudder ran down Andrew's spine when his eyes locked onto one of the men.

"Somethin' wrong, Pecos?" the man demanded as they stopped their horses beside Andrew's.

Andrew gulped. "Um... I..." He didn't go on, just stared at the man in horror.

He had a stone-hard face, brilliant, blue eyes, and a scar running from his nose to his ear. His tight blond goatee was broken in the middle by another scar which made him look rather sinister. In addition to his frightening face, he had a ridiculous amount of guns strapped all over him, maybe six or eight, and Andrew was certain he wouldn't have any problem using them.

Andrew tore his eyes away and looked at one of the other men. He instantly regretted it. These dudes were so creepy Andrew wished he could wake up right now. He'd never be mean to his mom again. He'd tell her he loved her, because he did. He'd promise to never climb a tree, ever again. He'd keep both feet on the ground, and he'd swear off painkillers for the rest of his life.

The second man wasn't wearing a hat, and his skin was as dark as the surrounding dirt, maybe darker. His hair was loose, flowing down his back in a shimmery, black wave, and Andrew guessed he was Native American, but he wasn't sure. His dark eyes were unfathomable, unreadable, but the worst part was that, in addition to a bow and a few guns, he was wearing so many knives Andrew didn't even try to count them.

Andrew shuddered, wondering what Pecos must look like if these were the type of guys he hung out with, and glanced at the third man. He actually looked normal enough except he had the widest and curliest mustache Andrew had ever seen. His eyes were a laughing brown, and his lips were curved in a slight grin. He even seemed to be wearing a normal amount of weapons, but Andrew couldn't be sure.

He'd never been around anyone who carried a gun or a knife before, let alone eight of them. He wasn't sure how he'd imagined these guys because he was positive the book hadn't been all that descriptive.

"Pecos?" the blond man asked again, a thread of annoyance in his tone.

*Listen you coward, you body thief, you slimy snake!* Pecos yelled. *Get the hell outta my body right this damn minute or I'm gonna truss you up and leave you for the coyotes!* How's that better than a knot? I mean, how're you gonna do it?

Pecos growled, and Andrew glanced between the three men, feeling trapped, like the time Chuck had pulled a prank, but Andrew had been caught holding the spray can.

He opened his mouth to reply to the blond man, but Pecos started yelling again, so loud that Andrew flinched. Shut up so I can think! Andrew snapped. *Shut up?! Shut up?! This is my body! You shut up, damn it!* Right now it's my body! So you shut up! *You ain't no man; you're just a coward!*

I'm not a coward or a man, so there! Andrew thought angrily. His head was starting to ache. There was just too much going on. Could your head even ache in a dream? I'm only thirteen, Andrew added. And I didn't steal your stupid body; why would I even want to? I just kinda ended up here. And it doesn't matter, 'cause THIS IS A DREAM!!!

This was getting weirder and weirder by the second. He'd

pay good money for his mom to wake him and tussle his hair. She could call him "baby" and sit by his bed all day asking him how he was, and he wouldn't even mind.

Pecos was still yelling, but Andrew tried to ignore him because the mustached man was talking.

"You alright, Pecos?"

"Um... yeah, just thinking," Andrew replied awkwardly.

"Thinkin' 'bout what?" the blond man snapped.

Andrew cringed. The blond guy freaked him out. He looked like the kind of guy who shot first and didn't bother to ask questions, ever. "I don't know... Just thinking."

The knife man had been watching Andrew or Pecos, whoever he was, intently, but now he spoke. "You wantin' to change your plan?"

Andrew grabbed at that. "Plan? What plan exactly?"

The blond man frowned deeply, but the knife man smiled slightly and replied, "The one you just made."

Andrew sighed; that had really cleared things up. "Let me think about it," he stalled. Help me out here, Pecos? *Ain't helpin' you, boy! You need to disappear.* I really wish I could, but I can't. I've never tried to wake up in a dream before; I don't know how to do it. *I done told you boy, ain't no dream,* Pecos said in a weary tone. Of course it is, but I still don't wanna get shot to death by your gun-happy friends. They'd like an answer, and I don't have any idea what they're talking about.

*Ain't gonna shoot me.* No, but they might shoot me, and see, I'm in your body in the middle of... of... Andrew looked around. There was nothing as far as he could see except dirt, rocks, little scrubby plants, and what he assumed were cactus clumps. He wasn't sure because he'd never seen actual cactuses before.

Why are we in a desert? *Ain't a desert, boy. Just a bit of dry land is all. We ridin' to stop the snake.* Andrew accidentally laughed. "Sorry," he said quickly. "Just thought of something funny. Still thinking," he added when the blond man opened his mouth to speak.

Four guys to stop one measly snake? You're kidding me right?! You're supposed to be a western legend! You fight things like tornados and rustlers and blue cows or something, right? *Watch it, boy…* Or what?

Andrew was beginning to enjoy himself. He hadn't had any fun in days; not since that stupid, wild, grey cat had knocked him out of the tree. Sure the cowboy dudes were scary looking; but it was a dream; and as such, nothing really bad could happen. And if it did, he'd just wake up. Like that one dream he'd had where he'd shown up to school naked. He'd woken just as the bell rang and right before everyone could file out into the hallway and laugh at him.

*This ain't a dream or a pleasure trip or a damn party! If you don't get outta my body right now folks're gonna die!* Andrew rolled his eyes. What did it matter if people died in a dream? It's not like they were real. *THIS IS REAL!!! Can't you feel it?!*

Andrew shook his head, annoyed that Pecos was so serious. It's too bad he hadn't had a baseball dream instead. One with Willie Mays and Derek Jeter and Babe Ruth. Andrew would pitch and see if they could get a hit. Now that would have been fun.

The only thing I can feel is the sun, Andrew complained. Is it always this hot? *That's just it, boy. When's the last time you felt the sun in a dream?* Andrew chose not to think about that. It was weird that he was so hot, that he was sweating, that he could feel the breeze cooling him down, but there was an explanation for that. His pain pills clearly had some terrible side effects. They were probably experimental. He shuddered, wondering what else they were doing to him.

*I can't believe this,* Pecos sighed. *You've gotta be the densest boy on earth.* Andrew frowned. I'm not dense! If I believed you, a figment of my imagination I might add, THEN I would be dense! *Fine, just keep on ignorin' your senses, and while you do, people'll die. Thanks to you.*

Whatever, let's get back to the plan. You're riding to stop a snake. Is that the whole plan? *Yep.* Andrew rolled his eyes. Great plan, super involved, covers all the fine points. *Boy...* "I'm good," Andrew said out loud. "Um, lead the way somebody." He figured it couldn't hurt to play along until he woke up. It was certainly better than counting the stars on his ceiling. Again.

The blond man glared at him, but knife man nodded, turning his horse and riding away. The other two followed him, and Andrew sat, watching them. Um, how do I make the horse go? *Not THE horse; her name's Dewmint.* Okay, how do I make Dewmint go? Pecos sighed. *Pick up the reins, tap with your heels, nice like.* Reins? *The leather straps,* Pecos ground out. Oh. Andrew picked up the reins and tapped with his heels.

Dewmint started walking, and Andrew gasped, clutching her mane with his hands. *What you doin'?* Trying not to fall off! *Ain't you never ridden before?* I've never even touched a horse before, let alone ridden one! Andrew was suddenly very aware how far away the ground was. Are all horses this tall? *Dewmint ain't that tall, just sixteen hands.* Hands? Pretty sure we measure in feet. *Boy...* Never mind; how do I go faster?

Andrew didn't actually want to go faster, but the others were already far ahead of him, and he figured he should probably catch up. Dream or no dream, he didn't want to get left behind in the desert or really dry landscape as Pecos called it. *Heels.* Oh. Andrew tapped his heels again, and Dewmint sped up.

Andrew closed his eyes in fear. But that was even worse, so he opened them again. This is stupid, he thought. Why am I scared? It's a dream! A super realistic dream, but a dream. *Never seen such an idiot in all my days, and that's sayin' somethin'.* Oh, shut up, Andrew snapped. You don't exist, and even if you did, which you don't, it's not possible to take over someone else's body. It's just not. That kinda crap doesn't even happen in movies. You know why? 'Cause no one would believe it!

Andrew tried to relax as Dewmint moved across the ground. He was still far behind the others, so he nudged her again. She sped up, and Andrew clutched the reins in terror. She was going so fast and everything was so bouncy, he felt like his back was breaking. He clenched his jaw to keep his teeth from clanking together with every step the horse took. *Downright embarrassin'. Of all the body thieves, I get a sissy, city slicker boy.*

Excuse me! I'm not a sissy or a… well, I guess I am a city slicker and a boy, but I'm not a sissy! So you take that back! *Ain't takin' nothin' back. What the hell you doin' here?* I told you already! I'M DREAMING!!! So stop asking!

If Pecos would just shut up, this could be the most epic dream ever. He was riding a horse, something his mom would never let him do; he was outside, instead of stuck in his room with a busted leg and no TV, riding through a landscape he'd never seen before; and he had guns, and they were probably loaded. *Don't you dare touch my guns, boy,* Pecos growled menacingly. Can't stop me, Andrew laughed.

He tried to look around, but it was hard because when he took his eyes off Dewmint's head, he felt like he was falling. But when he managed to look right for a second, he realized there were two more horses running behind him, reins attached to his saddle. He looked forward again and saw the others had extra horses too. Why do you have so many horses? *Ridin' hard.* So? *If you weren't a city slicker you would know!* Whatever.

Andrew glanced over Dewmint's head and saw waves of heat rolling off the dirt into the air. He'd never been able to see so far in all his life. He'd always been surrounded by buildings or trees. It felt so empty. He wondered if the desert really looked like this. He didn't think he'd seen many pictures of the desert, so he wasn't sure what his mind was basing this on. He heard Pecos sigh. *Ain't a dream, boy. It's real; as real as the nose on your, I mean MY, face.* Andrew shook his head. It's not real! It's a dream. But since you're clearly not gonna shut up, tell me more about your plan.

Dewmint was going really fast now, and Andrew was having a horrible time sitting upright. He kept sliding from side to side and having to wiggle back into the middle of the saddle. *Relax your back,* Pecos chided. Andrew tried, but every time Dewmint's hooves hit the ground, he jerked.

No wonder people don't ride horses anymore, he thought as he dragged himself upright. *Whadda you mean people don't ride horses?* Can you hear everything I think? *Mostly.* Well stop! It's annoying. *Whadda you mean?* Where I'm from, or when I'm from I guess, people drive cars and trucks and stuff. *Cars?* Like a… a wagon that doesn't need horses. Andrew shook his head with irritation. Why was he explaining this? It didn't matter if Pecos knew what a car was. He was going to disappear as soon as Andrew woke up.

Andrew pinched himself just to check, but he stayed right where he was.

He frowned, looking around in confusion. Everything was super, super real. The details of the landscape, Dewmint's mane, the heat of the sun, the smell of dust, the thirst in his throat, the ache in his rear, the voice in his head. All of it FELT real. But that would mean... He shook his head emphatically. Why was he even considering it?

So what about this snake you mentioned? Pecos chuckled softly. *You ain't gonna like the snake, boy.*

# BUY NOW AT AMAZON.COM

Interested in a gripping tale?
Check out M.M. **Boulder's**
psychological thrillers **today** at
Amazon.com!

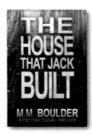

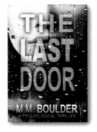

M.M. Crumley grew up in the woods of Colorado. She spent most of her time outside weaving stories in her mind while she explored.

About her writing, she has this to say:

"My characters are real to me, and on the page they become three dimensional. They are not stagnant. They change; they screw up; they conquer their fears. Sometimes they're unlikable. Sometimes they're broken. Sometimes they're on top of it all. Sometimes trouble finds them, sometimes they go looking for it, and sometimes that trouble defies explanation."

She also writes psychological thrillers under the name M.M. Boulder.

**Follow M.M. Crumley on Amazon.com to receive notifications of new releases or sign up for her VIP email at www.loneghostpublishing.com**

**Connect on Facebook:**
www.facebook.com/LoneGhostPublishing

Made in United States
North Haven, CT
30 March 2022

17701682R10171